"You think you got away with it, don't you?"

Diamond's eyes blazed with little points of green flame. "Well, think again, Adam Winter. I'll make you pay for what you did to my father."

Though Adam maintained his icy calm, a fire came into his eyes, turning them from silver to smoke. His fingers closed around her arm, and she felt his carefully controlled strength. When she tried to back away, he dragged her close.

The moment he touched her, he felt a flare of heat that he blamed on his temper. "Don't threaten me, Miss Jewel. And don't try to back me into a corner. If you do, you won't like what you find."

Though she trembled beneath his touch, Diamond lifted her head defiantly. "I'm not afraid of you."

"Well you should be, Miss Jewel.... And if you're wise, you'll stay as far away from me as possible."

Dear Reader,

Diamond is the first in Ruth Langan's new Jewels of Texas series, featuring four sisters who are brought together by the death of their father. Diamond is a beauty in the rough who believes that drifter Adam Winter is responsible for her father's death and is determined to bring him to justice, but her sisters have got other plans for the handsome Adam and their hard-nosed sibling. Don't miss any of this great new series set on a ranch in Texas.

In the third book of Suzanne Barclay's Lion Trilogy, *Lion's Legacy*, a Scottish warrior is hired to protect a tower from English raiders, but discovers that his benefactor has nothing to give him in return but the hand of his unwilling granddaughter. And in Emily French's second book, *Illusion*, the growing love between an ex-soldier and an heiress who have been drawn into a marriage of convenience is threatened by embezzlement and extortion.

Our fourth book for the month, *Twice Upon Time*, author Nina Beaumont's second Harlequin Historical time-travel novel, is an exciting tale of an ancient curse and a passion too strong to be denied.

Whatever your taste in reading, we hope to keep you coming back for more. Please keep a lookout for Harlequin Historical novels wherever books are sold.

Sincerely,

Tracy Farrell
Senior Editor

Please address questions and book requests to:
Harlequin Reader Service
U.S.: 3010 Walden Ave., P.O. Box 1325, Buffalo, NY 14269
Canadian: P.O. Box 609, Fort Erie, Ont. L2A 5X3

Ruth Langan

Diamond

Harlequin Books

TORONTO • NEW YORK • LONDON
AMSTERDAM • PARIS • SYDNEY • HAMBURG
STOCKHOLM • ATHENS • TOKYO • MILAN
MADRID • WARSAW • BUDAPEST • AUCKLAND

ISBN 0-373-28905-7

DIAMOND

Copyright © 1996 by Ruth Ryan Langan

This edition published by arrangement with Harlequin Books S.A.

® and ™ are trademarks of the publisher. Trademarks indicated with ® are registered in the United States Patent and Trademark Office, the Canadian Trade Marks Office and in other countries.

Printed in U.S.A.

Books by Ruth Langan

Harlequin Historicals

Mistress of the Seas #10
†*Texas Heart* #31
*Highland Barbarian #41
*Highland Heather #65
*Highland Fire #91
*Highland Heart #111
†*Texas Healer* #131
Christmas Miracle #147
†*Texas Hero* #180
Deception #196
*The Highlander #228
Angel #245
*Highland Heaven #269
**Diamond #305

†Texas Series
*The Highland Series
**The Jewels of Texas

Harlequin Books

Harlequin Historicals Christmas Stories 1990
"Christmas at Bitter Creek"

RUTH LANGAN

traces her ancestry to Scotland and Ireland. It is no surprise, then, that she feels a kinship with the characters in her historical novels.

Married to her childhood sweetheart, she has raised five children and lives in Michigan, the state where she was born and raised.

To sisters everywhere.

And especially to my sisters, Pat and Margaret.
Our threads have woven a rich tapestry of
family history.

And of course to Tom,
Whose love forever altered the fabric of my life.

Prologue

"You must eat something, Sēnorita Diamond." Carmelita Alvarez had been the cook and housekeeper on the Jewel Ranch for nearly twenty years. That gave her the right to issue orders to the eighteen-year-old daughter of the owner.

"No." Diamond peered out the window into the gathering darkness. "Not until Pa gets home."

Carmelita was well aware of the close bond between father and daughter. But she would give it one last attempt. "The food grows cold."

"I'm sorry." Diamond turned to the woman who hovered in the doorway, suddenly ashamed that she had allowed her fears to cloud her manners. "Is Rosario waiting to take you home?"

"Sí."

"Then you should go."

"But the food..."

"I'll warm it when Pa gets here. You know I can't eat without him. Go." She waved idly as the woman left, then began to pace.

Where was Pa? What was taking him so long?

She should have insisted on going with him. She was always at his side. But this time, he'd slammed his office door and stormed out, saying he'd be home later. His sudden shift of mood had frightened her. It was so unlike her father. She'd never seen him so angry.

She stopped her frantic pacing and resumed her watchful vigil. Pa would be home soon. Then they would settle down to share a meal. And Pa would take her into his confidence, as he always did.

On the banks of Poison Creek, the flickering flames of fire illuminated Onyx Jewel's handsome face, which was twisted into a mask of rage.

"I've always been a fair man. I expected the same from others." He pounded a fist into his palm. "Why?" It was the only strangled word he was able to manage over his building fury.

The other figure, draped in shadow, spoke not a word. But as Onyx turned away, a pistol was suddenly pressed into his back. A single gunshot rang out.

Onyx Jewel half turned, his eyes wide with shock and surprise. "Not . . . you."

And then, as the pain struck and realization dawned that he had been mortally wounded, he fumbled for his gun. Anticipating his move, his attacker's arm swung out, sending the pistol flying into the creek. Seized with a crippling pain, Onyx dropped to his knees and lifted a hand in an attempt to ensnare the offending arm.

The other figure sidestepped out of reach.

Onyx's lips moved, but no words came out. He fell, face down, and lay motionless.

After a lengthy pause, the figure stepped closer. A hesitant touch to Onyx's throat assured that his pulse had stopped.

As hoofbeats echoed, bearing a lone rider into the lengthening shadows, the blood of Onyx Jewel spilled from his lifeless body. The still waters of Poison Creek reflected a bloodred sky. Off to the west, the crimson sunset bled into the snow atop Widow's Peak. The whole of Texas seemed to be bleeding for its loss.

Hanging Tree Gazette
December 1, 1870
Rancher Murdered

Marshal Quent Regan was summoned to Poison Creek by a group of wranglers who found the body of Onyx Jewel, Hanging Tree's most prominent citizen, shot in the back. Marshal Regan promised to comb the countryside until the villain is brought to justice. Cal McCabe, foreman for the Jewel Ranch, announced that Onyx Jewel's daughter and only heir, Diamond, would continue operation of the cattle empire as her father would have wished.

Within days, the article was repeated in newspapers across the country. It wasn't often that news from the little Texas town of Hanging Tree made headlines in cities like Boston, San Francisco or St. Louis. But then, it wasn't often that a man of Onyx Jewel's stature was murdered, even in the rough-and-tumble state of Texas.

Jewel, a cattleman, had carved an empire of more than one hundred thousand acres out of some of the most primitive land in Texas. What was even more impressive was that he'd managed to do so without acquiring a long list of enemies. Onyx Jewel was not only Hanging Tree's wealthiest citizen, he was its most beloved. But someone had taken his life. Someone would have to pay.

Chapter One

Hanging Tree, Texas
December 3, 1870

"Remember. You're dealing with a vicious killer." Marshal Quent Regan's breath plumed in the frosty air. "From all I've heard, Adam Winter won't be taken without a fight. Stay alert. And stay alive."

Darkness still hung like a shroud over the land, though the first faint ribbons of light could be seen on the distant horizon. The six men, rifles at the ready, had dismounted nearly a mile back, leaving their horses tethered in a stand of trees. Given the reputation of the man they stalked, they were taking no chances. They wanted no sound to give them away. Their only hope of taking him alive was to catch him unawares.

"Arlo." At the marshal's whispered command, the men halted. "You and the others surround the place. He might have a lookout posted out back."

The stocky deputy nodded as he and three men crept to the far side of the cabin.

The marshal waited until they were in place, then moved stealthily forward, followed by a second man, whose glance swiveled from one side to the other, as if expecting at any moment to be blown away by blazing gunfire.

The marshal studied the small building looming out of the darkness. It couldn't really be called a cabin. It was little more than a shack, with four walls of rough-hewn timbers, the cracks gaping wide enough to admit a half-grown pup. There was a small window, where a hole had been cut in one wall in order to view approaching strangers. The door, swaying slightly, appeared to be tied shut from the inside. It would be an easy matter to kick it open and take the occupant by surprise, if luck stayed with them.

"Ready?" The marshal gave a final look around before driving his foot against the door. At the same moment that it swung inward, he and his partner dashed inside, rifles aimed and cocked.

"Don't move, Winter, or I'll blow a hole in you so big they won't even be able to find your chest." Marshal Regan used his voice like a weapon. He'd spent too many years dealing with the criminal element. Desperate men would do anything necessary to survive. They had to be subdued quickly, and made to understand that there would be no mercy.

By the dim light of glowing coals in the fireplace, a figure could be seen sitting up in bed, one hand snaking out toward his gun.

The marshal swept the pistol from the table beside the bed with the butt of his rifle.

The man leaped from his bed and tackled the marshal, driving him hard against the wall. The marshal gave a grunt of pain as a knee jammed into his midsection.

His deputy, seeing that the marshal was fighting a losing battle, brought his rifle into the stranger's back and snarled, "You move a muscle, you're dead."

The man turned on him and knocked the rifle aside as though it were a child's toy. But as he started toward his pistol on the floor, the marshal's voice stopped him.

"Stay right there, Winter. This badge says I have the right to shoot you without another warning."

"Badge?" The man froze.

"That's right. I'm Marshal Quent Regan."

"Why didn't you identify yourself right away? You could have saved us both a lot of trouble."

Seeing that the man was, for the moment, subdued, the marshal crossed the room and tossed the rifle propped up beside the bed to his partner.

At that moment the rest of the men crowded inside the little cabin, dragging a scruffy, stooped old man whose hands had been hastily tied behind his back. Though his blue shirt was faded and torn, it still bore the markings of the Union army.

"You were right, Marshal," the deputy called with a trace of pride. "We found this old coot sleeping out back in a wagon. Probably a lookout."

"Ain't no lookout," the old man said through his tangled whiskers. "Just can't stand to sleep inside. Gives me the sweats."

"Shut up, old man." The marshal turned to the figure across the room. "Let's go, Winter." He picked up a shirt from the foot of the bed and tossed it. "Put this on. You've got a long ride ahead of you."

"That so?" The voice was deep, roughened with a combination of anger and the last vestiges of sleep. "Where am I going?"

"You're going to hell, where you belong," the deputy called with a laugh.

Adam Winter took a step toward him, and all six men, despite the fact that their rifles were trained on him, took a step back. He was a commanding figure, exuding power and something even more frightening—raw fury.

"Would you care to tell me what this is about?" He kept his gaze level with the marshal's.

"It's about the murder of Onyx Jewel. I'm sure you've heard about it."

"I have. But what's that got to do with me?"

"You're sitting on land that borders the Jewel property."

Adam Winter remained silent. But the muscles of his arms bunched and tightened as his hands clenched at his sides. Every man in the cabin noted the movement, and their fingers tightened on their weapons.

"Last I heard, that was no crime."

"The water you need for your cattle is on Jewel property." The marshal nodded toward his deputy. "And Arlo here heard Onyx Jewel tell his foreman to see that your cattle were driven off his land and kept off his land."

"That doesn't make me a murderer."

"Maybe. Maybe not. That's for a judge to decide. But Arlo also heard you threaten to kill Onyx Jewel if he didn't stop damming up the river above your land. And, Winter, I don't know where you come from, but here in Texas, men have killed for a whole lot less than water. Now, get dressed."

"Looks like you're going to jail, Adam Winter," came the mocking voice of the deputy. "And the town's going to get to see what made it famous."

The hill overlooking the Jewel Ranch was barren and windswept, and resembled all the hills around it, except for the freshly dug hole. The entire town of Hanging Tree had gathered to watch Onyx Jewel's last ride. Despite the presence of the preacher in his somber black suit, the crowd appeared almost festive, with the men and women in their Sunday best, and the occasional lilt of an innocent child's laughter carried on the morning air.

Dust spewed from horses' hooves as a long line of wranglers led a procession from the ranch house, followed by a single wagon. Trotting alongside was a riderless horse. The ranch hands dismounted and formed two columns, standing at attention, while six cowboys lifted a simple pine box from the back of the wagon and carried it toward the grave. A lone figure, dressed like the other wranglers in boots and leather chaps, trailed slowly behind.

When the procession came to a halt, a slender hand lifted to remove the wide-brimmed hat, and a mane of fiery hair spilled loose to drift on the wind.

"It ain't proper for a lady to go to a funeral dressed like a wrangler," whispered town gossip Lavinia Thurlong.

"Especially to bury her own father," added neighbor Gladys Witherspoon. "But then, Diamond Jewel never cared what others thought. For that matter, neither did her pa."

"I could tell you things—" Lavinia began, but a look from her long-suffering husband stopped her.

Both women fell silent as the preacher's words carried over the crowd.

"...Ashes to ashes and dust to dust. Thus shall a man live his life so that, like Onyx Jewel, when he comes face-to-face with his Maker, he need not cower and hide, but lift his head proudly and answer the invitation to enter paradise." The preacher glanced around, meeting the gazes of several of his flock with a challenging look. "Let it be a lesson to all of us. We must live in such a way, as did Onyx Jewel, that we will not fear death when it comes to claim us."

Diamond Jewel stood alone, staring at her father's casket. It wasn't death she feared; it was living alone. Without Pa.

It didn't seem possible. They'd always been a team. Just the two of them. She couldn't remember anything about her mother, who had died when Diamond was just a baby. But she would never forget a single thing about her proud, handsome father. For all of her years, he had been the center of her life. She'd taught herself to walk like him, talk like him, even ride and shoot like him. How would it be possible to go on without him?

Two of the ranch hands helped lower the casket into the ground. At a word from the preacher, Diamond dug the first shovel of earth and scattered it over the casket. She had to swallow hard to hold back the lump that threatened to unravel all her hard-fought control.

"You aren't there, Pa," she whispered. "You're here beside me, just like always. Except now, I can't see you. But you're here. I just know it."

She stepped aside so that the others could pay their last tributes. Ranch foreman Cal McCabe looked grim as he shoveled dirt over the casket. Limping behind him was the trail cook. One big fat tear splashed down his cheek, and he rubbed it aside with the back of his hand.

Watching as each of the wranglers followed suit, Diamond felt the sting of tears burn her eyes, but she blinked them away, horrified at such a weakness. She sniffed. Pa wouldn't have cried. And neither would she. She was a Texan, born and bred. And a Jewel, as well. Pa said that made her special, but also gave her added responsibilities. He'd always taught her that she needed to be tougher, stronger, more honest, more disciplined. Right now she didn't feel like more of anything. She felt robbed of everything she'd ever loved. And helpless to do anything about it.

Helpless. That was the worst part. Nothing she could do would bring Pa back. Nothing.

She lifted her chin and stared straight ahead. She'd heard the whispers from the crowd, had seen their sideways looks, but chose to ignore them. How could anyone be concerned about clothes at a time like this? Only one thing mattered. Her father had been shot in the back. It was up to her to avenge that cowardly act.

She watched as the town banker, Chester Pierce, lifted a shovel of dirt and scattered it. He turned and drew her into his arms and she nearly gave in to the need to weep.

"Oh, Uncle Chet." Though he wasn't a blood relative, Diamond had always called him uncle. She drew in a breath and struggled for control.

"I know. I know." He patted her shoulder and continued to hold her close.

Chet Pierce had handled the Jewel finances through bad times and good. In the early days, he had loaned Onyx Jewel the money to add to his herd and meet his payroll. And Onyx had repaid him a hundredfold, banking his profits in town, despite the fact that larger banks in Eastern cities had offered more security. The friendship between the two men had benefited the town of Hanging Tree, since Chet Pierce was able to make loans to other, smaller businesses, thus expanding his own bank until it had become a powerful force in the state of Texas.

When the grave was covered with dirt, the young, charismatic minister, Reverend Wade Weston, stepped forward and caught the young woman's hand, speaking a few words meant to soothe. "Onyx rests in peace now, Miss Jewel."

"Peace?" The word was louder than she'd intended, distorted with fury. "My pa will never rest in peace until the coward who shot him is hanged."

"Vengeance is mine, sayeth the Lord."

"No, Reverend Weston." She snatched her hand from his, relieved to have a stronger, fiercer emotion nudge aside her grief. "I'll be the one to avenge my father's death. You can count on that."

Heads swiveled as a single horse galloped up the hill. The crowd parted for a tall, sun-bronzed man wearing the badge of a marshal. He strode forward until he reached Diamond.

"Thought you might like to know," Marshal Quent Regan muttered. "Early this morning, I arrested a man for the murder of your father."

Her head came up sharply. Her gaze narrowed. "Who is he?"

"Name's Adam Winter. Newcomer to Hanging Tree. Don't know much about him—" he rubbed at his tender shoulder, which he'd wrenched in his brawl with the prisoner "—except that he's said to be quick with his temper, and just as quick with a gun. I've asked my deputy to look into his claim that he owns the land just west of yours, where I found him scratching out a living. Maybe his claim of ownership is genuine. Then again, maybe not." He glanced at the banker for confirmation.

Chet Pierce shrugged. "Don't know much about this Adam Winter. He could be just a drifter and squatter."

"Where is he now?" Diamond demanded.

"In jail."

"I want to see him."

"Maybe you ought to wait. I mean, with the funeral and all..."

"I want to see him now," she said in a dangerously soft voice.

No one had ever argued with a Jewel when that tone of voice was used.

She turned and made her way through the tangle of curious townspeople, with the wranglers following. Most had worked for Onyx Jewel for years, and respected him. But even those who had recently hired on had soon learned that they were in the presence of an extraordinary man. Onyx Jewel had always worked alongside his men. With single-mindedness he'd carved an empire in the wilderness. And the young woman in their midst was a worthy heir. She had inherited not only his wealth, but his drive and determination, as well. There was no job she wouldn't tackle. And few men, with the exception of tough ranch foreman Cal McCabe, would dare to challenge her.

Diamond pulled herself into the saddle and took off without a backward glance at her father's grave. With the townspeople looking on, whispering at this strange turn of events, the wranglers followed, setting off at a thunderous pace.

As the earth trembled beneath the volley of hoofbeats, Reverend Weston felt a sudden wave of sympathy for the stranger who was about to taste Diamond Jewel's venom.

"This funeral service is concluded," he announced.

When he looked around, he realized his words had been unnecessary. The townspeople were dispersing as quickly as possible, so they wouldn't miss the expected fireworks in town.

"Adam, the deputy out there says they've already wired a federal judge to come and hold a trial." Zebulon Forrest was a gnarled, withered old man with cracked leather skin and a graying beard that disappeared inside a ragged shirt. Despite the fact that he'd been found sleeping in a wagon on Adam's property, the marshal had released him, after learning that the old man merely worked for Adam.

"Then it'll be up to the federal judge to find me innocent."

"Are you crazy? These people are getting ready for a hanging. Somebody killed the town hero, and they want to taste blood."

Adam Winter said softly, "It won't be mine, Zeb."

The old man clutched the bars that separated them and studied the man who reclined on the hard cot, his hat shielding the morning sun from his eyes. "From what I've heard, this town has a history of hanging men first and asking questions later. There must be something we can do to get you out of that cell."

Adam shoved the hat aside and turned his gaze toward his old friend. "I guess if life has taught me anything, it's that I can't change fate."

"Damn it, Adam." Zeb ran a hand through his hair in frustration. He knew what Adam Winter was thinking. Hadn't they been through hell and back together? Hadn't they been forced to watch too many good men die? Maybe they'd been helpless to stop all that, but this...this wasn't fate. This was just some federal marshal looking for a scapegoat. It was so unfair, the old man was itching to grab a club and start swinging. But there was no one to swing at. Except maybe Adam. Damn him for giving up without a fight. It wasn't like him.

"You've got to fight back," Zeb cried, trying to fire up some enthusiasm. "Fight like hell. Or else, they're going to use you for a sacrificial lamb."

Adam got to his feet and started across the cell, limping slightly. "Let it go, Zeb. There's nothing—"

Their heads came up as the door was thrown open and a cluster of wranglers trailed behind the federal marshal.

"There's your father's killer, Miss Jewel."

There was a moment of stunned silence.

"Leave me," came the hushed, slightly breathless voice

At once the others did as she commanded. When old Ze
tried to remain, the marshal caught him by the arm an
dragged him away to the outer office.

Diamond waited until the door closed. Then she yanke
off her hat and absently slapped it against her leg, sendin
dust flying. She peered through the bars at the man wh
stood facing her. She should have known he'd be a big ma
Taller even than her father, and broader of shoulder. Ony
Jewel had been nearly six feet of pure muscle, but he woul
have been no match for Adam Winter. The man who face
her had dark, shaggy hair, badly in need of a trim. It curle
over the collar of a tattered shirt. There was a stubble c
dark hair on his chin and cheeks, and she recalled that th
marshal had said he'd arrested him while he slept in th
shack he called a ranch. His eyes were smoky gray, and h
gaze held her even when she tried to look away.

Adam Winter studied the tall, slender figure. It had bee
a shock when she'd removed her hat. From a distance h
would have mistaken her for just another wrangler. But he
hair, the color of autumn leaves, was a glorious tangle tha
fell to her waist. In the sunlight streaming through the smal
narrow window he could see the way her shirt straine
against high, firm breasts. Her tiny waist and softly rounde
hips were encircled by empty gun belts. Her guns, no doub
lay on the marshal's desk, to be claimed when she was leav
ing. Up close her face was a small oval, with high cheek
bones and eyes that were more green than blue. Eyes tha
were studying him as though he were a rattlesnake.

"The marshal tells me your name is Adam Winter."

Again that voice, soft, breathless. But not from fear, h
realized. Not from nerves. From a deep, raging passion. I
was obvious that she was struggling to keep a tight rein o
her fury. But it would be no match for his own, if he al

lowed it to take hold of him. He cautioned himself to remember that this young woman was steeped in grief.

"That's right."

"Why did you kill my father? What did he ever do to you?"

"I didn't kill your father, Miss Jewel. The marshal arrested the wrong man."

"Quent warned me that you'd say that."

"Then why did you bother asking?"

"Damn you. You're so sure of yourself. So smug." Her eyes narrowed. He could almost see the sparks. One hand curled around the bars of his cell until her knuckles were white. "You took away the only thing that ever mattered to me in this world. I had to lay my father in the ground today." Her voice was layered with pain. "Do you know what that felt like?"

He held his silence, but something flared briefly in his eyes. Something that mirrored her pain.

She took no notice. She bent and pulled a pistol from her boot, then straightened and leveled it at him. "I ought to shoot you in the back, the same way you shot my father. But I want you to see me while I pull this trigger, Adam Winter. And I want to see your eyes when you know you're dying."

He moved so quickly she had no time to react. In one swift motion he caught her hand and pulled it through the bars, twisting until the gun slipped from her fingers and clattered to the floor of his cell. With his other hand he caught her roughly by the shoulder and dragged her close, until she was pressed tightly, painfully, against the bars of the cell.

"Little fool," he said between clenched teeth. "Do you really want the death of an innocent man on your conscience for the rest of your life?"

She could feel the strength in his hands as he caught and pinned her. Could feel his breath hot against her cheek. And could see in his eyes a terrible black rage that matched her own.

No man had ever dared to lay a hand on her in such a bruising, intimate manner. She was, after all, Onyx Jewel's daughter. Her father's reputation had always managed to insulate her from the tougher side of her countrymen. Now imprisoned against her will, she felt a strange heat slowly building within her. The heat of anger, she reasoned.

"Let me go." She was surprised at how difficult it was to speak.

"When I'm good and ready." Adam continued to press the bones of her hand and knew that, with one simple movement, he could snap them like the wings of a bird. His other hand grasped her shoulder, holding her firmly when she tried to pull back.

She was neither small nor fragile. But she was soft, as only a woman could be. Though she dressed like a man, she was unmistakably female. And for all her tough talk, a frightened, confused one at that.

All the anger, all the rage, seemed to drain out of him as quickly as it had filled him.

He released her and bent to pick up her weapon. As he straightened, he saw the way her eyes widened in fear. Almost at once the fear was replaced by a challenging look.

"Go ahead. Shoot me. But I won't turn tail and run. You won't get a second chance to shoot someone in the back, Adam Winter. If you shoot me, you'll have to face me while you do it."

She was startled when he handed her the gun through the bars of his cell. It was a calculated risk, he knew, but one he had to take. She could still turn the gun on him. But he was betting that her quick temper had already begun to cool.

Their fingers brushed and she felt another rush of heat. She pulled away as though burned.

"If you're smart, Miss Jewel, you'll put this back in your boot before the marshal sees it. I don't think he'd take too kindly to his prisoner being shot before the town has a chance to enjoy a good hanging."

It galled her to know that he was right. But in these few moments, she had lost her will to kill. Only now was she aware of how foolish, how rash, her actions had been.

With great reluctance she slid the pistol into her boot. "I intend to listen to every word spoken at your trial. And when they're ready to hang you, Adam Winter, I'll tie the noose myself."

His voice was rough. "I understand how you feel. I'd do the same to anyone who hurt my loved ones."

"Damn you, Adam Winter. Don't tell me that you understand. No one will ever know the pain I feel. I'll never forgive you. Never."

She turned and, pulling open the door, strode away, leaving the door to slam behind her.

In the silence, Adam stood, head bowed, hands clenched. It looked like Zeb was right. The town was ripe for a hanging. And without a doubt, so was Onyx Jewel's daughter.

Chapter Two

"What did Mr. Jewel say to you about the defendant' cattle, Mr. McCabe?"

Judge Bernard Thompkins spoke to the ranch foreman but his attention was captured by the rapt faces of the peo ple crowded around to witness the trial. As expected, th locals were spellbound.

He regularly traveled across Texas holding federal trial involving murder or bank robberies. He was well aware tha his stern demeanor and theatrical presence brought a bit o excitement to these otherwise drab little towns. As a youn man he'd dreamed of joining a band of traveling actors Instead, he'd joined his father's stuffy law firm, where he' toiled for thirty years. Though his hair was silver and hi middle thickening, his heart was still that of a young man And in truth, these past few years he'd been having the tim of his life in his very own traveling circus.

"He said to drive Adam Winter's cattle off our land an see that they stayed off."

The crowd murmured, and the judge rapped on his tabl for silence.

The trial was being held in the back room of Durfee' Mercantile. It was the only room big enough to hold th crowd that had gathered to watch Adam Winter face the music.

The judge's table had, until today, held Durfee's complete supply of petticoats, corsets and ladies' drawers.

The marshal and his deputy sat on either side of Adam Winter, who had been brought in with his hands and feet chained, in case he should attempt to escape. The marshal figured the chains also added weight to Winter's accusation of guilt. It didn't hurt that Winter had been in jail for over a week, with no chance to bathe, shave or change his clothes. Everything about the defendant shouted guilty.

A few chairs had been set up for distinguished onlookers, such as the mayor and his wife, the minister, the banker and, of course, Diamond Jewel. The rest of the townspeople were forced to stand shoulder to shoulder. Those who couldn't fit inside were milling about outside, listening through the open window.

It was a festive crowd. The men had been up since dawn to see to their chores so they could hurry into town. The women wore their Sunday best. Children of all ages swung from tree limbs and chased after one another. It was a fine day for a hanging.

"Deputy Arlo Spitz contends that Adam Winter threatened Mr. Jewel. Did you hear such a threat?"

"No, sir." Cal McCabe squirmed. A sworn oath was a sacred trust. And he wished to hell he could recall such a threat. He just wanted this over so he could return to the ranch. He much preferred riding the range to being confined in a courtroom.

At Cal's denial, the judge turned his stern gaze on the deputy seated beside the prisoner. Arlo flushed and swallowed, causing his Adam's apple to bulge in his throat like a bullfrog. He thought he remembered a threat, but then, he'd just been hoping the two men would get into a brawl. Nothing he enjoyed more than a good fight.

"Thank you, Mr. McCabe." The judge turned to a tall stick of a man with thin brown hair and eyes as sad as a hound's, peering balefully through round spectacles. "I suppose you'd like to ask a few questions, Mr. Burton?"

"Yes, sir." Rayford Burton got slowly to his feet. The moment he'd received Zeb's telegram, he'd dropped everything to come to the aid of his old army sergeant. Especially when he'd heard that the defendant was Adam Winter. After all, he owed his life to Adam. As a scared young recruit, he'd lost his nerve at the first sign of battle, and would have taken a bullet in the back if it hadn't been for the kindness of Adam Winter, a more seasoned fighter, who'd pulled him down behind a log and stayed with him until he discovered his courage.

With his limited legal training, Rayford spent most of his time these days in Pennsylvania drawing up wills for wealthy clients, or preparing bills of sale and eviction notices. Since his arrival in Hanging Tree three days ago, he'd asked hundreds of questions of the townspeople and made voluminous notes, hoping to appear as professional as possible. But he felt as lost as a six-year-old on his first day of school. He was still just that scared recruit.

"Mr. McCabe." He knew he presented a homely picture to the crowd, resembling a young Abe Lincoln. Though the President was dead now these past five years, his memory still conjured unpleasant memories for many in Texas whose sympathies lay with the shattered Confederacy. Because of that, Rayford Burton kept his face averted so as not to be too conspicuous. "I understand you argued with Mr. Jewel the day before he was shot."

Several in the crowd were heard to gasp.

The ranch foreman sprang to his feet in a rage. "Are you accusing me of killing my boss?"

"Sit down, Mr. McCabe." The judge rapped his gavel and glared at the witness.

Cal sank back in the chair, but his eyes were as hard as rock chips.

"Did you argue with Mr. Jewel?" Rayford Burton persisted.

"Maybe. I don't remember."

"I'll refresh your memory. You and Mr. Jewel had ridden to Adam Winter's cabin, along with the deputy, to caution Winter about letting his cattle roam off his property. When Mr. Winter complained about the water being dammed, Mr. Jewel ordered you to see that the dam was removed at once. And you flew into a rage, saying Adam Winter was lying. Is that correct?"

"You've got it all wrong. I wasn't mad at Onyx, I was—"

"You lost your temper, didn't you, Mr. McCabe?"

Cal glanced toward Diamond, who was staring holes through him. He'd have to answer to her later. "Yeah. I lost my temper. Everyone around here knows I do that a lot. But I didn't—"

"Thank you. That's all," Rayford Burton said as he returned to his chair.

"You're excused," the judge said. "I'd like to call Arlo Spitz."

The deputy avoided the marshal's eyes as he walked up and took the seat beside the judge's table.

There was no jury. Judge Thompkins wasn't about to put the fate of any man in the hands of wranglers whose loyalty could be bought for the price of a horse, or sometimes the promise of a job. Like all murder cases, this would be decided by the judge alone. And his word was right next to that of the Almighty.

When the oath had been administered, Judge Thompkins said, "Deputy, you've heard what Mr. McCabe said earlier. I'll ask you the same question. Did you ever hear Mr. Winter threaten Mr. Jewel?"

"Maybe not in so many words. But when Winter found that the water had been dammed up above his land, and that only a trickle was spilling into his stream, he was mad as a wounded bobcat. I wouldn't put it past a man with his temper to draw on an unarmed man."

Rayford Burton was on his feet immediately. "And what makes you think Mr. Jewel was unarmed?"

Arlo choked. "Why, he was shot in the back, that's why."

The judge's eyes narrowed. "Do you know something the rest of us don't know, deputy?"

"We didn't find Onyx Jewel's gun. And everyone around here knows that Jewel always carried a gun and was the best shot in the territory. If he'd had his gun, there's no doubt who would have been lying dead. That's why he was shot in the back by that no-good, cowardly—"

The judge said dryly, "Thank you for your brilliant observations, Mr. Spitz. And now, if you don't mind, I'll ask you to step down. Unless, of course, Mr. Burton has more questions for you." He turned to the young lawyer.

"No, sir. No more questions."

"Then I call Ezra Constable to testify."

The crowd glanced around in consternation. None of them had ever heard the name before. When the grizzled old Cookie stepped forward, there was a smattering of laughter.

"Is that not your name?" the judge asked.

"It's the name I was given at birth," the old man explained. "But I ain't been called anything except Cookie for so many years, nobody knows me by any other."

"All right. Cookie." The judge rapped for silence. "How long have you known Onyx Jewel?"

"Twenty years or more. Started with him as a wrangler, until I busted my leg. Tended to it myself, but it healed crooked, and I couldn't sit a horse without pain. So I took on the job of cooking for the wranglers."

The judge said, "I have no questions for you. But Mr. Burton here wanted your name on the witness list. So I'll let Mr. Burton ask his questions."

Once more Rayford Burton crossed the room. "I understand you and Onyx Jewel fought the night before he was murdered. And you told him to find himself another cook."

"Well, I . . ." The old man pulled a stained handkerchief from his pocket and nervously wiped it across his forehead. "I might have said something like that. But Onyx knew I didn't mean it."

"Do you often say things you don't mean?"

"Yes. No. Hell!" The old man's voice exploded. "Onyx wanted me to close up my chuckwagon and do my cooking in the main house. In the main house," he thundered for emphasis. He turned to the judge to avoid Diamond, who was staring wide-eyed at him. "Do you know what it would be like for an old cowhand to give up the trail and be confined to four walls?"

"So you quit," Rayford Burton said softly.

"Hell, yes, I quit. But just so Onyx would know how I felt. He knew I wouldn't really leave him."

"If he knew that, what good did it do to threaten?"

The old man stared at his gnarled hands. "No good. It was a foolish thing to do. But dammit, he hurt me."

"And you wanted to hurt him back." Rayford walked back to his seat, drawing out a long breath. "I guess shooting a man in the back would hurt him real good."

"You don't think...? You ain't saying...?" The old man was speechless.

"You can step down now, Cookie," the judge said. He glanced around the courtroom before saying, "I'd like to call Adam Winter."

The crowd both inside and outside the courtroom became ominously still. Since most of them didn't know the defendant, they had to base their information on rumors. And there were dozens of them. Rumors that Adam Winter was a professional gunslinger before retiring here in Hanging Tree. Rumors that he'd killed over a dozen men, and his poster hung in every sheriff's office from here to New Mexico Territory. Rumors that he was hard-drinking, hard-fighting and hard-living. The people of Hanging Tree were eager to hear every word from this vile outlaw's lips.

While the judge administered the oath, Diamond studied Adam Winter. Except for the dark growth of beard, his time spent in jail hadn't seemed to affect him in the least. Despite the bound hands and feet, and the soiled clothes, he held his head in an aloof, almost arrogant, manner.

"On the day of his murder," the judge began, "you argued with Onyx Jewel."

"I did." His voice when he spoke was as commanding as the judge's. Firm, with no hint of an apology.

His dark, penetrating gaze skimmed the courtroom until it came to rest on Diamond. She felt pinned by that look until, flushing, she lowered her gaze. Damn the man. He reminded her of a sleek mountain cat, all sinew and muscle, afraid of nothing and no one. At this moment, she believed every one of the rumors about him. If someone was foolish enough to shoot at him, he'd probably catch the bullet in his teeth and spit it back.

"What did you argue about?"

"Cattle and water."

The judge glowered at the defendant. "Would you care to elaborate, Mr. Winter?"

Even though Adam Winter turned toward the judge, he could feel Diamond Jewel's gaze boring into him. Though he hated to admit it, there was something about those haunted green eyes that got to him. His hands fisted against the chains that bound him.

"Onyx Jewel and his foreman brought back a string of cattle that had wandered off my land. Onyx warned me that if any more of my cows crossed onto Jewel property, they would be considered his."

"These cattle that wandered off your property, Mr. Winter. Had they been branded?"

Adam nodded. "They were."

"Then, during roundup time, couldn't they be culled from the herd and returned to you?"

"They could. But Onyx Jewel was no fool. He said he didn't build an empire by feeding other men's cattle, and then returning them fattened for slaughter."

"Were you angry when he threatened you?" the judge asked.

"Of course I was." Adam Winter's eyes narrowed. "I told him the cattle would never have crossed onto his land if his wranglers hadn't dammed up the stream, leaving my section dry and my cattle desperate for water."

"What did he say to that?"

"He claimed he didn't know about any dam. When he asked his foreman, Cal McCabe said he didn't know about it, either, and didn't believe me. So I invited them to ride with me to see the damage that had been done to my stream."

From her position in the front row, Diamond watched and listened. She could imagine her father's anger at the suggestion that he would intentionally interfere with a man's water supply. Out here, that was considered worse than being a horse thief. Onyx Jewel understood the importance of water better than most men. And why, she thought, bristling, would a man of her father's stature need to worry about the small amount of water Adam Winter's cattle would use? Why, he wouldn't have a care about a man like Adam Winter. After all, the marshal had said Winter's ranch wasn't even worth bothering about. How could this liar even suggest that Onyx Jewel would stoop to such a cowardly act?

"After they saw your stream, Mr. Winter, what did Onyx Jewel say?"

"After seeing the evidence, Jewel ordered his foreman to see that the dam was destroyed and my water allowed to flow freely. In turn, I gave Jewel my word that I would contain my cattle."

"Was he satisfied with that?" the judge asked.

"I'd say he was. Onyx Jewel and I shook hands and parted company."

"And his foreman, Cal McCabe? Was he satisfied, as well?"

Adam Winter shook his head. "McCabe said he didn't believe any of his wranglers had a hand in the building of that dam. They had no reason to. He suggested that I rigged the dam myself, to justify letting my cattle stray."

"Was McCabe angry?"

"He was," Adam said simply. "But I figured he and Onyx Jewel would work it out between them."

Judge Thompkins turned toward the young lawyer. "Do you have any questions, Mr. Burton?"

Rayford stood and walked toward the defendant, forcing those in the courtroom to follow his movements. He wanted to draw attention to Adam Winter's words. He stopped a few feet from Adam's chair.

"So you and Onyx Jewel parted company on friendly terms."

"We were far from friends. But at least we understood each other. And respected each other."

Respect? Though the word jolted Diamond, she found herself wondering. Would her father have respected a man like Adam Winter? Onyx Jewel had often boasted that he'd built his empire from a single tract of inhospitable landscape and some scrawny cattle. His humble beginnings were much like Adam Winter's. Her father would probably identify with a man like Adam. Still, she found herself rejecting the very idea that he would respect him.

Before she could continue that line of thought, she was interrupted by Rayford Burton's next question.

"How many guns do you own, Mr. Winter?"

Adam's eyes narrowed. "Two."

The young lawyer lifted them from the judge's table and held them aloft. "The marshal confiscated them the night he arrested you?"

"That's right."

"Would you tell me what they are, please."

"A Remington six-shot pistol and a Sharp's buffalo rifle."

The lawyer glanced at the defendant. "That's a lot of firepower, Mr. Winter. Were you expecting a war?"

Adam's expression never altered. But something blazed in his eyes. "I've learned the hard way that it's best to be prepared."

The judge seemed to be paying very close attention.

"Did you fire either of these guns on the night that Onyx Jewel was killed?"

"I did not."

Rayford Burton turned to the judge. "I have no more questions."

"You can step down, Mr. Winter," Judge Thompkins said.

The young lawyer turned to the group seated in the front row. "I'd like to ask Dr. Prentice a few questions."

The town doctor, as round as he was tall, with a tiny black mustache that looked as though it had been penciled over his upper lip, strode toward the witness chair. The judge administered the oath and he took a seat.

"I have just one question, Doctor. It's a simple one."

The crowd strained to hear.

"You examined the body of Onyx Jewel. Could he have been killed by a bullet from either of these weapons?"

Cosmo Prentice examined each gun carefully, then handed them back to the judge. In his familiar nasal voice he said, "Not a chance."

The crowd gave a collective gasp.

"The gun that killed Onyx Jewel was what I call a gentleman's gun," the doctor went on. "A small pistol that is worn in a man's sleeve, by a gambler, perhaps, or carried in a lady's handbag. It makes a very small wound in the flesh, both as it enters and exits the body. It's only good for close range."

"Thank you, Doctor. That's all." For the first time since the trial began, Rayford Burton felt his hopes rise as he returned to his seat.

The judge turned to the marshal. "Quent, you don't need to take the witness chair. Just remember that you're still under oath."

The marshal nodded as he got hesitantly to his feet. He was already beginning to sweat.

"Did you search Adam Winter's cabin and property for any other weapons?"

"We tore his place apart," the marshal said with obvious pride. "If there was another weapon anywhere on that hardscrabble piece of land, I'd have found it."

"So you don't think the defendant could have concealed another weapon?"

"Well, now..." The marshal began to backpedal. "I didn't say..."

"You said you tore his place apart."

The marshal swallowed, then nodded.

The judge made a steeple of his hands. "Thanks, Marshal." He glanced at the young lawyer, and the two exchanged a long, meaningful look.

Rayford Burton scraped back his chair and got to his feet. Despite his inexperience, he could see that the case against Adam Winter had just fallen apart.

"I ask, in view of the evidence, that you set this man free."

A rumble of dissent rippled through the crowd. When the judge rapped for silence, the people shifted their attention to him.

"I must agree with Mr. Burton. Since neither of the guns belonging to Adam Winter could have possibly been used to kill Onyx Jewel, I have no choice but to declare this man not guilty."

The crowd erupted into shouts. Several in the room cursed loudly at the judge's verdict. They had, after all, come to see justice done. And in their eyes, justice meant a verdict of guilty, and a hanging in the afternoon.

"Are you saying you're letting him walk free?" one man shouted.

Judge Bernard Thompkins rapped for silence. "That's exactly what I'm saying." He stood, knowing that his regal bearing and stern demeanor would have the desired calming effect. Enjoying the drama, he pointed a finger at the marshal, who looked as stunned and angry as the others. "See that this room is emptied, for the safety of the prisoner. Then unchain him. He's free to go."

Old Zeb Forrest pushed and shoved his way through the crowd until he was beside his friend. As soon as Adam's hands and feet were unbound, he thumped him affectionately on the shoulder.

"I knew you'd beat this," he muttered.

"Then you knew more than I did, old friend. Thanks for ignoring my wishes and sending for help."

Adam turned to shake Rayford Burton's hand. "I'm grateful. I can only guess how much work you dropped to come to my aid. I owe you a mighty big favor."

"No, sir," the young lawyer said. "Consider this just a small payment for the debt I owe you. Besides," he added with an embarrassed smile, "I've never participated in a murder trial before. I expected to be struck speechless. But the truth is, I felt more alive, more excited, than I can ever remember. Maybe, when I go back to Pennsylvania, I'll consider becoming a trial lawyer."

"If you ever decide to practice in Texas, you let me know," Adam Winter said. "From the looks of this hostile crowd, I may be needing your services in the future."

"Just ask. I'll be here."

The two men clasped hands again.

"Goodbye, sir," Rayford said.

"Safe journey," Adam murmured.

As Adam started to turn away, he felt fingers digging into his arm. He swiveled his head and found himself face-to-face with a furious Diamond Jewel.

"You think you got away with it, don't you?" Her eyes blazed with little points of green flame. "Well, think again, Adam Winter. If the court won't punish you, I will. I'll hound you day and night. By day, you won't be able to turn your back, or you'll find my bullet in it. By night, I'll see that you can't even sleep. If you let down your guard for even a minute, I'll make you pay for what you did to my father."

Though Adam remained icy calm, a fire came into his eyes, turning them from silver to smoke. A little muscle began working in his tightly clenched jaw. His fingers closed around her arm, and she felt the carefully controlled strength in him. It frightened her. But when she tried to back away, he dragged her close.

The moment he touched her, he felt a flare of heat and blamed it on his temper. His voice was a low rasp of fury. "Don't threaten me, Miss Jewel. And don't try to back me into a corner. If you do, you won't like what you find."

Though she trembled beneath his touch, she lifted her head defiantly. "I'm not afraid of you."

"You should be, Miss Jewel." He drew her fractionally closer, and she found herself staring into fathomless eyes. Then her gaze lowered to his lips, and she watched, mesmerized, as they curved into a dangerous smile. He caught her roughly by the shoulder.

At once she felt a rush of heat that left her shaken. How dare he put his hands on her? This dirty, unshaven, vicious killer.

"If you're wise, Miss Jewel, you'll stay as far away from me as you can."

He released her none too gently and took a step back. Rubbing her bruised arm, she backed away from him, bumping into Zeb. Startled, she nearly stumbled, but the old man steadied her. With an oath she pulled herself free of his touch and hurried away.

As she made her way through the crowd, Diamond shivered and came to a decision. She would not be frightened off by threats from Adam Winter. Despite the fact that his touch had been unsettling, she would not retreat. She would make him pay.

"Looks like you got her dander up," Zeb remarked. "Better watch out, Adam. Onyx Jewel's kitten has claws."

"That's no kitten, Zeb. That's a wildcat."

Still feeling the heat, Adam watched her walk away. His eyes remained dark with anger. But as he clenched his hands into fists at his sides, he noticed that they were none too steady.

It was merely the reaction from the trial.

It was not, he told himself sternly, because of that damnable little hellcat.

Chapter Three

Diamond stormed into the ranch house, still seething from her encounter with Adam Winter. Her hatred of him, and her determination to see him hang, had deepened with every mile. She fed the feelings, fanning the flames of hatred to blot out the pain of her loss. After all, anger was something she could deal with. But the empty hole in her heart left her numb and afraid.

As she entered her father's office, she skidded to a halt.

"Uncle Chet. What are you doing here?"

Chester Pierce came around her father's massive desk and opened his arms. "I know what you're going through, honey. I just want to make things as easy as possible for you. Your wranglers will want to be paid at the end of the month. Why don't I deduct the money from one of your accounts? You can return it to me later."

"Oh, Uncle Chet. Thank you." Warmed by his thoughtfulness, she rested her head on his shoulder. "But that isn't necessary. I've got weeks to worry about their pay."

"Suit yourself. But at least let me take your father's ledgers off your hands. A sweet girl like you shouldn't have to bother your pretty head with all those tedious details."

She felt tears sting the backs of her eyelids. As long as she had good friends like this, she would get through somehow. "Thanks, Uncle Chet." She brushed a kiss over his cheek. "But Pa taught me sums, and how to balance ledgers. I figure if I'm going to try to fill his shoes, I'd better start now."

"No one will ever fill Onyx Jewel's shoes," he said somberly.

It was the last straw for Diamond. Her eyes filled, and she latched on to Chester's arm, leading him to the front door. She had to flee before she embarrassed herself by crying in front of him.

"I'll never forget your kindness," she whispered as she gave him an affectionate hug.

She watched him stride toward his carriage. Then she flew up the stairs to her room, where she splashed cold water on her face from a basin, and began to pace. She would not give in to grief. Could not. Because if she did, it would be an admission that she was weak and helpless, and unworthy of her father's legacy. Instead, she would turn her grief into hard work. That, in Diamond's eyes, was a much more healthy outlet for these strange, wrenching emotions. And one that she understood.

Cal McCabe paced back and forth in front of the massive fireplace in Onyx Jewel's office. The ranch foreman had been summoned from the bunkhouse by Diamond, but when he arrived, the office was empty. Diamond had yet to show herself.

Just like her old man, Cal thought. He'd call you in and make you wait. And sweat.

He stalked to the window and stared out, hands jammed morosely into his pockets. He loved this place. Loved the vast, open spaces, the hard work, the camaraderie of the wranglers. Hell, he even loved the ornery, lop-eared cattle.

But he figured he was about to lose it all. Because of his damnable temper.

Onyx had always understood, but Diamond was another matter.

Sensing her presence in the room, he turned. Diamond was standing just inside the door, staring at her father's desk. She looked different, and it took Cal a moment to figure out why. Then it dawned on him. She was so still and quiet. Diamond Jewel had always been known for her vitality, her excessive energy. Her father had called her his frisky little mustang filly, always rearing, bucking, stomping, galloping. But now she stood, her whole body as still as death, while her gaze shifted from her father's desk to his boots in the corner.

She looked up to find Cal studying her, and struggled to pull herself together. "You defied my father. You publicly argued with him."

"I was defending my wranglers."

"They were Pa's wranglers, too, Cal."

"But they needed me on their side, Di. When Onyx saw that dam above Adam Winter's place, he flew into one of the blackest rages I've ever witnessed. You know how your father felt about any man who would deny another man water. It made his blood boil. He figured the dam must have been built by one of the wranglers who had a grudge against Winter. But I know my men, Di. I'd stake my life that it wasn't any of them."

She fell silent, and once again her gaze was drawn to her father's desk.

It was then that Cal noticed that her eyes were red rimmed. Why, she was close to tears. In all the years he'd worked here, he'd never seen Diamond cry. Even when she was seven and her attempt to ride her father's mean-tempered stallion had cost her a broken arm and several broken ribs, she hadn't shed a single tear. It had been up to Cal to hold her down while Doc Prentice set the arm, but she'd never made a sound. Which was more than could be said for her father, who had paced and cursed and threatened her with murder and mayhem if she ever did such a fool thing again. And then, when all her wounds had been tended and he was assured that she would mend, Onyx Jewel had gathered his little daughter into his big arms and wept.

And now she was struggling not to weep. For the father whose wounds could never be mended. For the lifetime that stretched out before her without the most important person there to share it.

For a fleeting moment Cal wished he knew how to be tender as Onyx had been. A little tenderness would probably be just the thing she needed, to realize it was all right to cry. But tenderness was alien to this Texas ranch foreman. He'd never been a father. Hell, he'd never even been in love. Being tough was all he knew. And so he cleared his throat and said gruffly, "I can be out of here in an hour, if that's what you want."

Her head came up in a challenge. "Just like that? Could you leave so easily?"

"I wouldn't like it, Di. I'd sure as hell miss this place. But if that's the order you gave, I'd have no choice but to obey, just as I'd obey your father."

Her lips pursed into a little pout, and for a moment he could see the little girl she'd been, not too many years ago.

"If I wanted you to go, I'd say so. Right now, with Pa and all . . ." She swallowed, but to her credit, her voice never wavered. ". . . I need you, Cal. And I expect you to keep me from making too many mistakes while I try to hold things together."

For the first time he relaxed, and, realizing that his hands had been clenched into tight fists at his sides, he opened them and flexed his stiff fingers. His breath came out in one long, slow stream. "You know you can always count on me, Di."

"Can I?"

He flushed, and knew that a seed of doubt had been planted by that damnable lawyer during the trial. It would take a while before Diamond was willing to trust anyone completely.

He watched as her eyes took on the familiar glint of fire. In the blink of an eye she was back in control. She took several tentative steps toward her father's desk, then turned.

"I'm not sure I agree with you about the wranglers. If Pa thought one of them was responsible for the dam, then I guess I think so, too. I expect you to find out who did it, and see that he's fired."

Cal sighed. There was no point in arguing with her right now. Besides, there was a chance, a slim chance, that she was right and one of their own wranglers was responsible. If so, he'd run him clear out of Texas.

"I'll make it my business to find out all I can."

She nodded and turned away, dismissing him. As he opened the door, she called, "Send Cookie in. We have a little matter to discuss."

"Di, maybe I'd better—"

"Now." She bit off the word just the way her father always had.

Cal left the main house and made his way to the bunkhouse. Inside, Cookie was pacing in his awkward, limping gait. A pipe was clenched tightly between his teeth.

"She wants to see you," Cal said softly.

The old man left without a word. Hat in hand, he made his way to the big house, down the hallway to Onyx's office. Not Onyx's anymore, the old man corrected himself mentally. Now it belonged to Diamond, and nothing would ever be the same again.

He knocked and entered, but after only two steps, he halted and stared.

Diamond was seated behind her father's massive desk. Though Cookie had never seen her there before, she looked as natural as though she'd been there all her life.

Without preamble she asked, "Why did Pa want you to give up the cook wagon?"

Cookie twisted the hat around and around in his stubby fingers. "Don't know, Diamond. Maybe he found somebody who could cook better'n me."

"You know that's not the reason. Tell me, Cookie." Her voice lowered, just the way Onyx's always did when he was determined to have his way. "Right now."

The old man couldn't quite meet her eyes. "My leg's been giving me more trouble than usual. Your pa found me doctorin' it out in the bunkhouse, and he decided that I'd be better off cooking in the big house, where it's always warm. Said he didn't want me sufferin' through another year of rain and wind and cold out on the trail."

"Oh, Cookie, I didn't know." Diamond started to rise, but he held out a hand to stop her. He was feeling a bit too emotional since the funeral to permit himself to accept any sympathy from this little female. Besides, he'd been around since she was born. He'd watched her grow from a filly to a mare. And right now, he was feeling as much pain as she was.

"I ain't no greenhorn that needs mollycoddling. And I ain't going to cook in no damned house, beggin' your pardon, Diamond."

"But Pa—"

His voice rose in anger. "I know your pa was trying to do what was right for me. But I know better'n anybody what's right for me. And what I need is to be out on the trail with the wranglers. And I'll tell you what I told your pa. Take me out of that chuckwagon, and I'll quit.''

Diamond didn't have the heart to remind the old man that he'd admitted his lie before the entire town. Cookie would die before he'd quit the Jewel Ranch. And now, everyone knew it.

"All right. Stay with the wranglers. But I want your word that when it gets to be too much, you'll tell me.''

His smile was radiant. "Oh, you can count on that, Diamond, honey. You'll be the first to know.'' He half turned, calling over his shoulder, "I got to go. The wranglers over by Widow's Peak are waiting for their grub.''

She nodded. "Tell Cal that I'll be gone for a couple of hours.''

Cookie thought about the fresh grave on a windswept hill, and the fact that she'd had little opportunity to grieve properly. "That's good, Diamond, honey. You go spend some time with your pa.''

After he left, she stared a moment at her father's rifle hanging above the mantel, then lifted it down, testing its weight in her hand.

"I'm going to spend some time,'' she muttered. "But not with Pa. I'm going to spend it tracking Pa's killer.''

"Sorry, Adam. I thought, with the creek flowing again, the cattle would stay put.'' Zeb shot a guilty look at the line of strays in the distance, ambling across Jewel land, foraging as they went. "I guess I should have skipped the trial and stayed here where I was needed.''

"It isn't your fault.'' Weary beyond belief, Adam tied his bedroll and hauled himself into the saddle. He'd barely taken time to eat. The beard that had grown during his time in jail itched. His clothes stuck to him like a second skin.

What he wanted was a shave, a bath and a change of clothes. What he'd have to settle for was a hard day in the saddle if he hoped to retrieve all his cows before dark.

"I'll drive the strays toward the bigger herd down by the creek. Once they discover water and range grass, they should settle down."

"Hope so. Can't get much done if we have to keep on chasing after those fool cattle every day." The old man turned back to the broken wagon wheel he'd been mending.

Adam urged his horse up a steep incline. Soon he was racing across a meadow of lush grass, determined to round up his latest strays and keep his word to a dead man.

Adam reined in his mount and watched as his cattle moved lazily ahead of him. All afternoon he'd had the strangest feeling that he was being followed. But a careful study of the trail showed no sign of a horseman. Still, he was a man who trusted his instincts. And all his instincts shouted that he wasn't alone.

Spotting nothing out of the ordinary, he turned to drink in the view. With the sun close to setting, the tips of the mountains in the distance seemed to take on a red-gold hue. The sand, even the rocks, glistened like gold. He knew he would never tire of the sight of all this untamed land. It soothed something inside him. Something wounded and raw that couldn't seem to heal.

He understood what it was that had drawn a man like Onyx Jewel to seek his fortune in this primitive place. There was room here. Room for a man, no matter what his past, to put down roots and build a life.

Roots. He shoved his hat back and wiped his forehead with his bandanna. Now, wasn't that a laugh? The last thing he wanted in his life was roots. All he wanted now was to be left alone to heal or hide as he chose. But there was no room in his life for any sort of permanence. Not now. Not ever. He'd learned to take it a day at a time.

A chill wind swept down from the north, and he drew his cowhide jacket tighter as he urged his horse into a trot behind the string of strays. He was grateful that they would soon clear Jewel property. Once they entered his own land, he could relax his guard.

Adam froze when he heard the unmistakable sound of a rifle being cocked. It was a sound that, once heard, was never forgotten. The hair on the back of his neck prickled as he adopted a lazy pose and nudged his horse behind a towering rock. As soon as he was safely concealed from view, his attitude altered. In the blink of an eye he took on the toughness of an outlaw. He pulled a small deadly knife from his boot and tensed in anticipation of the attack. A shadow of a horse and rider fell across the path. He moved with the cunning of a predator. In one swift motion he leaped, knocking the rider to the ground. They landed in a tangle of arms and legs. The two horses skittered nervously, and one ran away while their riders rolled over and over, locked in mortal combat.

As Adam pinned his opponent, his hand came into contact with a softness, a roundness, that could only be a woman's breast. In an instant all the fight went out of him.

"You!" He stared down into glittering green eyes that were brimming with hostility. His breath was coming hard and fast as he knelt up and grabbed the front of her shirt, hauling Diamond roughly to her feet beside him. "Woman, what in the hell are you doing, pulling a gun on me?"

With a sound of disgust she shoved his hand aside. Her own breathing was labored, and she struggled to form the words over the fury that threatened to choke her. For the past several hours her anger had deepened as she'd watched this hated man run his cattle over her land.

"It didn't take you long to break your word to my father, Adam Winter. His grave is barely dug and you're back driving your cattle across my land, fattening them on my grass. How many is it this time? A dozen? Two dozen? Fifty?"

"You little fool. If you've been following me, you can easily see that I'm rounding up my strays and driving them back toward my own land."

"Oh. Of course." Her voice dripped sarcasm. "I waited, and trailed you, giving you the benefit of the doubt. After all, the judge seems to think you're not guilty of anything. But if I recall, that shack you call a cabin is in the opposite direction from here. If you're driving them home, you're going the wrong way."

"I'm not driving them home. I'm driving them toward the creek, where the rest of my herd is grazing."

"Liar! You have an answer for everything, don't you? I can see that the only way to stop you is the same treatment you gave..." Without warning she uncoiled a whip that had been wrapped around her arm. In one sleek motion she swung her arm back and brought the whip down hard across Adam's shoulder.

It ripped away his sleeve, and with it, pieces of flesh, as it bit deeply into his shoulder. He swore viciously, savagely. But though the intense pain would have staggered most men, Diamond realized at once that she had met a formidable foe.

Adam caught hold of the whip and gave it a fierce tug, dragging her to her knees. In a flash he wrenched the offending weapon from her hands and stood over her. A great black rage filled him, and he flicked his arm, sending the whip snaking out behind him.

Diamond steeled herself against what was to come. But instead of retaliation, he tossed aside the weapon with a look of disgust. For long moments he stared down at her, and she could feel the tension that rippled through him.

After a moment he turned away. At once she scrambled to her feet and grabbed his arm. "This isn't over, Adam Winter. I'll never be satisfied until I've shot you in the back the same way you—"

He cut off her words abruptly by clamping a hand over her mouth and dragging her into the shadow of the rock. "Not a word. You understand?" he whispered furiously.

Her eyes widened with shock and anger. She lifted her hands to his chest to push him away. But before she could fight him, she realized what had him spooked. In her anger she'd missed the sound of hoofbeats approaching at a run.

She stopped struggling and went very still.

They stood pressed together, her hands still clutching the front of his shirt, his hand still firmly over her mouth. Their stance might have been as close as lovers, but there was a matching fire born of fury in their eyes.

"Your wranglers?" His lips were directly against her ear, and she felt a strange little shiver along her spine. It was not the nearness of this man, she told herself. It was fear, loathing. Nothing more. This dirty, unshaven trail bum was the man who had killed her father. The man who deserved only contempt.

He stared into her eyes and felt a rush of heat that left him shaken to the core. It had been a long time since he'd held a woman against his chest. Even one as angry as an untamed mustang caught in a noose. Despite the anger and the tension that hummed through him, he couldn't deny the feelings that pulsed. Her lips were soft beneath his palm. He felt the sexual jolt clear to his toes. The woman-scent of her touched something deep inside him. Something long-buried and half-forgotten.

Diamond tore her gaze from him and studied the line of horsemen, then shook her head. "I don't know those men. They aren't my wranglers."

"If you're lying..." He let the words die. Very carefully he released her. Pulling a pistol from his holster, he aimed it at the lead rider.

"Looking for me?" he called as he stepped from his place of concealment.

Diamond marveled at his fearlessness. Couldn't he see that he was one against half a dozen? If it had come from some other man, she would have believed he did it to draw attention away from her. But she refused to believe there was anything noble in what this man did. Besides, she needed no man's protection. Pulling a pistol from her boot, she stepped up beside him.

There was a string of surprised curses from the band of horsemen.

"Ride," commanded a deep voice. "We've been spotted."

At once the horsemen wheeled their mounts and raced away in a cloud of dust.

Diamond waited, expecting to see Adam Winter aim and fire at their retreating figures. If his reputation as a gunman could be believed, he would have no trouble shooting at least some of the strangers before they were out of range. But to her surprise, he merely watched until they were out of sight.

When the riders were gone, silence settled once more over the trail.

"They'll come back. And when they do, Adam Winter, I hope they leave your carcass for the wolves."

He turned back to her, and she was surprised to see the corner of his lips curl in a hint of a dangerous smile. "I thought you said they weren't your wranglers."

"They aren't."

"Then what makes you think they were trailing me?"

It took a moment before the blank look in her eyes was replaced with one of sudden realization.

"Who knows?" he added, sending a shiver along her spine. "You could just as easily be their target."

"Me!" She tried not to show the fear that had suddenly sliced through her veins like an icy blade. "Why would anyone want to kill me?"

Adam shrugged. "Why did someone kill your father?"

She was too stunned to reply.

"I guess when you learn why your father was killed, you'll have all your answers."

His words caused a flood of questions. Could Adam Winter be right? Could her life be in danger? Could her father's killer want her dead, too? But if that were so, it would mean that Adam Winter was not her father's killer. And she wasn't quite ready to accept that.

The two stared at each other for long, silent moments.

Adam holstered his gun, then bent to retrieve her fallen rifle. Noting that her horse had run off, he pulled himself into the saddle. "I'm heading to Poison Creek to see to my herd. You're welcome to ride along." He leaned down to offer a hand.

When she hesitated he said, "Suit yourself, Miss Jewel. If you'd rather walk back to your ranch..."

She shot him a hateful look. Damn the man for his arrogance. And damn him for knowing that he'd planted a seed of fear in her heart.

She wrapped the whip around her arm and saw the way his eyes narrowed. It gave her a small measure of satisfaction. At least she'd managed to inflict some pain along with a warning that she would not allow her father's death to go unavenged.

"Looks like I have no choice but to accept your generous offer." Her voice rang with sarcasm.

Accepting his hand, she pulled herself up behind him. He thrust her rifle alongside his in the boot of his saddle.

As the horse broke into a run, Diamond had two options. Hold on to Adam Winter, or risk falling.

Though she held herself stiffly, she was forced to wrap her arms around his waist. Her hand encountered the warmth of his flesh, and she felt a strange curling sensation deep inside.

Then she felt the warm trickle of his blood, from a wound she'd inflicted.

Through clenched teeth she muttered every rich, ripe curse she'd ever learned. And wondered how she would endure being this close to a man she despised.

Chapter Four

Adam seethed with fury at this strange turn of events. The last thing he wanted was to share the trail with the spoiled, temperamental daughter of the man he'd been accused of murdering.

Onyx Jewel's daughter. What a joke. She might as well be called his son. She fought like a man, dressed like a man. Hell, she even cussed like a man.

The wind whipped around them and she hunched close, pressing her cheek to his shoulder. Despite the cowhide jacket he could feel the softness of her breasts against his back, the press of her thighs to his. Not a man, came an unbidden thought. A woman. Despite the way she looked. Despite the way she talked. Despite the way she acted, she was every inch a woman. The touch of her hands at his waist had his throat going dry. The breeze flung wisps of her hair across his face, and he had the strangest urge to catch a handful and watch it sift through his fingers. Instead he grasped the reins tightly and urged his horse into a run, reminding himself that everything about this infuriating woman was repugnant to him.

As they came up over a rise, they looked down at Adam's herd, contentedly grazing on the tall grass along the banks of the creek. It was the sort of peaceful scene that never failed to stir the heart. In spite of the company he was forced to endure, in spite of the pain in his shoulder, Adam felt his spirits soar.

"Looks like they all made it."

Behind him, Diamond made a sound of surprise. "I didn't realize your herd was so large."

"Only a couple hundred head. But within a few years that could double or triple."

She heard the note of pride in his tone, and was reminded of her father's excitement each year at calving time. "Pa always took a personal interest in the calves. He used to say they were the key to a man's growth as a rancher."

"Your father was right. I'm counting on the spring calving to erase my debt to the bank."

As they drew closer to the creek, Adam reined in his mount and climbed from the saddle, then reached a hand to assist Diamond. As his hand closed over hers she felt the jolt. What was wrong with her? Why was she allowing this man's touch to shatter her cool control? She must be coming down with a chill. It was the only reasonable explanation.

She slid to the ground and turned away quickly, pretending to study the last rays of the sun as it dropped below the distant mountain peaks. "It'll be dark soon. Now that you've assured yourself that your cattle are back on your own land, I'd like to get back to my ranch."

Adam frowned. "I hadn't expected all those... delays along the trail." He saw the flush that touched her cheeks as he shot her a meaningful look. It gave him a measure of satisfaction. It seemed only fair that she accept some of the responsibility for what had happened back there. "I've decided not to leave the cattle alone here tonight. Those wranglers could pay another visit. And if they do, my cows are an easy target."

"Are you saying you're planning to spend the night here?"

"It looks like I have no choice."

She stuck her hands on her hips in a familiar gesture of defiance. "But what about me?"

His features never altered. But she thought she saw a flash of wicked humor in his eyes. "You're free to go. It can't be more than a couple of hours back to your ranch on foot." The smile grew until it almost reached his eyes. "If you'd like to stay, you're free to share my beans and biscuits, Miss Jewel. And my bedroll."

"How dare—" She bit back the angry words that were bursting to break free. When Pa had been alive, no wrangler would have dared to make a suggestive comment in her presence. He would have been fired on the spot. She'd felt so safe, so insulated, that she had been almost able to forget the fact that her sex was different from that of the other wranglers. With Pa's protection, she'd been free to ride the range, sleep under the stars, and work among the men without fear. Now, suddenly, she had something new to worry about. Something extremely unsettling.

It was another reason to hate Adam Winter.

He thought he'd have his revenge, did he? Well, she would show him that he couldn't frighten a Jewel. She would die before she'd give him the satisfaction of knowing that he held the upper hand.

In her sweetest voice she said, "How considerate of you, Mr. Winter. But I'm sure that once my horse returns to the ranch, Cal McCabe will have a dozen wranglers out searching for me. You can keep your beans. Carmelita's been aging a side of beef for supper. And as tempting as your bedroll sounds, I'd much prefer to sleep in my own bed tonight. Alone."

She spun away to escape this disgusting man, and climbed to the highest rock, eager for a glimpse of Cal and the wranglers who would be out searching for her. It would be only a matter of time until they spotted the campfire. She'd see how cool Adam Winter was when he was surrounded by dozens of her men.

For the first hour, she studied the countryside for any sign of her men and nurtured the hope that they would arrive at any minute. As she sat alone, the realization of her dilemma grew. She couldn't possibly spend the night here with Adam Winter. Maybe she should start out on foot, in the hopes of being picked up along the way by her wranglers. But if they didn't spot her in the darkness, she would have a long, painful walk home. And somewhere in the darkness was that band of strangers.

Finally, when darkness overtook the land, she was forced to concede that her wranglers weren't coming. Defeated, she climbed down from her perch and made her way to the campfire.

Adam was sprawled comfortably on his bedroll, his head pillowed on his saddle. He'd tied a bandanna around his shoulder to stem the blood.

Beans bubbled over the fire, causing her mouth to water.

"Hungry?" He didn't bother to open his eyes, which only added to her anger.

"A little." She eyed a tin of biscuits. "Did you bake those?"

"Yep. They're not bad, if you scrape off the burned bottoms."

"If you weren't planning on spending the night along the trail, how did you happen to have all this?"

"I've learned to carry everything I need in my bedroll. Flour, sugar, tobacco, whiskey." His eyes were still closed.

"Tobacco and whiskey." Her voice revealed her disdain. "I can see that a man like you wouldn't need much more than that."

He knew that she was trying to goad him into a fight. He didn't bother to take the bait. He was too weary.

"Why?" she asked more softly, dropping to the ground beside him.

"Why what?" He opened one eye and studied her.

"Why do you carry everything with you?"

"I've learned to be prepared for anything. If my cabin burns to the ground and my cattle are stolen, I'll still have all I need right here."

"Sounds like a man who's learned to expect the worst."

He sat up and began filling a tin plate with beans and biscuits, which he passed to her. "I've already seen the worst, Miss Jewel."

"But—"

"You talk too much. Just eat."

She didn't need any coaxing. As she took the first bite, she sighed with pleasure. She was too hungry to care that the biscuits were burned.

"I apologize that I don't have a side of aged beef, ma'am." Beside her, Adam took a long pull of whiskey from a bottle.

She ignored his barb. "You aren't eating?"

"You've got the only plate."

A grin touched her lips. "I thought you were prepared for anything."

"I guess life still has a few surprises to throw at me. I wasn't expecting company to share my campfire."

With a twinge of guilt she finished quickly, then passed the empty plate to him. "Here. Enjoy. I recommend the burned biscuits."

He ate his fill, then handed her a cup of steaming coffee. When she returned the empty cup to him, he filled it for himself and drank.

The sharing of plate and cup was an oddly intimate gesture. One that had her feeling awkward and self-conscious.

If Adam noticed, he gave no indication. Content, replete, he sat back and rolled himself a cigarette. Watching his hands as he expertly shook tobacco into a paper and sealed it, Diamond felt a sudden shaft of pain around her heart.

"Pa always rolled a smoke after supper. Then we'd just sit and..."

Adam could hear the catch in her voice, and remained silent, respecting her grief.

After a long pause he said, "It sounds like you and your father were closer than most."

She nodded, grateful that he'd given her time to compose herself. "From the time I was just a kid, Pa always took me with him on the trail. With a spread this size, we spent as much time in the saddle as we did at home. He never made me feel like I was in the way, or that I was too little to help. He always assigned tasks for me, and always praised me when I did them the way he wanted. Oh." A sigh welled up from deep inside her. "Those were the best times."

Adam stared into the flames of the fire, a pensive look on his face. He drew deeply on his cigarette and held his silence.

Diamond drew in a long breath. "I wish I'd told him," she said softly.

Adam turned his head.

She glanced at him, then away, but not before he saw the glitter of a single drop of moisture on her lashes. She blinked it away fiercely, embarrassed by this weakness.

"Fathers don't have to be told. They know." Adam took one last drag on his cigarette, then tossed the remains into the fire.

Standing, he shook out his bedroll. At once, an uneasiness came into Diamond's eyes.

Seeing it, he handed her the blankets and said, "Looks like your wranglers aren't coming to your rescue. Since you're stuck here, you'd best stay close to the campfire. From the bite of that wind, I'd say it's going to freeze tonight."

"What about you?"

He drew on his jacket and lifted his rifle. "I think I'll keep an eye out for visitors."

"I—" She swallowed and forged ahead, determined to say what was on her mind "—want you to know that just because you shared your food and bedroll with me, nothing has changed between us."

He pinned her with a look. "I didn't realize there was anything between us, Miss Jewel."

She chose to ignore the dry edge of humor in his tone. "Oh, but there is. Unfinished business. Even though the judge dismissed the charges against you, I still don't believe you. And until I'm convinced otherwise, I'll go right on believing that you killed my father."

He said nothing in his own defense. But she saw a hardness come into his eyes.

She watched as he strode into the darkness. For a few minutes she sat, staring into the flames. All she could hear echoing in her mind were his words meant to soothe. *Fathers don't have to be told. They know.*

The depth of Adam Winter's understanding had been unexpected. And disturbing. After all, he was still the only suspect in her father's murder. And if he was the one who'd pulled the trigger, he had no right to go on living. But if he wasn't . . .

"Oh, Pa," she whispered. "I'm so confused. I miss you so much. I wish you were here to tell me what to do."

Rolling herself into Adam Winter's bedroll, she listened to the sounds of the night. For as long as she could remember, she'd been comforted by these sounds. The lowing of cattle. The occasional howling of a coyote. The cry of a night bird. It was the music of Texas. A melody that stirred her heart and soothed her pain.

She found herself thinking about Adam Winter. What a strange man he was. Despite all her misgivings, he'd been as comfortable as a pair of old boots. Well, not exactly, she corrected herself. Whenever he got too close, she felt a distinct, uneasy stirring deep inside. An unsettling feeling that had her palms sweating, and her heart beating overtime. Maybe it was because he was a killer. Or maybe it was . . . something else. Something she couldn't quite put a name to.

She checked her rifle to be certain it was loaded, then placed it beside her in the bedroll. Just in case.

At last, tired in mind and body, lulled by the food and the warmth of the fire, she slept.

Diamond smiled at the lovely images in her dream. Pa was holding her hand, telling her it was all a mistake. He'd only left her for a little while. But now he was back. And she'd never be alone again. He'd help her work her way through the puzzle. He'd give her all the answers.

Without warning his image faded, and instead of Pa, she was staring into the smoldering eyes of Adam Winter. His lips were moving but the words made no sense. He seemed to be furious and out of control.

"No," she called out, rolling to one side, fumbling for her rifle. "Leave me alone."

He swore again, viciously. Before she could react he scooped her up, rifle and all, and began running. With every step she fought him, her arms flailing helplessly against his chest.

She felt a wave of pure terror. She was a strong woman, accustomed to taking care of herself. She'd always been able to rely on her skill with a gun and her ability to fight like a man. But she had never felt such strength in an opponent before. Despite the fact that she kicked and bit, twisted and turned, he never faltered as he half dragged, half carried her into the darkness.

Her mind was reeling. She was in the clutches of a madman. What had happened to send him over the edge? And why now, in the middle of the night?

Just as abruptly as the strange attack had begun, it ended when Adam dumped her unceremoniously on the hard ground.

Now she was fully awake. It was her turn to swear. Unleashing a string of oaths, she scrambled to her feet and caught him roughly by the arm. "Are you crazy? What in the—?"

Before she could finish, the night air was shattered by the sound of gunfire. She whirled and watched from the cover of darkness as the bedroll where she'd been sleeping was riddled with bullets.

"Who? What . . . ?" She wasn't even aware that she was clutching Adam's arm so hard her nails bit into his flesh.

As suddenly as the volley of gunfire began, it ended. In the eerie stillness that followed, a figure strode into the circle of light and kicked at the blankets. Finding them empty, he swore and called out something unintelligible. At once several more figures appeared.

"It looks like our gunmen are back. And this time they mean business." Adam tossed Diamond her rifle. "Get out of here. Take my horse and head for the safety of your ranch. And don't look back."

She watched in stunned disbelief as he stepped out of his place of concealment, effectively drawing attention away from her so that she could escape. " 'Evening, gentlemen."

His voice was as cold as ice. Diamond thought she had never heard anything so chilling.

"How nice of you to come calling. But you should have warned me. I hate surprises."

One of the men lifted his rifle and took aim, but before he could fire, Adam shot the weapon from his hand and sent him diving into the dirt.

Diamond stifled a gasp. The rumors she'd heard were true. Adam Winter was a fearless, cold-blooded killer. His hand had moved so quickly, she would have missed it if she'd blinked.

"I'd advise the rest of you to drop your guns." Adam continued walking closer.

Two more men took aim. Refusing to play it safe or back down, Adam stood straight and tall and without hesitation dropped the first one in his tracks. Before he could aim again, a single gunshot was heard and the second gunman pitched forward.

Another gunman, the leader of the group, aimed a pistol at Adam.

Adam kept on walking. "You might get off a shot in time," he said in that dangerously calm voice, "but then again, you might not." He came to a halt just a few feet away. "Are you a gambling man?"

"Not me," the gunman called, tossing aside his weapon and lifting his hands in a signal of surrender. "I only play sure things." His fear suddenly turned to relief as he stared past Adam and watched two shadows emerging from the darkness. "But right now," he said with a mocking laugh, "I'm sure of one thing. Unless you drop that gun, my partner will have to slit the lovely lady's throat. You wouldn't want that, would you?"

Adam whirled. A man dragged Diamond into the circle of firelight. One muscular arm was wrapped around her waist. At her throat he held the blade of a knife.

"Drop the gun," the stranger shouted, "or the woman dies."

Adam felt a trickle of perspiration. The gunman could be bluffing. This whole scene could have been set up by Onyx Jewel's daughter. Was this her way of seeking revenge? Had she lied earlier when she'd told him these men weren't her wranglers? The thought was immediately erased by the sight of the mangled bedroll. No matter who paid these men, they'd intended to kill the person asleep by the fire. And they had no way of knowing whether it was Adam or Diamond.

Whatever the outcome, he had no choice now but to see this thing through.

"Looks like you'll have to choose your victim," he said through gritted teeth. He saw the look that came into Diamond's eyes, and knew that she was both pained and enraged by his words. There was no chance to explain.

The gunman was clearly shocked. "You're willing to sacrifice the lady?"

Adam shrugged. "The choice is yours. Release her, and we'll talk. But if you harm the woman, there won't be time for talk. You'll be dead."

"He's bluffing," the other gunman shouted. "And even if he isn't, you can use her as a shield until you get to your horse. He can't shoot both of us. Come on. Move."

Adam showed absolutely no emotion as he stepped closer. "You listen to him, you won't walk away." Compelling gray eyes narrowed on the man. "How about it, stranger? Ready to risk your life?"

"My partner's right." Sweat streamed down the gunman's face. "You're bluffing." He pressed the blade of his knife to his hostage's throat until a small trickle of blood stained her shirt. Diamond whimpered as the blade sliced her flesh and pain flashed, white hot, through her.

Something dark and dangerous came into Adam's eyes. "You just sealed your fate," he said through clenched teeth. And as calmly as if he were taking target practice, he aimed his gun and fired.

The sound of the explosion roared inside Diamond's head and she waited for death to claim her. So this is what her father had felt. This searing pain, and then the darkness. She felt the arm at her waist go slack. At the same moment, the gunman began to pitch forward. Adam wrenched her free and pulled her aside, just as her captor fell to the dirt.

A horse whinnied and Adam whirled and fired, but the bullet missed the leader, who was dragging himself into the saddle. His horse took off in a cloud of dust.

Adam swore, then turned back to Diamond.

"What . . . ?" It took a moment for her to realize that she wasn't dead. At least not yet. She was amazed at how hard it was to speak. Her heart was still working overtime, the echo of it throbbing in her temples. She tried again. "What did you think you were doing?"

"Saving your miserable neck."

"Saving it! You told him to go ahead and kill me. And when his knife didn't finish me . . ." She gave a sound of disgust. "For a minute I thought you were going to shoot me instead of him."

He couldn't resist taunting her. "I'll admit, I did think about it. It took me a while to decide which one was the bad guy."

"But you just shot. As calmly as though..." Her eyes flashed fire. "You could have killed me."

"I had to move quickly, before his partner got a chance to go for his gun. Then we would have both been dead. Besides—" his look darkened "—you have no cause for complaint, Miss Jewel. As you recall, I told you to get out of here. If you'd done as you were told, you'd be halfway to your ranch by now, and I wouldn't have been forced to shoot all these men before I found out what they were after."

The short fuse on her temper matched his. "Listen, Adam Winter. You'd better get it through your head that I don't take orders. I give them. And if you think I'd run like a scared little rabbit from a gunfight, you can think again. My father taught me to shoot a rifle better than most men. And fight better, too."

Adam turned away from her in disgust. Once again this sharp-tongued female was bound and determined to have the last word. Because of her, he'd missed his chance to learn who these men were and why they'd attacked.

He circled the campfire, bending to each man to check for a pulse. Dead. All of them. And not one left to tell him what he wanted to know.

He turned back in time to see Diamond sinking slowly to her knees in the dirt. All the color had drained from her face.

She pressed a hand to her fevered brow. What in the world, she thought dazedly. This had never happened to her before. Through a blur she watched as Adam hurried over to kneel beside her.

"What's...wrong? What's...happening?" Her own voice seemed to fade in and out.

"I think you're about to faint, Miss Jewel."

"That's ridiculous." She was clearly outraged at the suggestion. "I've never fainted in my life."

With a muttered oath he tossed aside his rifle and began to tear away her shirt. "Let me see that wound."

"How dare—!" She brought her hand up to stop him, and found, to her consternation, that she was as weak as a kitten. Her hand was trembling so violently, she couldn't even make a fist.

He removed his bandanna and tied it gently around her neck.

"How bad...?"

"Could you just lie still for a minute and keep your mouth shut? Or is that too much to ask?"

She was surprised by the warmth and the gentleness of his touch.

"Stop fussing. It's nothing but..a little scratch," she protested.

"Um-hmm." He continued tying. When he was through he said, "I think we'll forget about staying with the herd. What you need is a warm bed and some of Zeb's hot stew. Come on. I'm taking you to my cabin."

"No. I...can't. Want to go...home."

Ignoring her protest, he lifted her in his arms and carried her to his horse. And hoped that he wouldn't have to listen to her litany of complaints all the way home.

But Diamond was beyond caring. She had already done the unthinkable. She had slipped into a dark, swirling tide of unconsciousness.

Chapter Five

Adam cradled the unconscious Diamond against his chest and held his horse to a slow, easy pace. He didn't like that jagged line of blood along her throat. Or her unnatural pallor.

Anger bubbled, hot and furious, within him. What in the hell was the matter with her? The damned ornery, obstinate little female almost got herself killed. Did she have a death wish?

Suddenly he remembered a fact that had, until this moment, escaped him. Or at least, until this moment, he'd had little time to sort it out. During the exchange of bullets, there had been one shot that hadn't been fired from his rifle. Yet all of the gunmen had fallen. That could only mean... His hand tightened at her shoulder. It had to mean that Diamond had remained, not merely to defy him, but to join him in the gunfight.

She'd saved his hide. But why, when only hours earlier, she'd tried to shoot him in the back?

Fool, he thought. He touched a hand to her pale cheek and allowed his fingers to linger a moment on the soft skin. Little fool.

He became aware of the heat of her body warming his own. Soon it became heat of another kind.

He was achingly aware of the woman in his arms and blamed it on the unusual circumstances. The gunfight, the sense of impending danger, had heightened his senses. That was why he was beginning to notice little things that had escaped his detection earlier. Like the fact that her skin, despite the harsh Texas sun, was as soft as a baby's. In the spill of moonlight he studied a sprinkle of freckles that paraded across her nose, and wondered if there might be more freckles on other...more intimate parts of her body. That caused his gaze to move lower, to the soft swell straining beneath her shirt. Heat stirred in his loins, and he forced himself to look away. But within moments his gaze was drawn back to her. To the tiny waist, looking incongruous with the heavy masculine gun belt encircling it. For all her tough talk and mannish swagger, she was softly curved in all the right places. He studied the way her hair fell over one eye in a most seductive fashion. There was so much about a woman he'd forgotten....

Suddenly he nudged his horse into a run. Now, more than ever, he wanted to get her to his cabin. Zeb was there. The old man would help him keep his mind off this damnable female and on more sensible things.

As he neared the cabin, he saw a dark silhouette rise up from the wagon bed and knew that Zeb had heard their approach. The old man leveled a rifle and peered through the darkness.

"It's all right. It's me," Adam called out.

At once the old man lowered his weapon and climbed down. "Good thing you called out a warning. I'm feeling a bit jumpy tonight."

Adam's voice took on a sharp edge. "Why? Did something happen while I was gone?"

Zeb shrugged. "Bunch of wranglers from the Jewel Ranch came by looking for their lady boss. Said her horse returned without her." He moved closer as Adam slid to the ground, cradling the woman against his chest. "Looks like you found her first."

Seeing that she was unconscious, he managed to hold back the questions that sprang to his lips as he walked ahead to hold open the cabin door. His questions would have to wait until later.

Adam strode inside and deposited Diamond on the bed.

"I'll need some warm water," he called. "And a clean cloth. And whiskey for her wound."

Zeb poured water from a blackened kettle into a small basin and set it on a bedside table, then found rags and a bottle of whiskey in a cupboard.

He peered over Adam's shoulder as the bandanna was removed, and sucked in his breath at the sight of the wound. "You going to tell me what happened?" he demanded.

"Gunmen attacked us in the night. Riddled my bedroll with bullets."

"Us." The old man studied his friend's bowed head as Adam washed away the blood. "You and the lady boss were sharing a bedroll?"

"You know me better than that," Adam said angrily.

Zeb chuckled. "Well, now, I don't know. She's a woman. You're a man. And you've been alone a long time now."

"If I wanted to ease the loneliness, I wouldn't choose a prickly wildcat with claws that could tear out my heart. Besides, have you forgotten? She's the daughter of the man I was accused of shooting."

"Hell," the old man cackled. "If you live as long as I have, you won't be surprised by anything that happens in this crazy world."

He waited a moment, watching as his friend poured whiskey onto a cloth and pressed it to her throat.

At the first contact Diamond gasped and pushed his hand away while she let out a string of oaths.

"Looks like that brought her around," Zeb said. "Sure can cuss, can't she?"

Diamond's lids flickered, and she stared up at the two pairs of eyes peering down at her. Her gaze fastened on steely eyes that were quickly becoming familiar. "What did you do to me now, Adam Winter? I feel like my throat is on fire."

"I think I liked you better when you were unconscious," he said dryly as he pressed the cloth to her throat again.

She gave a hiss of pain and glanced beyond him to Zeb. "Can't you stop him? He's trying to finish the job those gunmen started."

The old man shot her a reassuring smile. "He's just cleaning that wound, little lady. I know it stings, but Adam doesn't want to take any chances."

"A shame to waste good whiskey," Adam added. "But I wouldn't want to have your foreman accusing me of not doing all I could."

She grabbed at his hand. "I should have known you weren't doing all this out of the goodness of your heart."

He felt a rush of heat at the touch of her. "You can count on that." He stood abruptly and handed the cloth to Zeb. "Here, old man. See that she's made comfortable. I think I've had enough of her hissing and spitting for one night."

"Where're you headed?" Zeb called as Adam stormed across the cabin.

Adam didn't bother to reply. Instead he wrapped a blanket around his shoulders and stretched out on a rug in front of the fire. Within minutes he was sound asleep.

With the touch of her still warm on his hand.

"Here, little lady boss." Zeb plumped up the pillows and eased Diamond into a sitting position before handing her a steaming cup.

"What's in this?" She studied the liquid with suspicion.

"Just a splash of whiskey in some coffee. It'll ease the pain a bit and maybe help you sleep."

"I don't want to sleep. I want to go home."

The old man heard the note of weariness in her voice and knew that it wouldn't be long before she'd give in to the need to sleep.

"Adam will take you just as soon as he's had a chance to rest." He glanced at the blanket-clad figure stretched out in front of the fire. "He's been through a lot today."

"No more than he deserves. He should hang for what he did to my father."

"He didn't kill your pa, ma'am."

"And how would you know that?"

"Because I know Adam. If he disagreed with a man, he'd do it face-to-face. Adam has too much honor to ever shoot a man in the back." His voice lowered. "Besides, Adam's the fastest man with a gun that I've ever seen. He doesn't need to try any tricks. The man isn't alive who ever beat Adam Winter to the draw. And that's a fact."

She shivered, remembering the determined look in Adam's eyes when he'd faced the gunmen. Even though he'd been outnumbered, he'd never backed down. She felt a trickle of fear just thinking about the change in him. The look in his eyes had been that of a gunslinger, not a rancher.

Needing to talk, she told Zeb about the gunfight, and about the way Adam had reacted when her attacker had threatened to kill her. "He told him to go ahead. He refused to drop his gun."

"That was just a bluff," Zeb said softly. "The way Adam's mind works, he was buying a little time while he figured a way to save your life and his own."

"Maybe. Or maybe he's just a fool. My pa taught me to handle a gun. And I'm good at it," she said with a trace of

pride. "But he also taught me a healthy respect for anyone
who drew first. Adam Winter wasn't even smart enough to
be afraid."

Zeb chuckled. "Yep. That's Adam. Point a gun at him,
or threaten those he cares about, and he's a changed man.
But he doesn't go looking for trouble. Fact is, he'd rather be
left alone. Doesn't have much use for people these days.
Except me," he added with a twinkle in his eye. "And
sometimes I'm not even sure about that."

"Why would you bother with a man like that?"

"Adam's worth the bother." The old man poured a cup
for himself and eased into a rough wooden chair beside the
bunk. "He's a good friend," he stated simply.

"How long have you known him?" she asked as she
sipped her coffee.

"Six, seven years." He blew into his cup before he drank.

"That's not very long."

He gave her an appraising look before he said, "Long
enough to take the measure of a man. And Adam Winter
measures up better'n most."

"I suppose you have to defend him. After all, you work
for him."

Zeb looked up in surprise. "You think Adam pays me?"

"Doesn't he?"

He grinned, showing crooked teeth. "I don't work for
Adam, little lady boss."

"Then what are you doing here?"

He shrugged. "I'm just along for the ride."

She frowned. "I don't understand."

"Got nowhere else to be right now. So I offered to help
Adam get started. But he knows that one day he'll wake up
to find me gone. That's just the way I am. Can't stand
houses or walls or fences. And when I sleep, I like to sleep

under the stars and breathe air that's free. Don't ever want to answer to anyone else."

"And Adam Winter?" she asked as she drained her cup. "Is he like you?"

Zeb combed a hand through his beard. "Maybe. Can't say that Adam's like anyone else I ever knew. Been footloose a long time now. Tough for a man like that to settle down. And life's hardened him. But if anyone deserves to find a piece of land that he can call home, it's Adam."

Diamond's lids closed and her head bobbed, causing her to jerk upright. Seeing it, the old man drew a blanket around her shoulders and took the cup from her hand. He peered at the whip wrapped around her arm, then decided to leave it alone. "You sleep now, lady boss. You got some healing to do."

She had no energy left to argue. She was asleep before the old man let himself out of the cabin.

Adam moved soundlessly around the room, filling the kettle with water from a bucket, putting another log on the fire. But his gaze kept straying to where sunlight spilled through the small window of the shack, bathing the sleeping figure in a pool of liquid gold.

Seeing Diamond asleep in his bed bothered him much more than he cared to admit. He felt restless this morning, ill at ease. Tense and edgy and grouchy as a wounded bear.

He swore and tore his gaze from the woman. He needed to be busy.

Soon the aroma of coffee filled the air and he snatched up a square of linen before heading toward the creek.

Diamond stirred. Disoriented, she lay very still, sorting out the strange new sounds and smells. This wasn't her bed, nor was this her comfortable ranch house.

Realization dawned slowly. Adam Winter's cabin. She touched a hand to her throat. Though it was still tender, the torn flesh had formed a crust that would soon heal over.

Adam was standing across the room. Since he hadn't yet noticed that she was awake, she used the time to study him.

Dark pants rode low on his hips and molded his thighs. He was naked to the waist, and had evidently just finished bathing in the creek, since droplets of water still glistened in his dark hair. A straight razor made scraping sounds as he ran it across his cheeks and chin in smooth, easy motions. With each movement, the muscles of his back and shoulders bunched and tightened, causing a funny feeling in the pit of her stomach.

The shock of her injury must have made her fanciful. Though she had drifted in and out of consciousness during the ride here last night, she could recall the way she'd felt in his arms, warm and snug and...safe. And the way his heartbeat had kept time to hers, slow and steady and... reassuring. Those weren't the kinds of feelings she'd expected to experience with a man like Adam Winter. She must have been more dazed than she'd thought.

She forced her gaze upward. And realized that he was looking at her in the mirror.

The jolt was as powerful as if she'd been thrown from a wild mustang. For the space of several moments she couldn't breathe. Her heart forgot to beat.

He was frowning. But that was nothing new. He seemed to be always frowning around her. He didn't bother to turn around. "'Morning, Miss Jewel. How's your throat?"

Dry, at the moment. But she wouldn't admit that. "A little sore. But it's tolerable."

"Zeb left you some ointment. It's on the mantel. And I made coffee. It's strong, but it's hot. Help yourself."

She swung her feet to the floor and waited for a brief moment of dizzyness to pass. Glancing up, she could see him still watching her in the mirror. His eyes seemed lighter, almost silver this morning, and she blamed it on the brilliant sunlight. She got to her feet and, straightening her spine, crossed the room.

She applied the ointment, then tied Adam's bandanna around her neck. She cast a sideways glance at the man who was studying her in the mirror. She wasn't accustomed to being watched. Especially by a man like Adam Winter. She felt suddenly shy and self-conscious. Like a filly at an auction. And slightly light-headed. Something she'd never experienced before.

She took a few moments to study her surroundings. This wasn't at all what she'd expected. Though the cabin was small and sparsely furnished, it was neat and clean. Comfortable. That was the first word that came to mind. From the handmade quilt on the bed to the animal furs that softened the rough wooden floor and walls, from the child's wooden top to the dog-eared Bible on the shelf, it had a cozy feeling about it.

Tools leaned against a bench just inside the door. A knife, a saw, a wood shaver. And beside them lay a half-finished rocking chair that would be the match to the one in front of the fire.

It was apparent that Adam Winter was not one to be idle.

She wrapped a linen square around her hand and lifted the blackened pot from the fire. As she poured, she called, "Care for some?"

"Yes. Thanks." He wiped the last of the soap from his face and pulled on a clean shirt. As he was tucking it into his waistband, he turned. She found herself staring. Again she was forced to look away. But not before she'd had a glimpse of a hair-roughened chest and flat stomach that caused another uncomfortable feeling deep inside.

She handed him the steaming cup. As their fingers brushed she felt the warmth of heat all the way to her toes. She knew that her cheeks were probably flushed. That only made her blush all the more.

"Hungry?" he asked.

"A little." She was relieved when he turned away. But she would have been distressed if she'd known just how much her presence was affecting him.

"There's venison stew." He ladled some from a pot that sat on a warming ledge over the fire. "And yesterday's biscuits."

Diamond took a seat at the table and watched as he sat across from her. "Who does the cooking, you or Zeb?"

"We take turns." He enjoyed the sound of her voice. It was low, with a hint of breathlessness that whispered across his senses. He realized that all morning, while she'd slept, he'd been waiting to hear her speak.

"How about you, Miss Jewel? Are you a good cook?"

She shrugged her shoulders. "I've never tried, but I'm sure I'd be terrible."

"Never cooked?" He set down his cup and fixed her with a look. "You mean you and your mother never spent any time together in the kitchen?"

"I don't remember my ma. She died when I was just a baby. And Cookie has always been around to see that Pa and I had enough to eat."

"What do you do when Cookie is out on the trail?"

"I'm usually out with him," she admitted. Why was she telling him all this? She couldn't imagine sitting and talking with any other man this way. But with Adam Winter, it seemed the most natural thing in the world. She was practically babbling, and couldn't seem to stop herself. "We have a woman from town, Carmelita, who helps out at the ranch. She sees to it that I don't starve.''

"From the looks of you, I'd say you're a long way from starving."

The intimate way he studied her brought another flush to her cheeks. She looked down, fiddling with her spoon.

She forced herself to taste the stew and gave a sigh of pleasure. "Oh, this is good. Who made it?"

"I did. I prefer my cooking to Zeb's. All he really likes is meat cooked like shoe leather, and biscuits that could pass for cannon shot."

Despite her misgivings about being alone with Adam Winter, Diamond found herself chuckling.

Adam leaned back, sipping hot coffee. Her laughter was such a pleasing sound. He'd forgotten how musical a woman's voice could be. He'd forgotten too much about a woman. The smell, the touch, the taste...

"Zeb told me he doesn't work for you."

"That's right. He works with me. Although at times, I'd have to say he works against me."

Again her laughter, warm and lilting.

"He seems... colorful. He told me he doesn't like walls or fences."

"Or rules," Adam added. "Old Zeb says rules are for breaking."

"How about you?" Feeling stronger now, more relaxed than she had in days, Diamond carried the empty dishes to a basin of water and began to wash them. "Do you like to break the rules, too?"

"I guess in my lifetime I've broken most of them."

She was startled by the nearness of that deep, haunting voice. While her back was turned he'd walked up beside her and picked up a square of linen to dry the dishes. She felt a prickly feeling along her scalp, and scolded herself for her skittishness.

As she lifted another plate from the water, she was aware that her hand was trembling. She prayed that Adam wouldn't notice.

"So, you break all the rules. What good would rules be if everyone felt like you?"

"I guess . . ." Very deliberately he took the plate from her hand and set it down, all the while holding her gaze with his. He reached up and caught a strand of her hair, allowing it to sift through his fingers. It was something he'd wanted to do since he'd first seen that hair, all long and loose, spilling down her back in a riot of fiery curls. And it had been worth waiting for. It was every bit as soft, as silky, as he'd expected. "They'd have to write new rules."

At his look, his touch, Diamond's throat went dry and her heart began a wild dance.

All her life she'd been around men. She worked with them, rode with them. Was comfortable with them. But she'd never known a man like Adam Winter. And she'd never had a man touch her like this. As though she were soft and feminine and . . . beautiful.

She saw the way his gaze moved over her mouth, and knew, in that moment, that he was going to kiss her. His hand suddenly fisted in her hair. She lifted wet soapy hands to his chest, as if to hold him at bay. But he took no notice as he lowered his mouth to hers.

It was the merest whisper of his lips on hers, a slow, languid brushing of mouth to mouth. But she reacted as though she'd been burned. She would have pushed away, except that his hands closed over her shoulders, holding her still. And then, as his lips moved on hers, she was lost in a jumble of strange new feelings.

His kiss was easy, practiced. He tasted of horses and leather, with a tang of tobacco. Dark, mysterious tastes that had her blood heating and her heartbeat racing. There was so much strength in the hands that held her. A strength made all the more fascinating because she could sense the control he exerted. As though she were a fragile flower that would be crushed unless he took great care. It was an intoxicating, dizzying feeling.

"Why, Miss Jewel. It looks like—" his mouth moved ever-so-slightly against her lips, forming the words "—you're not accustomed to being kissed by a man."

"How dare—!"

He cut off her protest by increasing the pressure against her lips.

Her kiss was awkward. Uncomfortable. She fairly trembled beneath his touch. Her lips quivered under his.

She tasted wild and sweet and clean. As untouched as the snow that capped the distant mountains. His first thought was that he'd like to go on kissing her like this all morning, until she lost her fear and learned to savor, to enjoy. Oh, the things he could teach her.

His hand tightened at her shoulder and he deepened the kiss.

At once he realized his mistake. What the hell had he been thinking of? She wasn't just some sweet, unspoiled female. She was Onyx Jewel's daughter. And all that innocence was . . . a trap.

Suddenly he found that he couldn't think at all. The touch of her lips, so soft and cool, had crowded all thought from his mind. All he could do was feel.

Feelings long-buried came rushing back, and with them, the pain.

Oh, God, how could he have forgotten, even for a moment, the pain?

As abruptly as the kiss had started, it ended. Adam lifted his head and took a step back, breaking contact. His hands remained at her shoulders a moment longer as he struggled to compose himself.

There were so many things he'd forgotten. But it was just as well. It was dangerous remembering. Right now, he was remembering how desperately he could want.

Anger rose up, replacing all other feelings. Anger at himself for his carelessness. Anger at her, just for being.

Of all the women in the world, the last one he could ever desire was Diamond Jewel.

Chapter Six

Diamond took several deep breaths, grateful for Adam's hands on her shoulders. Without his support, she would probably have staggered.

It seemed very important that she not let him see how deeply his kiss had affected her. As he stared down at her, she felt compelled to say something to cover her awkwardness. But she could not bring herself to mention what they had just shared. It was too intimate. Too deeply personal. And she was in a state of total confusion.

Instead, she blurted the first thing that came to mind. "I want you to know that I never had any intention of shooting you in the back."

Adam regarded her in silence, though he had to dig deeply to bite back the smile that threatened. Did she have any idea how she looked, with her lips still moist and swollen from his kiss, her eyes too big for her face? Did she not understand how appealing she was? She was as open, as artless, as a child. And every one of those jumbled emotions she was experiencing was clearly visible in her eyes.

As he studied her, her face flamed and she lowered her gaze. "I was just going to let you know that I was following you . . ." She was babbling, she knew, but she couldn't seem to stop herself. It was better than standing here, feeling thoroughly confused and...thoroughly kissed. "By firing a warning shot."

He reached a hand to the bandanna at her throat, fingering the knotted ends, and felt the slight tremble she couldn't hide. It gave him a strange feeling to see his bandanna against her skin. Strange and...unsettling. "That would have been a mistake, Miss Jewel."

Her head came up sharply. "Why?"

"Because I don't take kindly to gunshots."

"But you were on my property...."

"And I don't take kindly to being followed. Oh, you were very good," he continued smoothly. "Though I sensed you, I never spotted you."

She felt a rush of warmth at his unexpected compliment. "Then how...?"

"You cocked your rifle. It's a sound I've heard too many times to ignore. And it almost cost you your life. I have a habit of returning gunfire with gunfire. And I rarely miss."

Suddenly the warmth of the kiss they'd just shared evaporated. Why had she wasted her time trying to explain herself to this infuriating man? He had managed to turn her words into another argument.

"I'd like to go home now."

"With pleasure, ma'am." He dropped his hand and took a step away. He was as eager to be rid of her as she was to leave. "I'll hitch the team. Zeb will take you in the wagon." And good riddance, he thought.

As he turned, he heard the sound of horses approaching, hard and fast. He caught up a rifle beside the door and said tersely, "Take cover."

Though her heart beat a little faster when she remembered last night's gunfight, she refused to heed his warning. Instead, she removed her pistol from the holster and joined him in the doorway.

Dust rose up in a cloud as dozens of horsemen thundered up to the little cabin. In the lead was Cal McCabe. His features were as dark as storm clouds.

When he spotted Diamond, he signaled to his men, who aimed their rifles at the man beside her.

"Drop your weapon and step aside, Winter," Cal shouted.

Just then Zeb came around the corner of the cabin and leveled a rifle on the foreman.

"Drop it, old man," Cal ordered. "You're outnumbered."

"Maybe," Zeb said, "but I'd like to raise the odds just a little. If I have to die, I'll take you and a few of your men with me."

"Cover him," Cal commanded his wranglers.

"I'll remind you that you're on my land," Adam said in an ominously calm tone.

"You bastard." Cal's eyes narrowed with fury. "If you've hurt her..."

"It's all right, Cal." Diamond holstered her gun. "We didn't know it was you coming. We expected trouble."

As she started out the door, Cal leaped from the saddle and covered the distance between them in a few hurried steps. He caught her by the arm, drawing her roughly behind him, protecting her with his own body.

"Cal, put the gun away. You don't understand," Diamond began, but her foreman was beyond hearing. Even as relief poured through him, his blood ran hot for revenge.

"Keep them both covered," he ordered his men. "Throw down your gun now, Winter. I won't give you another warning." To Diamond he said, "I'll send for the marshal. Adam Winter isn't going to get away with anything a second time."

"You'd better stop shouting orders and take the time to listen to the lady," Adam warned him. "The law says I have the right to protect myself. Especially on my own property. And right now, McCabe, you and your men are trespassing. That gives me the right to shoot first and ask questions later."

"I'd kill you right now," Cal interrupted, "but this time I want it all legal and correct, so that we're done with you once and for all, Winter. It's the way Onyx would have wanted it."

"Cal," Diamond called sharply as she finally managed to wriggle free of his grasp. "Listen to me."

Her commanding tone finally broke through his fury. Her foreman dragged his icy gaze from Adam to look at her.

"Adam Winter didn't do anything wrong. In fact, he saved my life." She stepped between the two men, who steadfastly refused to lower their weapons.

"Saved your life?" Cal McCabe looked from Diamond to Adam, and then back again. "What happened?"

"Last night we were attacked by gunmen."

"Gunmen!" His jaw clenched. "What gunmen?"

"Strangers. I've never seen them before. And I don't know what they were after. Five of them are dead. Up on the banks of Poison Creek. The sixth, the leader, got away."

"That's odd," he said, still regarding Adam. "We've been out searching all night, and we never passed any strangers on the trail."

"Are you calling the lady a liar?" Adam asked.

"I'm saying—"

"Enough." Diamond gave a sigh of exasperation. "Cal, I'm sorry that you spent the night looking for me."

"You know we'd go to hell and back for you, Di."

She placed a hand on Cal's arm, feeling her own tension dissipate. After last night's attack, she'd become suspicious of everyone. And that was dangerous. She needed her friends. And she needed to trust once again. "There was no way to get word to you."

Cal closed a hand over hers. "I'm just relieved that you're all right." He peered down into her eyes. "You really are all right? I mean, he didn't hurt you . . . in any way?"

Diamond felt the heat that began at the base of her throat and inched its way to her cheeks. Cal's concern was almost as deep as if he were her pa. She feared that if he looked too closely, he'd be able to see the change in her. Did a woman's skin glow, or her eyes shine, when she'd just shared a kiss with a man? Oh, she sincerely hoped not. But she'd had no experience in such matters.

"I'm fine. Really."

Cal looked up at Adam. "Sorry I misjudged you, Winter. I'd like to offer my thanks."

He stuck out his hand and Adam was forced to accept it. But each man continued to regard the other with guarded hostility.

"I'll need you to ride to town with us and file a report with the marshal." Cal lowered his rifle.

Adam nodded and lowered his own weapon. Turning to Zeb he called, "I'll probably be gone most of the day. After I deal with the marshal, I intend to ride out to the herd and make sure everything's all right."

He pulled himself into the saddle.

Diamond waited while Cal led her horse forward. As she mounted, she gave a long, deep sigh of relief. At least, for the moment, Cal McCabe and Adam Winter weren't about to kill each other.

But it was a tense, uneasy truce.

And a long way from any sort of peace.

The ride to town was the longest Diamond had ever endured. With Cal on one side of her and Adam on the other,

the air was charged with an electric current. Even the wranglers, sensing the hostility between the foreman and Adam
Winter, rode in silence. Despite the fact that Diamond had
been safely returned, there was no celebration. There was,
instead, a brooding sense that a killer rode in their midst.

Now that she was once more in her element, riding with
her men, she found herself replaying in her mind the incident in Adam's cabin. How could she have been so weak
and foolish? It wasn't at all like her to allow herself to be
manipulated by a man. And yet, that's exactly what had
happened. For a few brief moments, she had lost her common sense. It had been a momentary lapse. A mistake. But
it was over now. She was back in control. And she would
never allow such a thing to happen again.

They rode into town, past the stable and blacksmith's
shop, past Durfee's Mercantile, until they reined in their
mounts at the marshal's office.

Cal, Diamond and Adam dismounted and went inside,
trailed by the wranglers.

"Gunmen, you say?" Marshal Quent Regan listened to
Diamond's story in stony silence. He scraped back his chair
and leaned his palms flat down on the desktop, so that his
gaze was level with hers as she sat facing him. "And you
didn't recognize any of them?"

"Not a one."

He swiveled his gaze to Adam and narrowed his eyes. The
truth was, he still didn't trust this stranger. After all, someone had shot Onyx Jewel. Despite the judge's verdict, Quent
Regan had his doubts about Adam Winter's innocence.
"And you, Winter? You've never seen these men before?"

Adam shook his head. Since his arrival with Diamond
and her wranglers, he'd said not a word. Why bother? He

knew what the marshal thought about him. As well as every man in this room.

"Think harder," Marshal Regan prodded. "Maybe you had a run-in with them in some other town. Maybe in your travels before you settled here in Hanging Tree, you made an enemy. And that enemy now wants to even the score."

Adam met his look. "Maybe."

"Then you think they were after you, and Diamond just happened to be in the way?"

"I didn't say that."

Marshal Regan looked astonished. "Are you saying they were after Diamond?"

Adam gave a negligent shrug of his shoulders. "I didn't say that, either."

Some of the marshal's careful control began to slip. "Look, Winter. Just tell me what you know."

"I know they were hired guns."

The marshal straightened. "How would you know that?"

Adam showed no emotion. "They knew exactly where they were headed, and what they were supposed to do. Now, if they were hired to do away with me, it could be as you said. An old enemy who wants to even the score. If so, he'll do what he came here to do, and then leave. But if they were hired to do away with Onyx's daughter, then it means you've got a killer right here in your town. And when it's over, he won't be going anywhere."

The marshal bristled at the thought of someone in his town capable of such a despicable act. Still, he couldn't help seeing in his mind's eye the body of Onyx Jewel on the banks of Poison Creek. He'd been shot, point-blank, at close range. There was no doubt that there was a killer around. But one of the townspeople?

"Any names come to mind?" the marshal asked.

Again that infuriating shrug. "They didn't leave a calling card. And they didn't mention any names."

Marshal Regan's eyes narrowed. Adam Winter was a cool one. Too cool.

"Arlo," he called to his deputy. "Take a wagon out to Poison Creek and bring back those bodies. The rest of us are going to wait right here."

Two figures stood in the shadowy cave and stared down at the bodies littering the banks of Poison Creek.

"Six against two." The voice was a fierce whisper. "And the only ones who died are the ones who took my money. How do you explain this?"

The gunman flushed. "You told us this would be easy. We figured we'd just walk in and do the job. We weren't expecting a gun battle."

"Weren't expecting . . . !" There was a sudden, ominous silence. "For the money I paid you, I had the right to expect results. I hope you were smart enough to remove my money out of their pockets. They won't be needing it."

The gunman reached into his pocket and retrieved a handful of bills. "I've got it right here."

It was snatched roughly from his hand. After it was carefully counted, the shadowy figure said, "Remember, you won't see another dollar until I get what I paid for."

Horse and rider turned and were gone.

Despite the cold wind, the gunman realized he was sweating. He'd taken money for a variety of different crimes, including murder. But for the first time in his life, he'd felt that he was in the presence of evil.

The marshal was grim faced as he examined the bodies. The men were young, lean, tough. And, as Adam Winter had said, they had the look of professional gunmen. With the help of the deputy and several wranglers, the bodies were removed from the wagon and placed side by side in the marshal's office.

Marshal Regan turned to Diamond. "You didn't say how you happened to be at Poison Creek."

It was the question she had dreaded. And one she'd evaded from the beginning.

"I was out riding on the north ridge."

"Why?" the marshal asked.

"I—" she licked her lips "—needed to get away from the ranch house. And I came across Adam Winter driving some strays."

Marshal Regan's eyes narrowed. "Winter was on your property? In violation of his agreement?"

"Actually, he was trying to live up to his agreement. His cattle had strayed and he was driving them home. So I . . . began riding a short distance behind him." She felt her cheeks flush and refused to glance at Adam Winter. "Then, suddenly, we startled these gunmen, who were apparently trailing us, and they took off in the opposite direction."

"If they were trailing you, how did they overtake you?"

"We were stopped." Diamond's mind was racing. How was she going to explain this without lying? She hated lies. But now that she had told a single little one, she found herself mired in them.

Adam remained silent. This was Diamond's story. He'd let her tell it any way she pleased. Besides, he was beginning to enjoy himself. It was obvious that the lady was squirming.

"Stopped? Why?" Marshal Regan glanced from Diamond to Adam.

Diamond's foreman and wranglers did the same.

"I . . . fell off my horse."

"You fell!" Cal couldn't hide his astonishment.

"That's what I said. I fell." She put her hands on her hips and turned on her foreman. "What's wrong with that?"

"Nothing." He backed up a step at the murderous look in her eyes. "It's just that in all the years I've known you, Di, it took the toughest, meanest, wildest mustang to toss you out of the saddle. And Sunrise, why, she's just about the gentlest saddle horse we have."

Diamond was stuck with her lie. In her most commanding tones she said, "I guess something spooked her. The next thing I knew, I was on the ground and Sunrise had run off. Adam Winter offered to let me ride with him, but he explained that he was heading to Poison Creek. I didn't see that I had any other choice but to accept his offer."

"So, you went to Poison Creek to deliver strays. Then you must have been returning to your ranch when you were attacked," the marshal said.

"Not exactly."

"Where were you?" he asked with a sigh of impatience.

"On the bank of the creek. Lying . . . sitting by the campfire," she amended, grateful that Adam had left his bullet-riddled bedroll back at his cabin.

"You were lucky you weren't hit," Cal McCabe said softly.

"I would have been if Adam hadn't heard the horsemen coming and carried me off to the safety of some bushes."

Everyone turned to study Adam. The last thing they wanted to hear was that their suspicions about this mysterious man were wrong.

"And neither of you got hurt in the gunfight?"

"Just a little cut." Diamond felt her cheeks flush bright pink. Oh, she was no good at this lying business. Adam's bandanna suddenly felt like a noose around her neck. "One of the gunmen caught me and threatened to slit my throat if Adam didn't throw down his gun."

Cal McCabe swore. "The bastard. I'd like to get my hands on him. Did he hurt you?"

"Just a little cut."

"How did you get away from him?" the marshal asked.

"Adam called his bluff. And shot him before he could carry out his threat. But in all the confusion, the leader managed to get away."

"So, Winter, I guess you're a hero now," Marshal Regan said dryly. The word stuck in his throat.

Adam shook his head. "I just did what I had to to survive."

"Uh-huh." The marshal turned away, unconvinced. There was more here than either of them was admitting. And he hated loose ends. "You can go, Winter. For now."

He'd already decided to have Doc Prentice go over these bodies very carefully. After all, Adam Winter had already admitted shooting these men. If any of those wounds matched the ones in Onyx Jewel's body, he'd pay another visit to Adam Winter's ranch. And this time, hero or no hero, the town would have its hanging.

Adam stood and waited while Diamond and her foreman walked from the office, trailed by their wranglers. Pulling on his hat, he made his way to where his horse was tied to the hitching post. He looked up as the stagecoach rolled to a stop in a cloud of dust.

Small clusters of townspeople began to gather around in anticipation of the mail and supplies carried by the stage. The driver jumped down and held the door for a single passenger.

A young woman caught the driver's hand and stepped lightly from the coach. She wore a dark traveling coat in the latest fashion. The gown, which could be glimpsed beneath it, was palest pink. She hurriedly opened a pink parasol to shield her pale skin from the sun. In this rough Western town, where the inhabitants sported drab homespun clothes and leathery skin chafed by wind and sun, she made an impressive picture. A figure that was slender as a young willow. Hair the color of wheat. Cornflower eyes in the face of a porcelain angel.

"Please be careful with those trunks," she called in a cultured Eastern accent.

"Yes, ma'am." The driver lowered a trunk and a tapestry valise and piled them on the wooden walkway, out of the way of horses and wagons. "Will you be staying here in town?"

"I'm not sure." She glanced around uncertainly, then said, "Perhaps you could tell me where to hire a rig. I'd like to visit the Jewel Ranch."

At her words, Diamond paused, and all her men came to a halt behind her.

Adam, too, paused in the act of pulling himself into the saddle.

"I couldn't help overhearing." Diamond crossed the dusty patch of road and said with a smile, "My name's Diamond Jewel. I'm the owner of the Jewel Ranch. What could you possibly want out at my place?"

"Hello." The young woman returned the smile and offered her gloved hand. "I'm Pearl."

"Welcome to Hanging Tree, Pearl. What brings you to Texas?"

"Oh, dear." The young woman lifted one gloved hand to her mouth to stifle her little exclamation of alarm. "I can see that you don't know about me. I guess Daddy never mentioned me."

"Daddy?" Diamond stared at her without comprehension.

"I guess I should explain. My full name is Pearl Jewel."

"Jewel . . . ? But that's my . . ." Diamond's puzzled smile began to fade.

Before she could say more, the young woman continued. "I read in the Boston paper about the death of Onyx Jewel. He was my father. And I've come to pay my respects at his grave."

Chapter Seven

Dozens of townspeople had stopped in their tracks. Already there were little gasps of surprise, and murmurs of shock and disapproval. A crowd, hungry for more details, was beginning to close in around the two young women.

Diamond felt as if all the air had left her lungs. She couldn't breathe. Onyx Jewel's daughter? Impossible. That would make this cool, beautiful creature her...

A lie. It was all an elaborate lie. Pa. Pa would never...

With as much indignation as she could muster she managed to say, "I'm sure a great many people read about my father's death. And I would suppose the lure of quick money would bring a few fortune hunters to our town. But I assure you, Miss..." She couldn't bring herself to call this evil creature by the name she claimed. "I assure you, my father was an honorable man who had but one heir. Now, I bid you goodbye. I'm sorry you came all this way for nothing."

She turned away, clutching Cal McCabe's arm so tightly her nails dug into his flesh.

"I'm so sorry," came the cultured voice as Diamond mounted her horse. "I realize now that this must be a great shock to you, just as mention of your name in the newspaper was a shock to me. You must believe that I never intended to cause you pain. I have no interest in your ranch or fortune. But I cannot deny my birthright. I am a Jewel. Onyx Jewel was my daddy. I was overcome with grief at the announcement of his death. And I ask nothing more of you than the chance to visit his final resting place and pay my respects."

"You ask too much." Diamond stared down from the saddle like a queen from her throne. "He was my pa. Mine," she called with a catch in her voice. "For all my life, he was all I had. And I will not share him with you. Or with anyone. Especially now that he cannot be here to defend himself against such horrible lies."

"Please. I would not lie about something as sacred as my daddy. You must reconsider. I've come so far. And I will not leave until I've had a chance to visit Daddy's grave."

Diamond's tone hardened, as did the look in her eyes. "Stop calling him your daddy."

"But he was—"

"I can't force you to leave this town. But I'm warning you. If you so much as set foot on my property, I'll have you shot. Is that clear?"

Without a word the young woman lifted her head in a haughty gesture and met Diamond's harsh look.

At that moment, Adam Winter, watching from a short distance away, found himself amazed at the similarity between the two. Though their coloring was completely different, as was their manner of dress, there was something about that regal bearing, and the way each lifted her chin in defiance of the other.

"Well, what are you gawking at? Come on, Cal." Diamond and her wranglers urged their horses into a gallop, leaving the town and its curious, muttering occupants in their dust.

When the dust settled, Adam watched as the young woman picked up her valise and started walking. As she passed him, she compressed her lips together to keep them from trembling.

He nudged his horse into an easy gait. A smile split his lips. It had been one hell of a day, and it was only half-over.

He glanced back, to see the young woman disappear inside a boardinghouse at the edge of town. It looked like Onyx Jewel's chicken had come home to roost. And wasn't going to leave until she accomplished what she had come here to do.

Adam wondered if the town of Hanging Tree was big enough for two Jewels. Especially when one of them was a handful like Diamond. And the other was, for now, a complete mystery.

Adam brought his horse to a pause atop a ridge and cast one last look at his herd, peacefully grazing on the banks of Poison Creek. It was difficult to imagine this beautiful land harboring so much hatred and violence. But then, he'd known another time when the beautiful, peaceful hills of his beloved Maryland had run red with blood. Father against son. Brother against brother.

He wouldn't allow himself to think about the past. There was still too much pain. Instead, he would concentrate on a bright future. Next spring, with the calving, he could be, if not wealthy, at least solvent. And the year after that...

He spotted a cloud of dust in the distance and strained to see what caused it. After a few minutes it became clear. A small carriage, pulled by a single horse, was heading toward the Jewel Ranch. Even from this distance, he could make out the flutter of a pink gown, and the ridiculous pink parasol.

A smile touched his lips. Pearl Jewel had decided to ignore Diamond's threat, and was about to pay a call.

Wouldn't he love to watch that display of fireworks?

As he started to turn his mount toward home, he spotted, out of the corner of his eye, another cloud of dust. This one was much bigger.

He turned. And muttered a savage oath.

Several dozen wranglers rode in two columns toward the approaching rig. In their lead was a similarly dressed wrangler, whose fiery hair streamed behind her like a red flag.

Adam wheeled his stallion and spurred him into a run. He had to stop this nonsense before someone got hurt.

Straining at the bit, his horse ate up the distance, until he pulled up beside the rig. Pearl looked up in surprise and drew back on the reins. "If Diamond Jewel sent you to stop me—"

"No, ma'am." He wiped a sleeve across his sweaty forehead, grateful that he'd reached her in time. "I spotted you from that ridge and thought I'd better warn you. Diamond and her men are just over that hill. And they're headed this way. If you'd like, I'll escort you back to town."

She studied him for a moment. "Didn't I see you in town this morning?"

"Yes, ma'am. My name's Adam Winter."

"It's very nice to meet you, Mr. Winter. I am Pearl Jewel. And I thank you for your warning, and your kind offer. But I have no intention of turning back."

"But that could be dangerous—"

"Good day." She flicked the reins and the horse broke into a trot.

Adam kept pace alongside her. "Mind if I ride along?"

She peered at him from beneath her parasol. "Whatever for?"

"I've had a taste of Diamond's temper. I don't think you know what you're doing."

"I know exactly what I'm doing, Mr. Winter."

"Adam," he corrected her.

She smiled then. "Adam. As I told Diamond, I have no intention of leaving until I visit my daddy's grave. And no one, not even Diamond and all her wranglers, can stop me."

Adam had his doubts about that, but decided to keep his thoughts to himself.

As they came up over the top of the hill, they looked down on a solid wall of mounted wranglers, with rifles drawn. In their midst was Diamond. When she spotted Adam, her eyes flashed fire.

"So, this is how you plan to have your revenge, Adam Winter," she called. "By butting into other people's business. You should stick to your own problems. You have more than enough without taking on any more."

"You're right about that. But somebody has to try and knock some sense into that thick head of yours." He looked beyond her to her foreman. "What's the matter with you, McCabe? Haven't you told her that she can't simply shoot this young woman and walk away?"

"I've tried," Cal McCabe said tiredly. "But Di refuses to listen to me."

"And why can't I shoot her?" Diamond shouted. "She's trespassing. As I recall, you threatened much the same thing earlier today, when Cal McCabe and my wranglers rode up to your cabin. I'm entirely within my rights. And this time, there'll be no question. The whole town already heard me warn this . . . person to stay off my property."

Adam nudged his horse closer, until Diamond lifted her rifle and pressed it to his chest, holding him at bay. They sat astride their horses, facing each other.

Despite the anger that throbbed through her veins, Diamond felt her pulse accelerate at the nearness of him. Damn the man for whatever it was that caused this strange reaction in her.

"I'm not interested in how you'll justify this to the town," Adam said softly. "I'm here to remind you that if you carry out your threat, you'll have to live with the fact that you were responsible for the death of your father's daughter."

"Liar." Diamond's voice rose, and with it her temper. At this moment, she felt her fury slipping out of control. Fury with Adam for interfering. For taking sides. It was, she reminded herself, one more reason to hate him. "That woman is lying. She's not my father's daughter. And if you choose to believe her, you're a fool."

"You're the fool if you react in haste, Diamond. There are laws, even here in Hanging Tree. And lawyers and judges to see that justice is carried out."

"Oh, I'm aware of that," she said through clenched teeth. "I saw what the law and the judge did to my father's killer. Now, get out of my way, Adam Winter." She waved the rifle, but he refused to budge.

"For once in your life, stop and think before you act. How would you feel if you shot now, and discovered later that she was telling the truth?"

Diamond sent him a hateful look.

"I have proof of my claim." Pearl's voice, cool, composed, caused everyone to turn and stare at her. "And I would be happy to share it."

She opened the tapestry valise and withdrew a paper, then stepped from the rig and held it out to Diamond.

"And what is this?" Diamond's voice was filled with contempt as she slid from the saddle to confront this impostor.

"A document certifying my birth, and the names of my parents."

"Forged," Diamond scoffed, without even bothering to look at it. "Anyone with ink and paper can draw up a document. It doesn't mean a thing."

"There is more." Pearl removed several papers from the valise.

"What are these? More lies?"

"Letters. From my daddy to me." She thrust them toward Diamond. "I'm sure you'll recognize his handwriting."

Diamond snatched them toward her, eager to prove the lie. But when she caught sight of her father's large, scrawling script on the first page, she dropped it as though burned. "I will not dignify these forgeries by reading them." She tossed the letters down without another glance.

But the damage had been done; the seed of knowledge planted. And with it, the growing fear that there might be a kernel of truth in what this young woman was saying.

She watched as Pearl bent and retrieved the letters, brushing the sand from the pages as she did.

"I wish you had never come here," Diamond whispered. "I wish you would just go away and..." She stopped, her gaze arrested by the glint of something at Pearl's throat. A breeze ruffled the neckline of the pale pink gown, revealing a rope of gold, holding two stones side by side, one black, one a perfect luminous pearl.

"Oh, no." The words were torn from her lips.

"What?" Pearl pressed a hand to her throat in a gesture of alarm. "What is it? What has happened?"

"Your...necklace." With trembling fingers Diamond unfastened her rough plaid shirt. Nestled between her breasts was a similar rope of gold. On it were two stones, side by side. A black onyx, and a perfect, glittering diamond. "It was a gift from Pa when I turned sixteen."

Pearl lifted her necklace and touched it to her lips. "Mine also was a gift from Daddy for my sixteenth birthday."

Daddy. The word grated.

"Daddy told me that the necklace would remind me that he would always be at my side."

"Pa said the same thing to me." Confused, hurt, angry, and still desperate to deny what she sensed now was the truth, Diamond spun away and pulled herself into the saddle. She needed to put some distance between herself and this ... person.

"I'll allow you a quick visit to Pa's grave. And then I expect you to leave and never return. Is that understood?"

Pearl stared up at the haughty young woman, then nodded. As she climbed back into the rig and lifted the reins, she glanced toward the wall of silent wranglers, still holding their rifles. Then she turned toward Adam. In this whole vast land called Texas, he was the only one who had shown her the least kindness.

"I would like Adam Winter to go along."

Diamond's eyes glittered with suspicion. "Why?"

"Because I trust him."

"It figures. One skunk always sniffs out another." Diamond wheeled her mount. "Let's go," she called abruptly. "I want to be home by dark."

She and her wranglers started out at a fast pace.

"I hope you don't mind, Mr. Winter."

"Adam," he corrected her. "And no. I don't mind at all. I'm just glad I was able to slow things down awhile." He lifted a hand to shade the slanting sun from his eyes. "You'd better get moving. It looks like Diamond is in a hurry to be done with this."

Pearl had to whip her horse to catch up with the fast-moving horsemen. They made their way over hills, down gullies, across dry washes that during the rainy season would be swollen and overflowing. And then they paused on a barren, windswept hill. The mound of earth was still fresh. It had been topped off with several boulders. There was nothing else to mark the spot where Onyx Jewel lay.

Adam Winter helped Pearl from the rig, then stepped back to allow her to grieve in privacy. But as he turned away, he caught sight of the horror in her eyes. To an educated young woman from Boston, accustomed to ornate cathedrals and carefully manicured cemeteries filled with statuary and comforting signs of faith, this unmarked grave in the middle of a barren wilderness would seem uncivilized. Primitive.

He glanced at Diamond, who sat astride her horse, trying vainly not to look at the young woman who knelt in the dust. But when a cry was torn from Pearl's lips, it was obvious that a knife had twisted in Diamond's heart.

"Oh, Daddy," Pearl cried aloud. "I cannot bear the thought of you in this place. You deserved better." She touched a hand to the rough stones that marked the grave. "My heart is broken at the knowledge that I'll never see you again. Or hear your wonderful, deep laughter. I can't bear the thought that I'll never again be held in your warm embrace."

With a shiver of recognition, Diamond could hear her own voice saying the same words, although she had never spoken them aloud. But they were her words, her emotions. And they scraped against her already raw wounds.

She slid from the saddle and took a step closer, then stopped as Pearl moaned. "Oh, how cruel, that life should take first my mother, and now you, Daddy. I feel so alone. So helpless against what has happened. I'm angry. And I'm sad. And most of all, I'm frightened. Yes. Frightened. Even though I hardly ever saw you, you were the most important person in my world. Bigger even than life. Like bright sunlight piercing the darkness. Each time you came to me in Boston, my world became bright and wonderful. And I foolishly believed you would always be here for me. Now there is no more light or laughter. Now there is only..." Her voice broke, and she fell into a fit of sobbing.

Moved, Diamond stepped up beside her and awkwardly touched a hand to her shoulder. She felt Pearl stiffen at her touch.

"I . . . I know how you feel."

Pearl shook her head and said between sobs, "No one can know how I feel. It is as though the light has gone out of my world. Daddy was my rock, my anchor. I dreamed of him each night. Waited each day for his letters. He was the most important person in my life."

"Yes." Diamond's lips began to tremble and she immediately bit them until she tasted blood. "I know. We did everything together. Whenever he left on one of his buying trips, it was as though the world stopped. Then, when he returned, my life would begin again."

Pearl nodded. "Exactly. He could make me laugh when I was sad."

"Or when I was angry," Diamond added. "He used to say I inherited his quick temper, along with his love of horses and guns. But Pa could always tease me out of my temper."

"He had a wonderful laugh." Pearl felt a fresh round of pain as her throat tightened, and she swallowed back a sob.

"And so much strength." Diamond felt tears well up. But she would not permit them to spill over, to stream down her cheeks as Pearl's did. That was a weakness that a city-bred woman like Pearl could afford. But to a Texan there was no room for tears. "I feel like a stray caught in the hills during a snowstorm. And there's no one to rescue me. And no way to get back to the safety of my herd."

Amazingly, Pearl nodded, understanding completely. She squeezed Diamond's hand. "Since news of Daddy's death, I've felt lost and afraid. I know it makes no sense. I'm an educated woman. A teacher. I'm old enough to make my own way. But the word *orphan* strikes terror in my heart and I feel . . . Oh, I feel . . ."

A sob was torn from her lips, and Diamond answered with a heart-wrenching sigh. But something in her perverse nature would not permit her to give in to what she considered a weakness. She would not, could not, cry.

With Adam and the wranglers looking on in silence, the two young women turned toward each other at the same moment, opening their arms and coming together in a fierce embrace.

For Pearl, it was as though a dam had burst. She wept, openly, unselfconsciously. And all the while, Diamond murmured words meant to soothe. But each word thrust fresh pain through her heart. And each word brought a fresh round of sobbing from the young woman in her arms.

Pearl's tears flowed freely until there were none left. For the first time, Diamond spoke the words she'd held inside until now. It was as though, with this kindred spirit, she was free to speak what had been carefully hidden in her heart.

"I loved him with all my heart and soul. There will never be another like Pa."

Pearl nodded.

At last, cleansed, spent, they stepped apart.

They knelt side by side, and each young woman touched a hand to the soft earth. Their lips moved in silent words to the man who had meant everything in the world to them.

"I know Pa's burial site mustn't seem like much to a fine lady like you. But this was one of his favorite places." Diamond's voice held a trace of reverence. "He used to say that from here he could see for miles. And everything he saw belonged to him. The mountains, the hills, the creek, the sand, the cattle. But most of all, the land he loved."

"Then I'm glad you chose this spot for his final resting place," Pearl said softly. "In years to come it will be a comfort to me to know that Daddy is in a place he loved."

They fell silent again, each lost in private thoughts.

"If you don't mind, I would like to leave something here. Something very personal, that I know Daddy would have loved."

Pearl withdrew from her pocket a scrolled paper, tied with a pale ribbon.

"My diploma," she said. "Daddy would have been so proud. I want this to remain here with him."

She scraped away a little of the dirt and lay the scroll down, before anchoring it with earth.

At last, as if by mutual consent, Pearl and Diamond stood and, after one last glance at the grave, turned away.

Pearl glanced skyward and took note of the smudges of crimson that streaked the sky. "It's growing late. I had better return to Mrs. Potter's boardinghouse. If I linger much longer, I'll lose my way back."

"You're staying at Mrs. Potter's?" With the back of her hand Diamond wiped at a stray speck of moisture that had slipped, unbidden, from her eye.

Pearl nodded.

"Why don't you come back to the ranch?" Even as the words spilled from her mouth, Diamond regretted them. What in the world had happened to her common sense? She was shocked by her lapse. But, she reasoned, Pa would approve. And somehow, that thought gave her great comfort at the moment.

Pearl was equally shocked. "It isn't necessary to invite me into your home. That is not the reason I came to Texas. I came only to visit Daddy's grave, and to pay him a final respect."

"I know. And I'm glad now that you had your wish. But I'd like you to come home with me. Besides," Diamond added sheepishly, "I hate to eat alone."

"Really? So do I," Pearl admitted. Despite the tears that still clung to her lashes, she managed a smile. "I wonder if we will discover other things we have in common."

"I . . . doubt it." Diamond glanced at this immaculately groomed young woman, so unlike herself.

Suddenly, the two women seemed ill at ease. This very intimate scene they had just shared was over. They were, once again, two strangers bound by a single thread.

Diamond pulled herself into the saddle and glanced at Cal McCabe and her wranglers, aware that they had been allowed to glimpse something far too private and personal. "Well, what are you waiting for? Let's get started toward home. Cal, send one of the men into town for Pearl's bags."

She turned a last contemptuous glance at Adam, resenting the fact that he, too, had witnessed her private grief.

She seemed about to say something, then thought better about it and clamped her mouth shut. She'd tell him what she thought about him another time. For now, she would give him a wide berth. And hope he would do the same for her.

Adam helped Pearl into the rig. When she was seated she cast him a sideways glance.

"Thank you for intervening on my behalf, Adam. And for staying. It was very kind of you."

He mounted his stallion and tipped his hat to her. "You're welcome, Pearl. I hope you and Diamond take the time to get to know each other."

"Why?" she asked softly.

He glanced at the line of horsemen, and their leader, her spine stiff, her head lifted in that defiant pose. Already the haughty arrogance she wore like protective armor was back in place. "I think it's what your father would have wanted."

At the mention of her father, Pearl fought back the tears that threatened to blind her. With a nod, she flicked the reins and the horse and rig moved ahead.

Adam held his mount still, watching the strange procession winding its way toward the ranch house in the distance. He'd been right earlier, he thought. It had been quite a day. But for these two intriguing young women, it was far from over.

Chapter Eight

"**I** guess we could take our coffee over by the fire."

Supper was finished, and Carmelita had returned to her own little ranch with her husband, Rosario, leaving the two young women alone. And feeling stiff and awkward.

Diamond led the way across the room to a sofa flanking a large blackened fireplace, where a log blazed. Nudging off her boots, she lifted her feet to the hearth and gave a sigh.

Beside her, Pearl sat primly, her feet crossed at the ankles, her cup balanced delicately on her knees.

During their meal the conversation had been stilted and polite. Each had carefully skirted the edges of the topic that dominated their thoughts. But Onyx Jewel was clearly on the minds of both his daughters.

"It was nice of Mr. Winter to intervene for me today," Pearl said conversationally.

"You mean interfere."

Pearl heard the emotion that crept into Diamond's tone. "You don't approve of Adam Winter?"

"I don't trust him."

"Why?"

"He was accused of killing Pa."

"Oh." Pearl brought a hand to her mouth and looked stunned. "But if he killed Daddy, why is he still free?"

"He was found not guilty during his trial."

"Then he's innocent."

"I didn't say innocent," Diamond said bluntly. "I said not guilty." As briefly as possible she told Pearl about the trial, and the judge's verdict. Then, almost reluctantly, she added the details of how Adam had saved her life. "But in my eyes that doesn't mean a thing," she said. "I still have my suspicions about Adam Winter."

"His actions don't seem to be those of a killer. And I hope, not only for your sake, but for Daddy's, that the killer is found soon." Pearl sipped her tea and contemplated for long moments. "As for Mr. Winter, I thought he was a perfect gentleman."

Gentleman. The word grated. Diamond thought about the way he'd kissed her. She was pretty sure it wasn't a gentleman's kiss. Feeling a strange flutter in the pit of her stomach, she decided to change the subject.

"Tell me about your life in Boston." Diamond turned to study the young woman beside her.

"It's very ordinary." Pearl kept her gaze on the fire. "I live in a small, neat house with a lovely white fence. Whenever Daddy came to visit he..." Realizing how painful this must be for Diamond, her voice trailed off for a moment.

Beside her, Diamond sucked in a breath at the pain. Her father had kept a very important part of his life secret. Why? To spare her feelings, she surmised. But hadn't he known that one day the truth would come out and she would be hurt by it?

To cover the awkwardness Pearl continued, "There are many shops nearby. A seamstress, a hatmaker, a shoemaker, a fish market and several other markets where each day I buy what I need for my meals."

Her words pulled Diamond out of her painful reverie. "It sounds so strange. I can't imagine looking out my window and seeing shops and houses, and people walking along a street." She shook her head. "I don't think I'd like it at all."

"Mama loved Boston. Daddy talked about his life in the West, and I often used to daydream about joining him. But Mama warned me that I would probably wither and die in Texas. She said that it was a vast, lonely place, with few people one could call friends."

"Now that you've seen it, do you agree?" Diamond asked.

"Oh, no. Not at all. This part of the country takes my breath away. The mountains, the plains, the exotic rock formations. And the people, so open, so willing to say exactly what is on their minds." She sighed. "It is like no other place on earth."

Her words pleased Diamond. She tried to imagine what it must look like to this Boston woman. But it was impossible. She had no way to compare Texas with the rest of the world. To her, this was the only world.

"Mama was afraid, I think," Pearl said softly.

"Afraid of what?"

"Of losing me to the allure of Daddy's life. She knew I was enchanted by his stories of Texas. And so she reminded me that in Boston there are always friends to call upon when one is lonely. And lovely teas and parties."

"Is that all you do in Boston?" Diamond's eyes widened in surprise. "Go to teas and parties?"

"Of course not." Pearl laughed, and Diamond found herself warming to the sound. "I'm hoping soon to find work. Like my mother, I've studied at a school for young ladies, and I intend to become a teacher."

"School?" Diamond swiveled her head to stare at Pearl. "You studied at a ladies' school? What's it like?"

"It is a very large building, with the upper rooms used for dormitories. The lower rooms are used for classes. Many of the young ladies during my term came from far away and boarded there. But because I lived in town, I was allowed to go home each evening.''

''What did you study?''

''English, mathematics, history, biology. And a smattering of other sciences. And, of course, comportment. Most of the young ladies were expected to marry wealthy gentlemen, and were being trained in the womanly arts.''

Diamond had no idea what womanly arts were, but she thought she would like history and science. ''You must be very smart.''

The young woman shrugged. ''I never gave it much thought. Mama insisted that I get an education. It was just taken for granted that I would do as she said. But because I did not come from wealth, and was not part of a . . . proper family, I was being trained for a life of service.''

She looked over at Diamond. ''What about you? Didn't you go to school?''

''Until a few years ago there wasn't even much of a town in Hanging Tree to speak of, let alone a schoolhouse.'' She flushed. ''I suppose, after Boston, you still don't think it's much of a town.''

''Don't be silly. I think it's a lovely place. The stage driver was very kind to me. And Mrs. Potter couldn't have been sweeter when I asked for a room.''

Diamond chuckled. ''I'm not surprised. It isn't often she gets a chance to take in a boarder. Especially one that looks like you and smells so good.'' She breathed deeply. ''What is that sweet smell?''

''Lilac water,'' Pearl admitted. ''Would you like to borrow some?''

''Me?'' Diamond laughed harder, feeling suddenly more relaxed and carefree than she had in hours. Strange. She knew that she and Pearl could never be friends. But she had never had a close female friend before, except for Carmelita, and the housekeeper didn't count because she was so much older. Diamond hadn't known how easy it would be to talk with another female. "What would I want with lilac water?"

Pearl sipped her tea. "Sometimes, when I'm feeling sad, it makes me feel better just to touch a drop to my throat. It lifts my spirits. It feels cool and it smells so lovely."

Lovely. Diamond rubbed at her temple. That word again. Pearl seemed to use it a lot. And it suited her. The more she got to know this city girl, the more she realized Pearl was a...lovely person. She realized now that her first impressions were wrong. Pearl wasn't a charlatan. She was a grief-stricken young woman who had just lost her...father.

Father. She blinked back the sting behind her lids.

"You haven't told me about your education," Pearl persisted.

"There's not much to tell. We don't have a teacher here in Hanging Tree. No need for one. Mothers teach their daughters what they need to know, and fathers teach their sons."

"But you said your mother died when you were a baby. Who taught you?" Pearl asked.

"Pa." Diamond's voice warmed. "He taught me all I needed to know. There isn't a mustang alive I can't rope and ride. Pa used to say I could shoot almost as well as he could. And I can hold my own in any barroom brawl."

If Pearl was horrified by such accomplishments, she managed to hide it. "Can you read and write?"

"'Course I can. And Pa taught me sums so I could keep his ledgers."

"That's good. But there are some things only a woman can teach you," Pearl interrupted.

"Like what?"

Pearl's cheeks turned a becoming shade of pink. "Personal things. Female things. Like...taking care of your body. And dealing with men."

Now, that was a topic that had Diamond's complete attention. Could it be that Pearl might have some advice for dealing with these strange new feelings she'd been having whenever she got too close to Adam Winter? At once she dismissed the thought. After all, she hardly knew this young woman. How could she bring herself to discuss anything so intimate, so confusing?

"And only another woman can teach you about having babies," Pearl added.

"Well, I won't need to know about those things," Diamond said emphatically.

Pearl seemed genuinely shocked. "Why?"

"I'll never marry and have children. I'm never going to let any man take Pa's place in my heart."

For long minutes the two young women looked away, staring into the fire, deep in thought.

Pearl glanced around at the strange mix of furnishings scattered about the substantial room. There were ornately carved high-back chairs from Mexico, paired with elegantly embroidered footstools from Europe. The rug underfoot was Turkish, and the curtains at the windows were Irish lace. Yet the young woman who took such splendor for granted seemed as simple and unaffected as a child. "How did you come by such exotic things?"

"Pa found a lot of these things on his buying trips to...the East and to California." It suddenly occurred to Diamond that he had found more than furniture on his "buying" trips. He'd found someone to ease his loneliness, and eventually another daughter. Oh, Pa, she thought with sudden, wrenching sadness. I thought I knew everything about you. But I didn't really know you at all.

She struggled to gather her scattered thoughts. "Pa said the ports were crammed with all manner of imported things, if a man knew where to look."

"Some of these appear to be quite expensive."

Diamond shrugged. The cost of a thing had never interested her. Nor had she ever, until now, thought to question the value of her surroundings. "Pa used to say that the cattle business had been very good to him." She looked up. "But it was never the money that drove him. It was his desire to be the best. I understood that. It's the same with me. I won't...I can't," she corrected herself, "allow Pa's death to mark the end of the Jewel empire. For Pa's sake, for my own, I have to carry on Pa's work."

Pearl heard the note of urgency in Diamond's voice, and realized that this young woman was desperately trying to convince herself that she could manage alone.

"Death is never the end," she whispered. "It is merely a passing."

"I try..." Diamond swallowed. "I try to imagine that Pa is right here beside me. But..."

Again the two young women turned away, uncomfortably aware of the fact that the grief each carried in her heart was shared by the other. And yet, except for the brief moment at the grave, they seemed determined to grieve alone.

After a few minutes Pearl struggled to stifle a yawn behind her hand, and Diamond realized with a twinge of guilt that this delicate-looking young woman had just endured an exhausting journey without a word of complaint.

"I'm sorry. You're tired." She took the empty cup from Pearl's hand. "Let me show you to your room."

Pearl offered no objection as she got wearily to her feet and followed Diamond up the stairs and down a long hallway.

"Carmelita said she prepared this room for you before she left." Diamond opened the door and allowed Pearl to precede her.

Like the rest of the house, the room was impressively large. A log blazed on the fire. Pulled in front of it was a rocking chair draped with a comfortable quilt. The bed was bigger than any Pearl had ever seen. Made of rough-hewn logs, it dominated one side of the room. A fur throw was draped at the foot of the bed. The blankets had been turned down to reveal snowy linens. Beside the bed was a table on which rested a pitcher and basin.

"It's a lovely room."

"Well . . ." Diamond was suddenly uncomfortable once again. "If you need anything, I'm in the room next door."

"Thank you, Diamond. Good night," Pearl called as she crossed the room.

"Yeah. 'Night."

Too agitated to sleep, Diamond returned to the sofa and curled up in one corner, staring into the flames as though they somehow held the answers to all her questions.

Why had she invited Pearl into her home? It was completely unlike her to open up to a stranger. But after the intimacy of shared grief at Pa's grave, it had seemed the most natural thing in the world. Besides, she consoled herself, it wasn't anything permanent. Tomorrow she would show Pearl the ranch. She had a sudden need to introduce Pearl to Pa's life here in Texas. And then, her curiosity satisfied, Pearl would return to her home in Boston. And Diamond could resume her life as she'd known it.

There was another, more perplexing problem than Pearl. One that she didn't want to deal with tonight. But it nagged at the edges of her mind.

Adam Winter. It wasn't surprising that the thought of him always caused her blood to heat. After all, he was still the

prime suspect in her father's murder. But why did Pearl insist on trusting him when he was a complete stranger?

And why did the very mention of his name cause that little curl in the pit of her stomach?

Annoyed, she got to her feet. What she needed was a ride,
alone in the darkness. Always, whenever she was troubled,
she found her spirit restored, her energy renewed, by a sol-
itary nighttime ride.

"Ye're quiet tonight." Zeb pushed back from the table
and wrapped his hands around a cup of coffee.

"I was thinking about Diamond Jewel."

The old man chuckled. "I'm not surprised. She's a fine-
looking filly."

Adam bristled. "I wasn't thinking about how she looks."

"'Course not. A noble fellow like you." Zeb's laughter
rumbled in his chest. "Especially now that she's shared your
bedroll."

"We didn't share it, old man. She slept in it alone. I found
a spot some distance away where I could keep watch for the
night."

"Don't try to tell me you kept your eyes on the trail the
whole time."

Adam grinned. "I may have cast a glance or two her
way."

"Uh-huh." The old man blew into his cup and said, "So
what were you thinking about just now?"

"About the latest twist in her life. While we were in town
today, a young woman arrived from Boston claiming to be
Onyx Jewel's daughter."

"You don't say?" Zeb's head came up. "Looks like Onyx
Jewel was interested in more than just horseflesh." He
sipped in silence, then asked, "How'd the little wildcat take
the news?"

"About the way you'd expect. She threw a fit and threatened to shoot the young woman if she came on her property. Later, she invited her to spend the night at the Jewel Ranch."

"Well, that beats all." Zeb drained his cup and headed toward the door. "But like I've said, when you've lived as long as I have, you won't be surprised by anything."

When the door closed behind him, Adam drew his chair up to the fireplace and began to mend a broken harness. As he worked, his thoughts kept returning to the scene at the grave.

It had been good for Pearl to grieve. As for Diamond... from the way she'd held in her tears, it appeared that she considered crying beneath her. Too damned ornery to allow herself the luxury of grief.

Grief. He'd had his share. There were too many graves. And too many memories. In order to survive, he'd had to bury his memories along with the dead.

He paused in his work to roll a cigarette. Leaning back, he drew deeply and closed his eyes. The memory of Diamond, leading her wranglers like a fiery little general, caused him to smile.

She was the most contradictory little female he'd ever met. Tough as nails. He'd feared, for the first few minutes of that confrontation, that she would make good her threat to shoot Pearl. He'd been prepared to do battle if necessary. Even if it meant throttling her within an inch of her life. Yet, when that same little wildcat had held back her own tears at her father's grave, he'd had the strangest desire to take her in his arms and comfort her until she gave in and sobbed her heart out.

What the hell was the matter with him? Why was he getting involved in her fight? She'd made her feelings about him very obvious. She disliked him, mistrusted him, and intended to do everything in her power to blame him for her father's murder.

He drew smoke into his lungs, then slowly exhaled, watching the stream drift toward the ceiling. The truth was, whenever he thought about Diamond Jewel, he thought about the way she tasted. Wild. Sweet. Enticing. And about the way she'd felt in his arms. Soft. Warm. Seductive.

Zeb was halfway right. He'd spent a great deal of that night watching her sleep. And more than anything, he'd wanted to share her bedroll.

He stood and tossed the last of his cigarette into the fire. Then he pulled on his sheepskin jacket and headed for the door. There was no sense trying to sleep now. What he needed was to find some tough, demanding work for the next hour or so. And exorcise the images of one damnable little witch from his mind.

The night was cold, the air crisp and clean. A full golden moon hung in a star-studded sky.

Diamond gave her horse its head and felt the wind lash her hair and sting her cheeks as she and her mount raced across the flat range.

This was what she needed. She was weary of thinking. She wanted only to be free. Free from worry, from doubt, from all troublesome thought.

Free from this stranger who called herself Onyx Jewel's daughter.

Free from Adam Winter.

She urged her horse faster, leaning low over the mare's neck, until she felt as though they were flying. It was a glorious feeling. Horse and rider moved as one, skimming across the grassy plain. When at last the mare began to slow, Diamond sat straighter in the saddle, her eyes glowing, her lips parted in a wide smile. As her horse crested a ridge, she slowed to a walk.

"You are one fine horsewoman, Diamond Jewel."

At the sound of Adam's voice, her smile froze.

She turned her head, seeking him in the darkness. He sat astride his black stallion, blending into the shadows of a stand of trees. It was only when he nudged his horse closer that she could make out his figure.

Her heart was beating overtime. She blamed it on the exertion of the ride.

"Are you following me?"

Her voice had that same breathless quality he'd first heard in the jail. It had the same effect, whispering over his senses, causing his blood to heat.

"A man would have an easier time trying to follow the wind."

As his horse moved closer, she held her mare still, even though she was tempted to turn and run while there was still time.

"You're on my property." She moistened her lips with the tip of her tongue.

He watched the movement, and his hands tightened on the reins. "I heard some wolves. Thought I'd see if they were having a midnight feast on a couple of cows. I've been losing a lot of cattle lately."

"I heard them, too." She nodded over her shoulder. "I saw a couple of shadows moving over there. I figured I scared them off. They don't take too kindly to people."

"Unless they sense a weakness," Adam muttered. "Then you'd better beware."

She lifted her head in a gesture he'd come to recognize. "Are you warning me about the wolves? Or about you?"

He caught her chin in his hand. His gaze burned over her mouth, sending a flare of heat racing along her spine. "That depends. Do you have a weakness, Diamond?"

She tried to pull away, but he was too quick. His hand found her shoulder and he drew her closer. Their two horses stood still, as though sensing the importance of the moment.

She had the strangest urge to melt into him, to feel his arms around her, holding her close to his heart. Instead, she held herself stiffly, her gaze meeting his defiantly.

"I detest weakness. Pa taught me one rule to live by."

"And what is that?" His thumb traced the outline of her lips, sending another rush of heat coursing through her blood, until it flowed like molten lava.

"Here in Texas, only the strong survive."

"Then you needn't worry, Diamond." He drew her fractionally closer, until his lips were mere inches from hers. "You're the strongest woman I've ever met."

Up close she could see his eyes, dark and dangerous. She knew, with certainty, that he was going to kiss her. And she knew just as certainly, after that earlier taste of his lips, that she had no defense against him.

"I have to go."

"Not until I kiss you," he muttered.

"No." She pushed against the solid wall of his chest, attempting to free the whip that she carried coiled around her saddle horn.

His lips curved into a smile. If she'd thought he looked dangerous before, she knew that he was doubly dangerous when he smiled like that. A tiny thread of feeling curled along her spine. Fear? she wondered. Or anticipation?

"Now you've done it. You see, there's always been an ornery streak in me that just could never stand being told what to do," he murmured as his lips covered hers in a savage kiss.

His hands at her shoulders weren't gentle. Nor was his kiss. His mouth moved over hers, taking, taking, until she sighed and found herself giving in to the strange new feelings that swept through her.

If the tender kiss between them in his cabin had caused tremors, this mating of mouth to mouth caused thunder to rumble and lightning to strike. She was helpless against such an onslaught. All she could do was hold on and hope to survive. But she could feel herself slipping, slipping....

Her fingers curled into the front of his shirt, and a sound issued from deep in her throat. A sound that was almost primitive, as the kiss deepened, and his arms came around her in a fierce embrace.

The swift surge of desire left him stunned. Her lips were soft and warm, and slightly parted. Her breasts were flattened against his chest. Adam combed his fingers through the tangles of her hair, then, unable to get enough of her, changed the angle of the kiss and took it deeper, then deeper still, until she gasped and pushed against him.

Diamond tried to break away, but his arms were locked around her. His gaze swept her and she felt another rush of heat at the way her body strained toward his. Her gaze was no longer defiant. Her eyes were no longer cool and resentful. She couldn't hide the desire that simmered just below the surface.

He wanted her. And if she were another sort of woman, he'd take her here, now. But Diamond Jewel was an innocent. And not the sort of woman a man could take and then discard. She was the sort of woman who made a man think about vows, and permanence, and roots.

The knowledge left him shaken.

He lowered his hands and lifted the reins. His stallion tossed his head and moved several steps away.

"Pleasant dreams." He touched a hand to the rim of his hat.

"Go to..." She wheeled her mount and set off at a gallop in the direction from which she'd come.

He watched until she was out of sight. Then he rolled a cigarette and struck a match to the tip. His hand was none too steady.

He swore, loudly, savagely. He couldn't decide who made him angrier. Himself. Or Diamond Jewel.

Chapter Nine

"So." Carmelita bustled about the kitchen, a crisp white apron tied just below her ample bosom. Beneath it she wore a colorful scarlet blouse and long tiered skirt in brilliant colors. Jet black hair, streaked with gray, was pinned up in a knot, but stray curls had already pulled loose and swung like corkscrews around her flushed cheeks. "You and the *señorita* have made the acquaintance."

"Um-hmm." Diamond popped a handful of chopped chili peppers into her mouth and reached for another until Carmelita rapped her hand with a wooden spoon.

She wished she could talk to the housekeeper about Adam. She needed a woman's advice. But it wasn't something she could bring herself to talk about.

"She told me about her life in Boston. I told her about my life here in Texas."

"And now?" the housekeeper asked. "Has she satisfied her curiosity? Does she go back home?"

"In a day or two." She'd reached the decision in the small hours of the morning, while she'd lain awake agonizing over Adam's kiss. For some strange reason, she rather liked the idea of having another young woman around. Maybe, if the opportunity presented itself, she'd talk to Pearl about men.

"I thought, since she's come all this way, I'd show her around the ranch."

"That's nice." Carmelita snatched away a plate of freshly baked corn bread before Diamond could break off a hunk. "Can't you wait until breakfast is ready?"

"I was just going to see if it was done."

"It is done to perfection. Now go. Sit down. I don't need you underfoot."

With a sigh of exasperation, Diamond crossed the room and took a seat at the huge wooden table. She idly traced the indentation of her initials, scratched into the wood years ago, when she'd first been given a knife by her father. She was restless, edgy. And all because of a certain irritating man.

"Remember this?" she asked.

Carmelita glanced over, then nodded. "*Sí.* Your father threatened to take away your favorite pony if you ever did such a thing again."

"In defense, I told him I'd learned it from him. Pa had carved a mark into the wall every year on my birthday to show how much I'd grown. I thought it was all right to carve my initials into the wood in the same way."

"He was so angry," Carmelita said with a laugh. "But when he'd had time to think about it, he admitted that you were just giving him a compliment by imitating him. Oh, he was so proud of you."

Diamond felt an ache, raw and deep, around her heart.

Carmelita glanced up in time to spot a figure in the doorway.

Pearl looked as though she might flee at any moment. On her face was a look of intense suffering. It was plain that she had overheard. The housekeeper realized that her words had been the cause of this stranger's pain. Though these two young women had shared the same father, they had led very different lives. One had enjoyed a great deal of her father's attention, and had been his pride and joy. The other had been denied all but a few stolen moments of his life. And had been kept a secret. A deep, dark secret. As though born in shame.

"Come, Señorita Pearl." Carmelita beckoned her, her voice conveying her regret. "You will need a good meal before you begin your day."

She turned to the stove to tend to the eggs, just as Cal McCabe sauntered in through the back door. When he spied Pearl, his easy smile turned into a puzzled frown. He didn't know what to make of this prissy little city-bred female.

He snatched his wide-brimmed hat from his head. "'Morning, ma'am."

She nodded shyly as she crossed the room and took a seat beside Diamond.

"'Morning, Cal," Diamond called. "Care to join us?"

"I ate with the wranglers. But I'll have some coffee." He took a seat, stretching his long legs beneath the table.

Diamond noted the dark circles beneath Pearl's eyes. "How'd you sleep?"

"Not very well. I heard a howling in the night. A wolf, I think. And it had me so frightened, I couldn't get back to sleep."

Diamond averted her gaze. The mention of wolves had her thinking about Adam again.

"Probably just a coyote," Cal explained. "I suppose, to a city woman, they'd be fearsome."

Pearl blushed at his derisive tone.

Seeing it, he added lamely, "They make a mournful sound, ma'am, but they're harmless."

Diamond accepted a platter of eggs from Carmelita and spooned some onto her plate before passing it to Pearl.

Pearl stared at the colorful concoction. "What is this?"

"Eggs," the housekeeper said as she poured coffee for Cal. "You don't have eggs in Boston?"

"I've never seen eggs like this before. There's something in them."

"Chili peppers," Diamond muttered before taking a big bite. "Carmelita makes the best eggs in Texas."

Pearl looked doubtful as she managed a taste. Intrigued by the unusual flavor, she helped herself to more. And quickly reached for a glass of milk. "Oh, my. They're...hot."

Even when she'd drained her milk, she could still feel her tongue burning.

Across the table, she could see Cal struggling not to smile as he sipped his coffee in silence. That only made her feel all the more awkward.

Diamond continued eating, unaware of Pearl's discomfort. "I thought you might like to see some of the ranch today, before you leave."

"You mean, you'd like me to stay on?"

Diamond shrugged. "You may as well. At least for a day or two. After all, you did come clear across the country, didn't you?"

Pearl felt her spirits begin to lift. She had been dreading the thought of endless miles in the cramped stagecoach until she reached the railroad line at Abilene. She'd been hoping against hope that she could remain in Texas for a day or two, just to rest and recover from the grueling journey. And now, she would be granted her wish.

"That's very generous of you, Diamond. I'd like very much to see Daddy's—" She saw Cal's head come up sharply, and wanted to call back the word. But it had already been spoken aloud. All she could do now was try to cover her mistake. "...I'd love to see your ranch."

"Can you sit a horse?" Cal asked.

"Not very well, I'm afraid," Pearl admitted. "In Boston I was able to walk to most places. When I needed to go any distance, I hired a horse and cart."

Cal drained his cup, then pushed back his chair and got to his feet. "I'll have one of the wranglers hitch up your rig. And I'll saddle Sunrise for you, Diamond. Unless, of course," he added with a knowing grin, "you'd like a gentler horse. I'd hate to see you get thrown again."

Diamond's cheeks flooded with color. Once again, it seemed, her lie was coming back to haunt her. And judging by the silly grin on Cal's lips, he'd recognized it.

She nearly choked on her food as she said, "Sunrise will do just fine."

"By the way, she seemed a bit lathered this morning. Did you ride her last night?"

"I . . . yes. I needed to get away for a while by myself."

"Alone, huh?" He studied her intently for a moment, and she felt her color rise. "Let me know when you're ready to go," he called as he tipped his hat to Carmelita and ambled out the door.

Pearl took another bite of eggs, bracing herself for the burning sensation on her tongue. When it came, she gave a laugh of pure delight. She was suddenly having the time of her life. She was eating food she'd never tasted before. And she was about to be given a glimpse of a whole new world. Her father's world.

Diamond remained silent and tight-lipped. Cal's question had brought back all the feelings she'd experienced last night in Adam's arms. Feelings that left her anxious. And restless. And definitely out of sorts.

"How much of this is your land?" Pearl sat in the rig and lifted a hand to shade the sun from her eyes. In order to keep up with Diamond, she'd been forced to give up the dainty parasol, which lay forgotten on the seat beside her, and use both hands to hold the reins.

They had come to a halt atop a steep hill, affording them a view of the rolling hills and valleys below.

"All of it."

"All of it?" Pearl turned to Diamond in amazement.

Diamond nodded. "As far as the eye can see, there's nothing but Jewel land." Her voice rang with pride. "Except," she added grudgingly, "for a little speck of land over that rise that belongs to Adam Winter."

"And the cattle?" Pearl gazed at the vast herd, so large it covered the surrounding land like a great black swarm of locusts, devouring everything in its path.

"A thousand head or more. There will be twice as many come spring," Diamond said, "when the calves are born and the strays rounded up."

"How can you possibly make room for more?"

"This is Texas." Diamond slid from the saddle and held the reins easily in one gloved hand while she surveyed her father's legacy. "Pa said this land was made for cattle. They'll graze on lush grass all summer, and by fall, when we round them up for the drive to Abeline, they'll be sleek and fat and worth nearly fifty dollars on the hoof."

Pearl shook her head at the wonder of it. Diamond made it all sound so easy. But from what she had seen, Pearl knew that it took dozens of men and a great deal of hard work and money to operate a ranch of this size.

"Your foreman said he was sending a man out to one of the line camps. What does that mean?"

"Our ranch is so big, we had to build camps along the far perimeters." Diamond pulled herself into the saddle, and began leading the way across the hill to a path worn smooth by Cookie's wagon wheels. Pearl followed in the rig. As the path widened, Diamond was able to ride alongside, making conversation easier.

"Those are called line camps. They're not much to speak of. A cabin, and a corral for the horses. One of the wranglers will live in a camp for six months or more."

"What does he do way out there?" Pearl asked in wonder.

"What does he do?" Diamond chuckled. "Everything. Doctor a steer, pull cows out of bogs, dehorn cattle, lead them through blizzards, handle roundups, and patrol the border to keep the cattle from straying."

Pearl lifted a hand to her mouth in a gasp of surprise. "What a strange, lonely life."

Diamond shrugged. "I guess," she mused, "to someone from a city like Boston, it must seem like a strange way to live. The truth is, some men wouldn't have it any other way. They thrive on the isolation. Others can't stand the loneliness, and they leave. But there's always someone willing to take their place. It's just the way of the cowboy."

"And why has your foreman sent a man out there?"

"To take supplies. And make sure our wrangler isn't sick or injured. Once a month, weather permitting, someone rides out to a different line camp. This month he'll visit the northern camp. When he returns in a few days, our wrangler will give me a report on how things are going—"

At the sound of a horse approaching, Diamond cautioned Pearl to be quiet. Then she withdrew her rifle from the boot of her saddle and aimed it at the trail ahead.

Within moments a horse and rider came into view. Her finger tightened on the trigger when she recognized Adam. At once her heart began to beat a little faster, and she cursed herself for her weakness. Was this going to happen every time she saw him?

"Good morning, Diamond," he called.

"What's good about it?"

His lips curved in a dangerous smile. "I see you're in pleasant humor." He addressed a welcome to Pearl. "This is a pleasant surprise. I wasn't expecting to see you here. I figured by now you'd be halfway to Abeline, Miss Jewel."

Diamond's temper flared. "You're on my property, Adam."

"So I am. Again."

He turned his head, and she felt the heat of his gaze as surely as if he'd touched her. Or kissed her. The very thought brought a tingle to her lips.

"But this time, it isn't my cattle that brought me here. It's yours."

He turned and nodded back down the trail. A few minutes later a dozen or more cows came into view. Behind them rode Zeb.

"'Morning, ladies." Zeb lifted his hat in a courtly gesture. "Thought we'd return your cattle, lady boss. So's your wranglers won't think we're stealing."

"I'll have a word with Cal about this. One of our wranglers should have caught these strays before they got this far."

"Don't worry about it," Adam said. "No harm done."

"Maybe. Maybe not. But you don't have time to haul my cattle home every time they stray." She nodded over her shoulder. "If you drive them that way, Zeb, you'll see my herd on the other side of this rise."

"Yes'm." He glanced at Pearl. "And who might this young lady be?"

"This is Pearl..." She still couldn't bring herself to speak the full name aloud. It seemed somehow disloyal to all her childhood memories to call this young woman by the same name as her own.

"I'm Pearl Jewel," came the soft, cultured voice.

"Howdy, ma'am. Zebulon Forrest. Folks call me Zeb."

"It's nice to meet you, Zeb."

He replaced his hat. "Well, I'll just drive these—"

A shot rang out. The bullet exploded in the dirt between Diamond and Adam, sending sand spewing around their horses' feet. Reflexively Adam reached out, dragging Diamond from her mount. He held her in his arms as easily as if she weighed nothing at all, while he expertly turned his horse, shielding her body with his own. When she was safely behind the wagon, he dropped her to the ground, just as a second shot rang out. In the next instant, Adam hauled Pearl from her perch on the wagon. She was tossed into the dirt beside Diamond.

"Stay down," Adam commanded as Diamond started to reach for her rifle.

He slid to the ground, a pistol in his hand. Pearl remained behind him, peering around cautiously. But Diamond, furious at this blatant attack, grabbed her rifle and started forward.

At that moment they heard the sound of hoofbeats thundering away.

By the time Diamond had raced to the top of the rise, with the others following, the horse and rider were out of sight. All that could be seen was a brief glimpse of a dark horse and a figure in a cowhide jacket before the woods closed in, blocking horse and rider from view.

"What . . . ?" Breathless and terrified, Pearl struggled to get the words out. "What was that all about?"

"I'd say someone was out to kill." Adam holstered his gun and turned a meaningful glance toward Zeb. "The only problem is, am I the intended victim?" He slowly turned to narrow his gaze on Diamond. "Or is it you they're after?"

* * *

It took Diamond a full minute to steady her jangling nerves. When she did, she was more angry than frightened.

"No man would dare to trespass on my land and threaten me. Besides, the only time these things happen is when you're here, Adam Winter. You have to be the one they're shooting at."

"Could be. And if it's true, all you have to do is stay away from me and you won't get hit in the crossfire." His eyes narrowed. "But then again, since you might be the target, you'd be wise to take extra precautions until this gunman is caught."

"What extra precautions?" she demanded.

"Don't ride alone. Especially after dark."

At once she felt her cheeks flood with color, and hated him for daring to mention such a thing.

If he was aware of her discomfort, he gave no indication. "Have a couple of your wranglers with you at all times. And stay away from remote areas, where a gunman could easily hide behind rocks or buttes." His voice lowered. "I guess the best thing you could do is stay on your ranch until this gunman is caught."

Her eyes blazed. "In other words, I ought to turn tail and hide like some useless little female?"

"Now, Diamond, that isn't what I was—"

"Why should I believe you?" she demanded. "Maybe you're just doing this to make everyone believe in your innocence."

He shrugged, feeling his temper rise. "Believe whatever you want. Right now, I intend to accompany you back to your ranch, whether you like it or not."

Her anger exploded. "I can take care of—"

"Please, Diamond." Pearl grasped her arm, eyes wide with fear. "I'd feel a whole lot safer if you'd allow Adam to ride with us."

Despite her anger, Diamond felt a sudden wave of sympathy. While she'd been merely annoyed at this inconvenience, Pearl had probably been scared out of her wits. "You haven't had much of a welcome to Texas, have you?"

Pearl struggled to smile, but she couldn't hide the slight trembling of her lips. "Please don't apologize. It's more than I'd hoped for. You gave me a place to sleep, and a glimpse of a life I've only dreamed about. For that, I'll be forever grateful. But right now, I'd feel a lot better if Adam would see us home."

In syrupy tones Diamond said, "I hope you're happy, Adam Winter. It looks like you managed to convince one of us that you're worthy of trust."

Just then she glanced down at the small, silver object in Pearl's hand. Her jaw dropped. "Is that a gun?"

Pearl's cheeks flamed and she thrust the little pistol into the pocket of her gown. "A friend in Boston warned me that I would have need of protection in the wilds of Texas."

Without a word Diamond pulled herself into the saddle and watched as Adam helped Pearl to the seat of the rig. Seeing his hand at Pearl's elbow brought a bitter twinge of feeling. Jealousy? she wondered. Impossible. She'd never known such an emotion in her whole life. Still, at the sight of the little derringer, she was experiencing all sorts of doubts about Pearl. And Adam.

When Adam had mounted, Diamond pulled her rifle from the boot of her saddle and aimed it at him. She saw his eyes narrow slightly.

"I don't take kindly to a gun being trained on me."

"And I don't take kindly to a watchdog being forced on me. I'll allow you to ride with us as far as the ranch. But only because Pearl asked. As for me, Adam Winter, keep in mind that I don't believe you, I don't trust you, and most of all, I don't need you."

She nudged her horse into a gallop, leaving Pearl and Adam in her dust.

"Zeb," Adam called. "Drive Diamond's strays over that ridge, then return to our herd." His tone was rough with anger. "I'll get back as soon as I can."

He looked up in time to see the old man's eyes twinkling with suppressed laughter, his lips split into a wide grin. "That little lady boss sure does have a temper," Zeb shouted as he started after the cows.

"She doesn't mean anything by it," Pearl said in Diamond's defense. "I think she's just shaken by what happened, and she's more comfortable with anger than gratitude."

"One night under her roof and you've got her figured out, have you, Miss Jewel?" Adam asked.

Pearl smiled demurely. "I know her better than I expected. You see, she's just like my daddy. He could be very funny, and he was the most charming man I'd ever met. He was also loyal and generous to a fault. He loved to laugh, and his laughter was contagious. But he was uncomfortable with any display of what he considered the weaker emotions. He had a difficult time saying thank you. And it would have been impossible for him to publicly grieve. I see so much of Daddy in Diamond."

Adam shot her an approving glance. "You're wise beyond your years, Miss Jewel." He nudged his horse into a trot. "We'd better get going if we're going to catch up."

She flicked the reins. "It seems to be all I've been doing since my arrival."

At his sideways glance she explained. "Catching up."

"You're not alone, Miss Jewel." He squinted at the figure up ahead. "The whole of Texas probably has to struggle to keep up with Diamond."

Chapter Ten

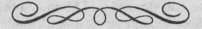

Diamond kept her horse on a steady course toward home. Though she refused to slow down, or to look over her shoulder, she knew that Pearl and Adam were following. It gave her a measure of satisfaction to know that the smug Adam Winter was forced to eat her dust.

Twice now he'd caught her off guard with his kiss. And twice she'd behaved like some silly, moonstruck female. No more, she told herself. From now on, she would be in control of her emotions.

She could hear the deep rumble of his voice as he rode alongside Pearl's rig, patiently answering her questions. For some strange reason, the sound of his voice caused an odd flutter deep inside.

It was nothing more than nerves, Diamond scolded herself.

Though she hated to admit it, even to herself, she was still feeling uneasy about what had happened back there. Could Adam be right? Was she the target of the unknown gunman? She shivered. But why? Why would anyone want to harm her? At once, the thought came unbidden to her mind. Hadn't someone wanted her father dead?

Someone shot Pa in the back.

It wasn't too difficult to take that to the next logical step. If someone wanted Pa dead, didn't it stand to reason they might want his daughter dead, as well? But why? Why?

Oh, Pa. Why did you have to keep so many secrets? Why couldn't you have trusted me with them?

If her father had just told her why he was so angry that night, and who was meeting him, the mystery would be solved. But he had stormed out, his mouth twisted into a tight, angry line, without saying a word. And now he was gone. And his secrets died with him.

And Pearl. How could he have kept such an important secret all these years? When Diamond thought about all the nights spent on the trail together, talking endlessly about the future, she felt a terrible pain around her heart.

You could have told me, Pa. I would have been able to accept it from your lips.

And was it mere coincidence that Pearl was carrying a little pistol like the one Doc had said killed Pa? Could he have died at the hand of his own daughter? Could Pearl actually hate him because he hadn't been a good enough father?

She shoved aside her wide-brimmed hat and rubbed her temple. All these vexing thoughts were giving her a headache.

She was relieved when the ranch came into view. She slowed her mount, drinking in the sight. The house, as solid and sturdy as the man who had built it, had a calming influence. After all, she was home. What could harm her here in her father's place, surrounded by men loyal to his memory?

Seeing the look of pleasure on her face, Pearl slowed the rig and lifted a hand to shade her eyes.

"Your home is beautiful, Diamond. It's even more wonderful than I'd imagined. You're very lucky."

Diamond glanced at the young woman, then at the horseman beside her. His face was expressionless, but she thought, for just a moment, that she had seen a flicker of some emotion in Adam's eyes.

"Yes, I am. I just wish I'd realized it sooner, when Pa was still . . ." Annoyed at her lapse, she flicked the reins and her horse started forward, eager for the promise of food and water at the end of the trail.

Pearl snapped the leather and the rig rolled smoothly alongside. Adam followed more slowly, his gaze trained on the surrounding rocks and hills. He fought back a sense of frustration. There were a hundred places where a determined gunman could hide. With a headstrong woman like Diamond Jewel, it would take an army to protect her. And even with that, she would probably find a way to slip out of their grasp and get herself into trouble.

Their arrival did not go unnoticed. Within minutes a dozen horsemen, with Cal McCabe in the lead, rode out to meet them.

"What are you doing here, Winter?" McCabe shouted.

"What you ought to be doing. Looking out for Diamond's safety."

"What is that supposed to mean?" Cal's tone hardened.

"It means that there was more gunfire."

Cal went pale. "Are you all right, Di?"

"I'm fine. But it happened on my own property. It's getting too close, Cal."

"Tell me about it."

"Pearl and I were up on the west ridge, overlooking Adam's spread. He and Zeb crossed our path."

"And how did that happen, Winter?" Cal demanded.

Seeing the dark look in Adam's eyes, Diamond quickly replied, "They were returning some of our strays—"

"Our strays," Cal interrupted. "This is something new, Winter. I'd have expected you to try to keep them."

"Please, Cal. Let me finish. A bullet was fired that landed right between us."

"Between you and Winter." Cal's gaze narrowed on Adam.

"That's right." Adam's voice held a challenge.

"So, once again, we don't know if the gunman was aiming at you or at Di." Cal couldn't keep the anger from his tone. "I suppose nobody got a look at this invisible gunman."

"Right again." Adam's voice frosted over. He noted that at least half the horses were dark, and that Cal and many of the wranglers were dressed in nearly identical cowhide jackets. Any one of them could have been the shooter. "Where were you when all this was going on, McCabe?"

The foreman exploded. "Are you suggesting that I had something to do with this?" His fingers closed over the gun at his waist.

At once, Diamond reached out and placed a hand on his sleeve. "Don't, Cal. That won't settle anything."

"Maybe. Maybe not. But it'll make me feel a whole lot better," he muttered.

"The last thing I need is to have those around me fighting. Don't you see? Right now, what I need most is your cool head and your steady hand."

Slowly, with great reluctance, he lifted his hand away from his holster. Ignoring Adam Winter, he said to Diamond, "I was over on the north ridge, seeing to the herd there. Cookie passed me on his way to take grub to the men. You can ask him yourself."

Diamond squeezed his arm. "I don't need to check out your story, Cal. I'd trust you with my life. Come on. Let's go home."

He held back. "What about Winter?"

Diamond glanced at the man who sat as still as a statue alongside Pearl's rig. She knew that that stillness masked a grim determination. He'd been prepared to do battle if Cal had drawn his gun. Even though it would have meant fighting a dozen wranglers.

"Adam insisted on seeing us home. I think the least I can do is repay the favor." She turned. "It's been a long ride, Adam. I hope you'll stay for lunch."

Adam touched a hand to the brim of his hat, surprised and pleased at the invitation. "Thanks. I will. As long as you promise not to do the cooking."

That remark brought a grin to the faces of several of the wranglers. Seeing them, Diamond felt a sudden rush of anger. Why was it, even when she was trying to be nice, Adam Winter seemed to take delight in humiliating her?

Cal, too, was angry. But it wasn't Adam's humor that had him seething. It was the fact that this drifter had wrangled an invitation into Onyx Jewel's home. It wasn't right. After all, though Diamond may have forgotten that Winter had been arrested for her father's murder, Cal never intended to forget. Or forgive.

"We'll see you to the ranch," he called to Diamond. "But then I think the wranglers and I will head on out to that ridge and see if we can find any trace of your attacker."

"Fine." Diamond turned away to hide the flush on her cheeks. The thought of taking a meal with Adam had her pulse racing. But at least, she assured herself, they wouldn't be alone. She would have Pearl and Carmelita to help carry the conversation. "The sooner we eat, the sooner Adam can get back to his cattle." And she could get rid of the strange, uneasy tingle that inched along her spine whenever he was near. "Come on."

"Yes, ma'am." Adam's smile deepened.

At the ranch house, Diamond found herself forced to endure Adam's touch as he lifted a hand to help her down from the saddle. At once she experienced a rush of heat. Was he aware of her reaction? Were her cheeks flushed? Were her eyes too wide? Oh, if only she knew how to handle all these strange new emotions.

"Thank you," she muttered as she broke contact and turned away quickly.

Adam assisted Pearl as she stepped from the rig.

"Oh, my." She touched a hand to her lower back and gave a long, deep sigh. "All those miles by coach seem to have caught up with me."

Diamond glanced over with a contrite look. "I'm sorry, Pearl. This was pretty careless of me. I only wanted to show you the ranch. But I shouldn't have taken you so far."

"Please, Diamond. Don't apologize." Pearl crossed the distance between them and stopped, suddenly awkward. It was a gesture that seemed out of place between family members. But they still had a long way to go before they would be completely relaxed in each other's presence. "I wouldn't have missed it for the world. Though," she added, "I would have preferred a less . . . eventful ride. I was really terrified back there. And so impressed by the cool, calm way you and Adam dealt with it."

Diamond gave an uneasy laugh. "Maybe Adam was calm. My heart was pounding."

"Truly?" Pearl shook her head. "I would have never guessed. You're an amazing woman."

The two young women strolled into the house. Adam, trailing behind, found himself agreeing with Pearl's remark. Diamond really was a remarkable woman. Instead of being concerned with her own safety, she'd been more concerned with retrieving her rifle, in order to return the gunfire. She was truly unique.

Cal and the wranglers wheeled their horses, intent upon backtracking on Diamond's trail. But as he rode away, Cal turned in the saddle and kept a flinty gaze on Adam. He didn't trust Winter. And he couldn't, for the life of him, figure out why he was hanging around.

What he didn't know was that Adam was asking himself the same question.

"Good. You are back just in time." Carmelita looked up from the oven, where she was lifting a pan of steaming corn bread.

The wonderful fragrance wafted through the kitchen, along with the sweet, spicy smell of onions and chilis.

"I've brought company," Diamond called. "Carmelita, this is Adam Winter."

Carmelita eyed him speculatively. So this was the man who had the whole town of Hanging Tree buzzing. What she had heard about him was true. There was a look of danger about him. But he appeared dangerous in more ways than one. True, he wore his guns like a man accustomed to using them. And that gave him an aura of power. But he was devastatingly good-looking, as well. Tall. Dark. Mysterious. Slightly aloof. And that only added to his appeal.

"Señor Winter. Welcome. I have missed cooking for a man. Sit," she commanded. "You will eat while it is hot."

"She means it," Pearl said in an aside. "My eggs were so hot this morning, I thought my mouth was on fire."

Adam found himself grinning as Pearl cast a wary glance at the platter of thin strips of beef laced with onions and red and green peppers.

"You are new to Texas?" Carmelita asked as she paused beside Adam with a basket of corn bread.

"Yes, ma'am." He helped himself to some and passed it on to Diamond.

"And where was your home before?"

Adam was aware that Diamond was watching him carefully. "Maryland."

"Why did you leave this...Mary-land?" Carmelita stumbled over the word as she filled his glass with water.

He drained it, and was rewarded with a second glass almost at once.

"After the war, there wasn't anything left of my home."

"The war has been over for several years," Carmelita said as she pressed the platter of beef into his hands. "Why did it take you so long to settle in Texas?"

"I...had some things to take care of. And then I just drifted for a while. When I found this place, it felt good. It felt right. And I decided to try my hand at ranching."

"So. Do you think you will stay?"

Adam shrugged. His tone roughened. "Who knows? I've learned to take things a day at a time."

Beside him, Diamond was strangely silent. She had thought that the size of his herd had meant he'd made a commitment to this land. She should have known better. A man like Adam Winter, a drifter, a loner, was in it only for the money to be made. And then he'd move on, driven by some inner demon. Pa had always had disdain for such men, who took from the land and never stayed around long enough to give anything back.

Her thoughts were interrupted by Pearl's cool, cultured voice. "Do you have family back in Maryland?"

"No." He bit the word off before lifting a cup of coffee to his lips.

Something in the way he said it caused Carmelita to turn from the stove. But he merely gave her a fleeting look and said, "This is the best food I've eaten in a long time, ma'am."

"You do not find it too hot?" she asked.

"I spent a little time in Mexico. I guess my mouth got used to spices. I've missed them."

The housekeeper beamed at his words and urged him to take a second helping.

"Maryland seems as foreign to me as Boston," Diamond remarked. "What's it like?"

"I guess, if I were to describe it in one word, it would be *gentle*." Adam turned toward her, and she noted a softness in his eyes.

Even his voice had softened, and she found herself amazed at the transformation. His eyes, which had always seemed so cold and hard, were the color of the pearl gray ridges of Widow's Peak she saw each morning through her window when she awoke. Without his usual frown, he was positively handsome.

"My farm was set amid green, rolling hills."

"Was it large?" Pearl asked.

"I suppose so. By Maryland standards. I farmed a hundred acres of rich soil, and had a herd of several hundred dairy cows. I owned another hundred acres that was given over to tenant farmers. But compared with the Jewel land here in Texas, it would seem small indeed."

"Did you farm it alone?" Diamond asked.

He shook his head. "My father and two brothers owned neighboring farms, and we all shared the hard work of planting and harvesting."

That would explain the hard, muscled body, Diamond thought. The press of that body against hers had been exquisite torture.

At that moment he turned toward her, and she felt her cheeks redden. Could he read her mind? Did he know what she'd just been thinking? As if in answer he muttered, "Did you lose your appetite?"

"What? Oh." She stared down at her plate and realized she hadn't eaten a thing. Lifting the fork to her mouth, she felt the need to say something. "What is the weather like in Maryland?"

"As a farmer, I'd have to say perfect for growing crops. Like ranchers, farmers are held hostage to the weather. It's generally warm in summer, cold in winter. But I don't think it has the extremes that you find here in Texas. Even the weather is gentle."

Gentle. There was that word again. And Diamond found herself fascinated by this unexpected gentle side of Adam Winter. It was a side she wouldn't have expected from the hardened loner she'd first met in jail.

"Do you think you will return one day to your Maryland?" Carmelita asked.

At once the softness was gone. "No. I won't be returning."

Diamond was instantly intrigued. What had wiped the smile from his lips and his eyes? What had happened in Maryland to send him halfway across the country in search of a new home?

Eager to deflect any further questions, Adam said, "Tell me about your home in Boston, Pearl."

While Pearl spoke fondly about the city of her birth, Diamond fell silent, studying Adam's hard, chiseled profile. What was it about this man that set her heart racing, her blood pounding? As if sensing her scrutiny, he turned and pinned her with a look.

"Isn't that right, Diamond?" Pearl asked.

"I..." Feeling lost and foolish, Diamond flushed clear to her toes.

"You see how modest she is?" Pearl insisted. "I was telling Adam how kind you've been since my arrival. This sort of hospitality was more than I ever hoped for."

Diamond's flush deepened. "I . . . wasn't exactly feeling hospitable when you first introduced yourself."

"But that's because you had no warning. And here I'd thought that you'd known all along about me, even though I'd only learned about you from the newspaper account of Daddy's death." Pearl gave Diamond her sweetest smile. "I've been asking myself how I would have responded in your place. I'm sure I would have reacted exactly as you did, if I'd suddenly learned a burning secret that had been kept from me for a lifetime. And the secret, finally revealed, was that I had a sister."

Sister. The word grated. Diamond felt her temples begin to throb once more. The tension was returning. She scraped back her chair. "If we're finished with lunch, I'm sure Adam will want to return to his ranch."

Adam couldn't help smiling at Diamond's reaction. She was as transparent as an artless child. And at the moment, the child in her was rebelling against the many surprises in her life. "You're right. Zeb will have a few choice words for me about leaving him with all the chores."

The three women walked with him along the cool, darkened hallway. As they passed the large parlor, he noted the sumptuous surroundings, which seemed so out of place in this harsh, primitive land. It was obvious that Diamond Jewel, despite the fact that she could ride and rope and shoot like a man, had been raised like a pampered princess.

They stepped out onto the wide veranda, and Diamond found herself sandwiched between Adam and Carmelita. As always, the nearness of him overwhelmed her.

She turned to him, eager to send him on his way. "We've kept you from your chores long enough. Thank you again for seeing us home." She stuck out her hand awkwardly. When he took hold of it, she felt the sizzle all the way up her arm. It was all she could do to keep from snatching her hand away and backing up. Instead, she stood her ground, and forced herself to meet his eyes.

"You're welcome." If he felt anything at their touch, he kept it well hidden. His voice was cool and confident; his words impersonal. "Always happy to help out a fellow rancher." He released her hand and turned to the housekeeper, who was wiping her hands on her apron. "Thank you for the fine meal, Carmelita. It was the best I've had in a long time."

"Then you must come back again. Only next time, if I know in advance, I will make you something very special. With every spice I can find."

He chuckled. "I'd like that."

Diamond couldn't believe her eyes. Carmelita was actually blushing like a girl.

"Goodbye, Pearl," Adam said as he shook her hand. "I'm glad you're getting a chance to see some of Texas. When do you leave?"

She glanced at Diamond, then looked down at the toe of her shoe. "I don't know. Tomorrow, I suppose."

"Then I wish you a safe journey," he said before turning away.

Just then they caught sight of something quite extraordinary. An ornate carriage, all silver and gilt, with a pair of matched white horses, was rolling toward them. It was an amazing sight, rarely seen in Texas. A carriage like that would only be at home in the streets of San Francisco or New York.

The horses, with manes and tails fluttering like flags in the wind, pranced in unison. Dust swirled as they came to a halt at the foot of the veranda.

As the others watched, the driver, an elegant young woman, set aside the reins and prepared to alight. Jet black hair, sleek and straight, fell to below her waist. Almond eyes sparkled in an exquisitely beautiful face. Her gown of shimmering green Chinese silk, with high mandarin collar and frog closings, fell to her ankles. The skirt was slit on either side, revealing a length of shapely leg as she stepped from the carriage.

"I was given directions to this ranch by your marshal," came a soft, slightly accented voice. "Which of you is Diamond Jewel?"

"I am." Diamond took a tentative step forward, unable to take her eyes off the lovely, delicate creature who had just arrived in a fairy-tale carriage.

"Ah. Then I am so pleased to meet you. I am Jade."

"Jade." Diamond smiled in spite of her curiosity. The name perfectly suited this young Oriental woman. "Why did you ask directions to my ranch, Jade?"

The young woman's smile faded slightly. "I see. You do not know about me."

"Know...?" Diamond felt a sudden rush of panic as she recalled a similar conversation.... Was it just a day ago? A string of curses flitted through her mind. Oh, no. This couldn't be happening again. It couldn't. The last time she'd heard these words, the outcome had been ...

"I left my home in San Francisco as soon as I read about the murder," the young woman explained in her musical voice. "I am Jade Jewel. And Onyx Jewel is ... was," she corrected herself with a catch in her voice, "... my father."

Chapter Eleven

Adam stood to one side, watching the scene unfolding before him. Diamond had gone rigid with shock. She stood, hands clenched at her sides, staring at this tiny, delicate stranger. All her feelings were mirrored in her eyes. Shock. Anger. Fear. Rejection. But to her credit, she held back her protest and allowed the young woman to speak.

"Though I saw him only infrequently, my father was the most important person in my life. When I read about his murder, I left San Francisco at once."

"And you came all this way alone, just to see his grave?" Diamond demanded.

Jade nodded. "It would bring great dishonor to Father's memory if I did not come here to pay my respects at the place where he is buried. Besides, I could not stay away. He was, after all, my father."

"I suppose you have some proof of your claim?"

"Proof?" Jade seemed insulted at the thought of anyone questioning her integrity.

In that moment, as she lifted her chin defiantly, Adam could see the resemblance between this young woman and the two who faced her. If they had one thing in common, it was a determined, defiant nature. And apparently, an impulsive one.

Jade returned to the carriage and retrieved a delicately embroidered satin bag. She opened it to reveal several documents.

"As was the custom, my birth was recorded." She held up a scroll on which were a series of Chinese characters.

"I can't read that," Diamond reminded her.

"Ah. Of course. It says that a female child was born to Ahn Lin, the daughter of Hu Nan, and Onyx Jewel, the son of—"

Diamond held up her hand to interrupt. "That isn't necessary. Since I can't read your language, I have no way of knowing if what you say is true."

Jade looked stricken. "But why would I lie? Such a thing would dishonor my father." She rummaged through the satin bag and removed several letters. "These were missives from my father through the years." She held one up. "As you can see, he had managed to learn some of my mother's language."

Diamond examined a letter. She could make out an occasional Chinese character sprinkled among the words. But despite the presence of foreign words, the handwriting was definitely that of her father.

Pearl, who had remained silent throughout this exchange, studied the letter. "I am forced to believe her," she announced.

"Thank you." Jade managed a tentative smile. "And who are you?"

"My name is Pearl. Pearl Jewel. I came here from a place far away, Boston, when I heard about my—" she couldn't bring herself to say "our" "—father's death."

"Another daughter?"

Now it was Pearl's turn to look stricken. She should be accustomed to such insults. But each time one was hurled, it inflicted pain.

"Forgive me," Jade said softly. "The newspaper account mentioned only a daughter named Diamond. It made no mention of another. Since you have come all this long distance, you understand why I had to do the same." Jade glanced at Diamond, whose features were still stiff and unyielding. "What can I say to make you believe me?"

"There's nothing you can—"

"The necklace," Pearl blurted.

Diamond shot her a questioning glance.

"Don't you see? If Jade is truly Onyx's daughter, he would have given her a necklace like ours."

"You mean this?" Jade reached inside the high open collar of her gown to remove a gold chain on which resided two stones, side by side. One was jet black, the other jade. "Father presented me with this on my sixteenth birthday," the young woman said. "He told me that it was to remind me that he would always be beside me."

Pearl revealed her necklace, then nudged Diamond, until, reluctantly, she did the same.

"I know how shocking this is," Pearl whispered. "I am more than a little stunned myself. But we must do the right thing and... accept her as Daddy's daughter."

We. When, Diamond wondered, had *I* become *we*? She bit her lip, wondering how many more surprises she would be forced to endure. But then, prodded by Pearl's determination, she managed to put aside her worries, at least for the moment. With Pearl nudging her forward, she was forced to step off the veranda and pretend to make this stranger welcome.

"I guess," she muttered halfheartedly, "I'd better get used to the idea of having... a few surprises in my life."

Diamond and Pearl came to a halt in front of Jade and extended their hands. The young woman bowed before accepting their handshakes. It was done quickly. A clasp of hands, and then the three stepped apart and faced one another awkwardly.

Diamond nodded toward the man and woman still on the porch. "This is Carmelita, our housekeeper and cook. And this is our...neighbor, Adam Winter."

Jade bowed in greeting.

"Well." Carmelita cleared her throat of the lump that had settled there. Like Adam, she could see the resemblance in these three young women. Though they were very different, she could see Onyx Jewel in each of his daughters. Clearly flustered, she managed to say, "You must eat and refresh yourself after your long journey, Señorita Jade. Come inside. I will fix you a meal."

"Thank you." Jade held back. "If you do not mind, I would first like to visit my father's final resting place."

"I'll take you there," Diamond offered.

"That might not be wise," Adam said.

She looked up, annoyed at his intrusion. "Why?"

"Cal and the wranglers aren't back yet. You can't ride out there alone."

Diamond's eyes blazed. "Are you suggesting that it isn't even safe for me to ride to my father's grave?"

"Yes, ma'am, I am."

"Adam Winter, you can go to—"

"Yes, ma'am. My thoughts exactly. And I'm sure I'll get there soon enough." Though his face remained impassive, his eyes were warm with laughter. "But if you're determined to visit your father's grave right now, I'm afraid I'll have to ride along."

"I don't need someone riding shotgun every time I go for a ride."

"Until Cal McCabe comes back, that's just what I intend to do."

The two faced each other, neither willing to give an inch. But, though Diamond wasn't accustomed to yielding, she could see that she had met her match in Adam.

She turned on her heel. "I'll saddle my horse. Pearl, you can ride in the carriage with Jade."

Adam watched as she headed toward the corral. Then, in quick, easy strides, he caught up with her.

"Now what do you want?" she demanded.

"Settle down. I'm just going to fetch my horse. Mind if I walk along?"

She turned away in disgust. It was clear to her that Adam Winter wasn't going to let her out of his sight for a moment.

And for some odd reason, that made her more uncomfortable than the thought of an unknown gunman stalking her.

"This is Pa's grave." Diamond led the way to the top of the windswept hill.

Jade, holding a small earthen jar in her hand, stood very still, studying the mound of earth topped with stones. It seemed a primitive burial, compared with the colorful rituals of her people. There had been no ancient ones to pray and chant, no incense, no dragons dancing. And there were no ashes to mingle with the earth and wind, to scatter over the ocean, to carry the spirit home to the bosom from which it sprang. But she did not wish to offend her father's other daughters, who obviously approved of this stark burial.

Though she said not a word, the bleak look on her face spoke volumes.

Pearl, whose own first glimpse of this mound of earth had left her shaken, said softly, "According to Diamond, this was Daddy's favorite place."

"Ah. Then this final resting place was chosen to honor our father in a special way?"

Diamond swallowed, then nodded. "I figure Pa is happy here, with a view of the land he loved." She was uncomfortable sharing her grief with these two, and seeing the grave brought a fresh round of pain. "Would you like to be alone, Jade?"

"Oh, no. I think Father would be pleased to see us together." Jade removed the stopper from the earthen jar and began to sprinkle ashes over the grave.

"What are you doing?" Pearl asked in alarm.

"These are my mother's ashes. I have kept them on a small altar to honor her memory. When I heard of Father's death, I knew that it would please her to have some of her ashes mingled with those of the only man she ever loved. I only wish that I had some of Father's ashes, so that I could place them on the altar with Mother's."

Pearl shivered, and it was obvious that she thought the custom barbaric. But for some strange reason, the thought pleased Diamond, who could not remember her own mother. Jade's exotic customs touched some romantic place in her heart that she hadn't even known existed.

"I think Pa would like that," she said.

For the first time, Jade smiled. "Then, if you do not mind, I will take some of the earth from Father's grave, and mix it with the ashes in this urn."

"I'll help you." Grateful for something to do, Diamond knelt and began to scoop a small portion of sand from the mound of earth. While Jade held out the urn, she allowed it to sift through her fingers to mingle with the ashes.

Pearl knelt and began to pray. Jade stood, clutching the earthen jar to her chest and chanting in an ancient tongue. Diamond dropped to one knee and touched a hand to the pile of rocks while staring out across the land. Pa's land. *My land,* she thought fiercely. And then, even as that thought came, another nudged it aside. Was it truly her land now? Or did a part of it belong to these two strangers, who called Onyx Jewel their father?

She was fairly certain that legally she was the legitimate heir to her father's estate. But more important than the legal issue was a deeper, more personal one. One involving heart and soul. What would Pa have wanted her to do about these two?

The thought tore at Diamond's composure. Oh, why had she been given this burden?

Tears coursed down Jade's cheeks, though she adamantly refused to make a sound. It was clear that she did not wish to display her grief in front of the others. But the harder she tried to hold back the sobs, the more the tears forced their way out, until, with a little moan, she dropped to her knees and buried her face in her hands.

Pearl, whose tender heart was touched by the scene, knelt beside her and touched a hand to her shoulder, whispering words meant to soothe.

Diamond stood alone, watching with a frown. When the two young women's cries became loud, heart-wrenching sobs, she bit her lip and turned her head away. She would not allow herself to join in this public display. What good were tears? Would they bring Pa back? Would they rid her of this terrible pain around her heart?

Adam waited beside the ornate carriage, his gaze sweeping the rocks and hills for any sign of a gunman. But every so often he found himself staring at the slender figure in the garb of a wrangler. Once again she had turned inward, finding the will to deny her own grief. She was distinctly different from the other two young women. Neither fragile nor ladylike. Still, the mere sight of her took his breath away. He found himself replaying in his mind the kiss they'd shared in the moonlight. The taste of her, so wild and sweet, lingered on his tongue. At the first touch of her, the memory of every other woman had been wiped from his mind.

Right now, seeing the way she held herself apart from the others, he wanted nothing more than to take her in his arms and comfort her. To tell her it was all right to weep. And to console her when the tears had run their course. Instead, he stood alone and watched from a distance.

Pearl sniffed and wiped at her eyes with a lace handkerchief. Beside her, Jade lifted the earthen jar to her lips and pressed a kiss to it, then hollowed out a small section of earth and placed the jar in it. Pressing the sand around the base, she stood.

"If you do not mind, I wish to leave my mother's ashes in this place. I know it is where she would like to be."

Diamond nodded, oddly touched, and thought about her own mother's burial plot, not far from the barn. Maybe one day she would have it moved to this spot.

"We'd better get back to the house." She cast a wary eye on the clouds overhead. "We're in for some weather."

Jade walked to her, once again bowing slightly. "I wish to thank you for allowing me to visit my father's grave. And now I will bid you goodbye."

"Where will you stay?" Pearl asked. She had assumed a proprietary role toward the newcomer, remembering her own sense of loss and confusion upon her arrival at this wild, primitive place.

Jade gave a negligent shrug of her shoulders. "I will find a room in the nearest town. And then I will return to San Francisco."

Diamond swallowed. Before she had time to think, the words just spilled from her lips. "There's plenty of room at the ranch. Would you like to spend the night with us?"

Jade smiled through her tears. "I would like that very much. Thank you."

"It's...settled, then." Diamond glanced at Adam. "Thanks for your company. But I think we can manage to find our way back to the ranch alone."

"I'm sure you can. But if you don't mind, I'll just ride along, anyway."

"But I do mind. I'm—"

They heard the report of a rifle at the same moment that a bullet sent dirt spraying around their feet.

Adam moved instinctively, gathering the three women in his arms and shoving them to safety behind Jade's carriage. "Don't move," he called as he removed his gun from his holster and studied the surrounding rocks.

"The bullet came from that direction." Diamond pointed her pistol, eager for the chance to return the gunfire.

Adam dropped to one knee, squinting against the setting sun. He felt a tingle along the back of his neck. Once again, the bullet had landed directly between him and Diamond. From the cover of those rocks, it would have been impossible to do that intentionally. That shot had not been intended as a warning. The shooter had wanted one of them dead.

But which of them?

Adam was a man who'd learned to trust his instincts. And all his instincts told him that the gunman was getting closer. And more desperate.

He studied the rocks. Nothing seemed out of place. There was no movement. Not even a single shadow flickered. The gunman, once again, had made good his escape.

Adam got to his feet, holstering his gun. "Come on," he said. "I'm taking you home."

This time, though she still brandished her gun, there was no word of protest from Diamond. But when she looked at

Pearl and Jade, both young women were holding small silver pistols in their hands.

"Where did you get that?" Diamond demanded of Jade.

"It was my mother's," the young woman said. "I always carry it on my person for protection."

Diamond's eyes narrowed. "Protection from what?"

"From any threat." Jade nodded toward Diamond's pistol. "Is it not the same for you?"

"I—suppose so." Diamond holstered her gun. But her mind remained troubled. Another pistol like the one that had killed her father. Carried by another stranger claiming to be his daughter.

The three young women were silent and grim as they made their way back to the ranch house. Once there, Diamond was surprised to see Adam dismount.

"You've done your duty. You've seen us home. Now what do you think you're doing?"

"I don't see any sign of Cal or the wranglers. I'll just stay until they return. I don't want the three of you to be alone here."

"You certainly can't believe that the gunman is going to try to enter my home."

Adam took her arm and escorted her to the door. "Right now, I don't know what to think. Just go inside."

She glanced at Pearl and Jade, who brushed past her as they entered the house. Her lower lip jutted in defiance. "I'd rather stay out here. I don't want to go inside."

Despite the danger, he couldn't help smiling. "I can see that. You'd like to avoid any contact with those two. It looks like your father left you quite a mess to clean up."

She sighed, and for the first time, gave in to a momentary display of weakness. "Oh, Adam. What am I going to do?"

He tousled her hair, then allowed his hand to linger a moment, enjoying the feel of silk against his rough palm. "You're going to go in there and be your usual smiling, charming self."

She gave out a string of oaths that had him roaring with laughter. "All right," he said when he'd managed to stop laughing. "So you're not going to smile and charm them. But at least you can entertain them with your rich vocabulary. I'll bet those two young women haven't heard most of those words before."

She shot him a look of disgust.

In a more sober tone he murmured, "I know this isn't going to be easy. You're going to be pretty busy for a while, just figuring out how to get along with two strangers. But remember this, Diamond. Your father loved them. And if you want to cherish his memory, you need to get to know them better. Maybe you'll learn things about your father from Pearl and Jade that you never would have known otherwise."

"I don't need those two to tell me about Pa."

"All right. But what about them? They didn't have as much time with him as you did. Maybe, while they're here, you could give them a glimpse of his life. Something they could carry with them when they leave."

She tilted her head up, and her lips nearly brushed his. The movement had them both going very still. She tried to step back, but his fingers brushing her scalp stopped her.

She felt his gaze burn over her mouth and saw a hunger in his eyes. Her throat went dry and her heart began a painful hammering.

"Are you always this smart?" she whispered.

His hand fisted in her hair, but he managed to keep his tone light. "Sometimes I'm even smarter."

She leaned fractionally closer, until their bodies were almost touching. "And while I'm busy learning how to put up with these strangers who claim to be family, what are you going to do?"

"That's easy." He allowed a strand of her hair to sift through his fingers. The urge to kiss her was so strong, he had to call on every ounce of willpower to resist. "I'm going to stable the horses and check the house and outbuildings. Then I'm going to have a second helping of Carmelita's corn bread."

"I should have known." She pushed against him, breaking the spell. "This whole scheme wasn't about my safety. You were just looking for an excuse to sample more of Carmelita's good cooking."

He stood very still, afraid to touch her. "And I should have known you'd find out the truth sooner or later."

She turned away. But Adam continued standing in the doorway, feeling his entire body vibrating with need.

He'd manage to resist her for a while longer. But he could feel a storm brewing. And it wasn't just in the clouds.

"You are quiet." Carmelita placed a slice of corn bread and a steaming cup of coffee in front of Adam.

He had checked out the house and outbuildings, and had found nothing out of place. He'd taken his time rubbing down the horses and stowing Jade's carriage in the barn. Now there was nothing to do but wait. But this was the hardest part. Being forced to spend time watching Diamond, and not being able to touch her.

"I don't believe in talking unless I have something to say."

"Diamond told me about the gunman. Do you suspect anyone?"

He shook his head. "It could be anyone." Hell, he thought, it could even be Cal or one of the wranglers.

"Do you think it is you they shoot at? Or is it Diamond?"

He'd been pondering that same question for the past hour. What if the intended victim wasn't Diamond at all? If he was the one the gunman was stalking, his presence here could prove to be a terrible mistake. The longer he stayed here, the greater the chance that he could bring harm to Diamond and these innocent women. But he couldn't take the chance of leaving them alone.

"I hope it's me," he muttered before lifting the cup to his lips.

"Why do you say that?"

"I like the odds better. I'm used to looking over my shoulder. And I've been shot at before. Diamond, on the other hand, is headstrong and careless. I get the idea that she led a sheltered life here on the ranch."

Carmelita smiled gently. "She would not like to hear you say that. In many ways she has known great freedom. She has done things that few young ladies have done. For the most part she has lived the life of a frisky young colt. But it is true. Her father shielded her from many things."

They both glanced across the room, where the three young women sat together, looking distinctly uncomfortable with one another.

"Perhaps he shielded her from too many things. Now she is completely unprepared for what has been given her," Carmelita added before walking away.

Adam rubbed the back of his neck. Who was ever prepared for what life tossed at them? He certainly hadn't been prepared for a hellion by the name of Diamond.

He looked up at the sound of an approaching horse and cart. "Are you expecting anyone?" he asked.

With a shake of her head, Diamond got to her feet and headed for the front door. Adam followed, his gun drawn.

At the sight of a tall figure dressed in a black suit, Diamond threw open the door and sauntered onto the porch. "Uncle Chet. What brings you out here?"

"'Evening, Diamond." He tipped his hat and bent to brush a kiss across her cheek.

His smile faded when he caught sight of Adam behind her. "Winter. What are you doing here?"

"He was—"

"Paying a neighborly call." Adam's tone was brusque.

"Yes." Diamond recovered quickly. "He was paying a call."

"Odd that you should entertain the man accused of murdering your father."

"I wasn't entertaining him, Uncle Chet. I was just..." Seeing Adam's slight shake of the head, she let the words die. Linking her arm through Chester's, she said, "Come on in. Carmelita is fixing supper."

"I can't stay." He walked inside, then turned toward her father's office. "I just came to pick up the monthly ledgers."

"Oh, dear." Diamond stopped short.

"What's wrong?"

"Nothing. But so much has happened, I forgot about them."

He gave her shoulder an affectionate squeeze. "No harm done, my dear. I'll take them with me and have them tallied by tomorrow."

Diamond was struck by a sudden inspiration. Working on her father's ledgers would give her the perfect excuse to escape Pearl and Jade whenever the conversation got too intense. She had been wondering just how she could avoid spending the entire evening with these two strangers.

"I'm afraid I can't let you have them, Uncle Chet."

He lifted a brow to study her. "What are you saying?"

"I insist upon doing Pa's books myself. I guess I see it as a test of how well I can manage on my own."

"But that isn't necessary, Diamond. I'm perfectly willing—"

"I won't hear of it." She gave him a bright, breezy smile. "I'm so sorry you came all this way for nothing, Uncle Chet. Are you sure you won't stay for supper?"

"No." He couldn't hide his frustration. "It will be dark before I arrive home." He gave a sigh of disgust. "I suppose I'll see you soon?"

"Of course, Uncle Chet. I'll stop by the bank in a few days."

"Good night, then, my dear."

He pressed another kiss to her cheek, then shot a withering look at Adam before walking out the door.

"I'm afraid Uncle Chet wasn't too happy to see you here," Diamond said.

"I seem to have that effect on a lot of townspeople," Adam remarked.

Diamond shrugged. "You can hardly blame them. They just want Pa's killer caught and punished."

She turned, relieved to have something besides revenge to occupy her time until supper. "If Carmelita comes looking for me, tell her I'm in Pa's room."

Adam caught her arm and dragged her close. "Need some help?"

She hated the way her heart leaped to her throat. She was forced to swallow twice before she could manage, "No, thanks. But I'm sure Carmelita will be thrilled for your company."

His voice was low, seductive. "It isn't Carmelita I want to spend time with."

Her eyes widened in surprise. He could read the jumble of emotions in their depths. Shock, at his unexpected admission. Pleasure, that she could evoke such feelings in him. And slowly, gradually, invitation.

"And why would you want to spend time with me?"

She was teasing him. Flirting. It was the first time in her life she'd ever done this. And the realization made her blush furiously.

Mortified, she lowered her gaze, allowing her lashes to sweep down, hoping to hide what she knew he would see in her eyes.

With great tenderness he lifted her chin and forced her to meet his gaze.

"Because you fascinate me, Diamond. You're unlike any woman I've ever met."

She was certain he could hear the pounding of her heart. "I'd . . . better get at Pa's ledgers."

Very carefully he lowered his hand to his side, where he clenched it into a fist. He had to remember to stop touching her. It always made him . . . uncomfortable.

He crossed to the front door and stood watching until the banker's rig disappeared over a distant ridge. Already the storm clouds were gathering overhead. Chester Pierce would be drenched before he made it back to town.

Adam turned to stare at the closed door to Onyx Jewel's office. He frowned as he thought about what he'd like to do behind that closed door.

Still frowning, he made his way down the hall toward the kitchen in the back of the house, where female voices could be heard in animated conversation. He hoped Cal McCabe and the wranglers returned soon. He needed to put some distance between himself and Diamond Jewel.

Chapter Twelve

"Supper is ready."

Diamond looked up at the familiar sound of Carmelita's voice outside the door. She was grateful to close the ledgers and stash them in her father's desk drawer.

She made her way to the kitchen. When she caught Adam's glance, she immediately looked away. But she could feel the heat of his gaze, even though she adamantly kept her own averted.

"We missed you," Pearl admonished her as they took their places around the table.

"I have to get the ledgers ready for Uncle Chet at the bank."

"Uncle Chet?" Jade looked puzzled. "Father never mentioned a brother."

"He isn't really my uncle. But I've known Chester Pierce since I was a baby. I've always called him my uncle."

"I see. And why must you prepare ledgers for him?" Jade accepted a tray of thinly sliced roast beef and pork swimming in rich gravy. She took a small portion, then passed the tray to Adam.

"Because he has to know how much money I'll need this month to pay my wranglers."

"Is it not the same amount every month?"

"It's always different. Cal often takes on extra help when the work begins to pile up. Every spring, during calving, we hire extra wranglers. And every fall, for roundup and branding, we add even more. And when we start the drive to the stockyards in Abilene, we need to leave extra help here to see to the ranch chores." Diamond rubbed at her temple. "I just never thought doing sums would be so tiring."

"Maybe I could help," Pearl offered. "I was considered something of an expert at mathematics while I was a student."

"You mean it?" Diamond couldn't hide her surprise and her pleasure. "You wouldn't mind?"

"I'd be happy to. It would be my way of thanking you for your hospitality."

Diamond looked relieved as she helped herself to corn bread fresh from the oven. "Then, as long as you're willing, we'll tackle those ledgers first thing in the morning." She glanced at Jade. "And then, Jade, if you'd like, we'll go on a tour of the ranch before you leave."

The young woman's lips split into a wide smile. "Thank you. I would like that."

"Just so long as you take Cal and several of the wranglers along," Adam warned.

Diamond shot him a quelling look. "Thank you for that reminder. I wouldn't want to go out without my wet nurse."

Adam grinned and chose to ignore her sarcasm. As he bit into the beef he looked up and asked unexpectedly, "Carmelita, are you married?"

The housekeeper blinked, then nodded. "*Sí*. His name is Rosario."

"Rosario is the luckiest man in the world," he muttered. "This is the tenderest, tastiest beef I've ever had."

She actually giggled before pressing the platter into his hand for another helping.

Across the table, Diamond practically groaned in disgust. Couldn't Carmelita see that he was using his charm?

Adam turned his smile on Jade. "You're a long way from home, Miss Jewel. Tell us about your life in San Francisco."

This brought a smile from the young woman. "My mother and I made our home in a suite of lovely rooms looking out over the city. From my bedroom I could see the ocean, and the ships like the one that had brought my mother to this country from China."

"Did you go to school?" Diamond asked.

"I did not attend school, but my mother saw to it that tutors were brought to me, to teach me everything from science to embroidery."

"Did you learn your lessons in English or Chinese?" Pearl found herself thoroughly enjoying the meal, since it seemed to have few spices. It was almost as good as the beef her mother used to cook.

"Both. I can converse in several Chinese tongues, as well as English and French. It was considered essential to know the language of many distant lands."

"Why is that?" Diamond asked.

"Because San Francisco is a busy, exciting port. People come from all over the world. Those who do business there must be prepared for many foreign languages."

"Did you live right in the city?" Adam asked.

Jade nodded. "Father tried to persuade Mother to permit him to buy us a house in the country, away from the bustle and noise of the city." She paused and realized that this revelation had caused Diamond's mouth to drop. She cursed herself for her clumsiness. She must remember to keep mention of her life with her father to a minimum. "But Mother had no interest in the countryside. Her life was intertwined with that of the people of the city."

"Was your house as big as this?" Diamond helped herself to more beef.

Jade smiled. "We did not live in a house. We lived on the top floor of Mother's business."

"Your mother worked?" Pearl sipped her tea, then touched a napkin to her lips. "What was her business?"

"She was the proprietor of the Golden Dragon," Jade said proudly.

"The Golden Dragon?" Diamond frowned. "Your mother bought and sold gold?"

"No." Jade's smile grew. It was clear that she took great pride in her mother's accomplishments. "The Golden Dragon was the largest pleasure palace in San Francisco. It is where my father met my mother."

"What's a pleasure palace?" Diamond asked.

Adam coughed.

But before he could say a word, Jade asked, "You mean there are no such things in Hanging Tree? A pleasure palace is a place where men go to forget the worries of the day."

"You mean a saloon?" Diamond's frown turned into a smile. "Your mother owned a saloon?"

"I suppose one could call it a saloon. A man can buy a drink. But he can also buy other pleasures."

"What kind of pleasures?" Pearl asked.

"Cards or dice. Or perhaps the company of a beautiful woman."

Pearl's cheeks went from pink to scarlet. Her eyes widened in surprise, then narrowed in horror. This woman, who called herself Daddy's daughter, had a mother who ran a... The thought was too horrible.

Diamond, on the other hand, seemed to take no notice. "That's nice," she commented idly. She shoved aside her plate, clearly unaware of what Jade was talking about. "Carmelita, did I smell apple pie?"

The housekeeper had lowered herself onto a chair and had buried her face in her apron. At Diamond's question, she managed to lift her head and compose her features. "*Sí*. I will cut and serve it right away."

Across the table, Adam watched the various reactions to Jade's simple description of a pleasure palace. Diamond, in all her innocence, didn't have the slightest inkling of what Jade had just revealed. She still thought Jade's mother had owned a saloon. Pearl on the other hand was scandalized. Her features were still contorted in shock. As for Jade, she merely sipped her tea and kept her gaze averted. Her mother's business was a fact of life. Nothing more.

It would seem, he thought with a grin, that Onyx Jewel's family tree had just sprouted a fascinating new limb.

It had been raining for nearly an hour. A cold, stinging rain that chilled clear to the bone. If the temperature dropped, it would turn to snow.

Adam was sipping his fourth cup of coffee and polishing off his second piece of pie, when he heard the sound of approaching horses.

"The wranglers are back," Carmelita announced.

At the sound of booted feet along the hall, Adam looked up to see Cal standing in the doorway, dripping water from his hat and duster. The foreman snatched his hat from his head. When he spotted Adam, his lips turned down into a frown.

"I didn't expect to see you still here, Winter."

Adam offered no word of explanation. He merely drained his cup while the foreman turned to study Jade.

Seeing his puzzled look Diamond hastened to explain. "Cal, this is Jade. She's . . . That is, Pa was her . . ."

Seeing her dilemma, Jade said in her softly accented voice, "I am Jade Jewel, from San Francisco. Onyx Jewel was my father."

For a moment Cal looked thunderstruck. His eyes mirrored his shock. Then, recovering, he managed a bland smile as he extended his hand. "Welcome, Miss Jade. I'm Cal McCabe, Diamond's foreman."

An awkward silence settled over the room.

"Will you have coffee?" Carmelita asked.

"No, thanks. Cookie brought grub to the wranglers in the south pasture, and I joined them."

"Did you see any sign of our gunman?" Diamond asked.

"None. Maybe he's gone for good."

"Afraid not," came Adam's low response.

"What does that mean?"

"There was another attack." Adam was rewarded with a look of stunned surprise from the foreman.

Cal turned to Diamond. "Where?"

"At Pa's grave." Before Cal could admonish her she explained, "We took Jade there after she arrived. She came all the way from San Francisco to pay her respects."

"Was it the same as before?" Cal asked.

Diamond nodded. "The bullet could have been aimed at Adam or at me. It landed between us."

"And I suppose nobody saw the gunman." He didn't try to mask the sarcasm in his tone.

Diamond shook her head.

He met Adam's steely look with one of his own as he said to Diamond, "It seems odd that the only time you're shot at is when you're with Winter."

"I know it's strange." Diamond's tone was sharper than she'd intended. There was just too much happening. Sisters arriving. Bullets flying. And Adam Winter. Especially

Adam. He was causing her to think about things she'd never thought of before.

She was losing control. The one area of her life that she could still control was the ranch and its foreman. "I'll talk to you tomorrow, Cal. Right now, I think I'd like to turn in."

"Right." His tone was equally abrupt. "Good night."

He stalked from the room.

Diamond waited until his footsteps receded. Then she turned to Adam. "Good night, Adam."

He thanked Carmelita for the dinner, then bade goodnight to the three young women. At the door he took Diamond's hand in his. He could feel the way she tried to pull back, but he had anticipated her action. His strength was too much for her.

"A word of advice," he murmured. "I know you value your freedom, Diamond. But don't be foolish enough to take any midnight rides. At least until this gunman is found."

Her eyes blazed, but she managed to say simply, "I'm quite able to make my own decisions. Good night, Adam."

He turned away in disgust. As soon as the door closed, he headed toward the bunkhouse.

Several of the wranglers were seated on their bunks, mending harnesses. In one corner, a cowboy was whittling on a block of wood. A group of wranglers had gathered around the fireplace, swapping stories. Laughter punctuated the steady hum of voices, and drowned out the sound of the downpour outside.

Adam spotted Cal standing by a window, morosely staring at the rain that streaked the pane.

"I'd like to talk to you, McCabe," he called.

His words caused the wranglers to fall silent. Cal's head came up sharply. After a moment he shrugged and pulled on his leather duster before following Adam outside. The cowboys remained silent for a moment longer, then began to talk among themselves again, but in a more subdued manner.

Cal stepped into the rain, pulling the door shut behind him. "What do you want now, Winter?"

"I think you'd be wise to post guards around the ranch," Adam said without preamble.

"Do you?" Cal's eyes narrowed. "And what else do you think, Winter?"

"I think you'd better assign a couple of wranglers to keep an eye on Diamond. She's just headstrong enough to do something foolish, to prove that she's not afraid of this gunman."

Cal's tone quivered with indignation. "Since when did you become an expert on Diamond?"

"What's wrong with you, Cal? You know I'm right."

Cal jabbed a hand against Adam's chest, catching a fistful of his shirt. "I know that I don't trust you, Winter. And I don't want your advice. Now go on home. And leave Diamond to me."

Adam's voice was surprisingly soft. And chilling. "Don't ever put a hand on me, Cal. Unless you want to lose it."

It was all the invitation Cal needed. He could hardly see through the red mist of fury that clouded his eyes. He went for the pistol at his waist, only to find that Adam was already pressing the barrel of his gun to his chest.

"Drop it," Adam ordered.

Slowly, purposefully, Cal's fingers uncurled, allowing the pistol to fall to the ground. He lifted his head, prepared to die. Instead, he was surprised to see Adam toss his own gun aside and unfasten his gun belt.

"What're you doing?" he demanded.

"You've been spoiling for a fight ever since you first met me. I'm about to give you your wish. But not with guns," Adam added. "You're going to have to fight me like a man, with only your fists."

Cal's hand went to the buckle of his gun belt. "With pleasure," he said. As soon as his gun belt dropped, he lunged at his opponent, landing a solid blow to the side of Adam's head.

Adam shook his head to clear it, then managed to dodge Cal's second attempt. Caught off-balance, Cal was unprepared when Adam's fist landed in his midsection. The foreman doubled over for a moment. Enraged, he attacked with a string of blows about Adam's head and chest. Though some landed in the air, several found their mark, and Adam was soon gasping for air.

Hearing the sounds of shouting and scuffling, the door to the bunkhouse was thrown open and the wranglers spilled out into the darkness. Seeing that it was a fair fight that didn't require their intervention, they formed a ring around the two men. Oblivious to the rain, they shouted words of encouragement to their boss.

The opponents were evenly matched. Though Adam was taller by a head, Cal's years of wrangling had made him hard and tough. He'd never backed away from a fight in his life, and this was one adversary he'd been itching to engage.

"You keep away from Diamond," Cal shouted as he smashed his fist into Adam's chin. "I don't trust you. And I don't want you coming around here again."

"Then see that you do your job." Adam retaliated with a blow to the nose that had Cal swearing. "A wild creature like Diamond needs a keeper. That's the only way she's going to stay alive."

"It's not Diamond I'm worried about, Winter." Cal gave a grunt of pain as another blow landed in his gut. He answered with a fist to Adam's chest that had him gasping. "It's you. None of this mysterious gunfire started until you came into the picture."

Adam butted his head into Cal's chest, driving him backward into the mud. "And I suppose I'm hiring someone to shoot at me? Or maybe I'm doing the shooting myself, and then appearing mysteriously after the fact."

Cal sprang to his feet and charged at Adam. Both men toppled, and began to roll around and around, fists flying. "All I know is, Diamond doesn't need you, Winter."

"It's time you took a look at her, McCabe." Adam momentarily lost his voice as a blow landed in his face. Recovering, he shouted, "She may be your boss, but she's still just a confused, frightened girl."

"Girl!" Cal's fist slammed into Adam's shoulder and he pinned him to the ground. "I've seen the way you look at Diamond. That's no girl you're seeing. It's a woman. And if her pa was alive, he'd have your hide. And since Onyx isn't here to look out for her, I'll just have to—"

As he raised his fist, a shot rang out, causing both men to freeze.

"All right," came Cookie's voice from the doorway of the bunkhouse. "That's enough. Now, I want both of you to get up off the ground and take two steps backward."

Neither man moved.

Cookie fired another blast from his rifle, sending mud and water spraying around their heads. Slowly, reluctantly, Cal lowered his fist and scrambled to his feet. When Adam stood, the two men faced each other, their fists clenched, their chests heaving.

"The fun's over," Cookie called sharply to the wranglers. "Get back inside now. Go on about your business."

The men returned to the bunkhouse, grumbling that their night's entertainment had ended so abruptly.

"Look at you," Cookie called, stepping forward between Cal and Adam. "Down in the mud fighting like dogs. And for what? Sounded to me like the oldest of all reasons. A female."

"That's not what this was about," Cal began, but his words were cut off when Diamond, her white nightshift fluttering like a moth's wings in the darkness, came sailing toward them. In her hand was a pistol.

Behind her, looking absolutely terrified, were Pearl and Jade, cowering beneath the cover of Diamond's leather duster.

"I heard gunshots. What's happened? Is anyone hurt...?"

Diamond stared at the two men, their faces streaked with mud and blood, their clothes torn and dirty and plastered to their skin. "Cal! Adam! What in the...? Whatever are you doing out here?"

"You go on back inside now, Diamond," Cookie said, waving the rifle. "This isn't any of your business."

"Not my business?" Diamond became indignant. "Everything that happens here on the ranch is my business." She turned on the two men. "Look at you. Instead of searching for the gunfighter, you're fighting each other. And you don't think this is my business?"

"But this is men's business, Diamond," the cook managed to say with as much patience as he could.

"Men's...? I don't understand."

Just then, Jade, who had been studying the faces of the two warriors, gave a mysterious woman's smile. Touching a hand to Diamond's arm she whispered, "Come inside, please. I will explain."

Diamond gave one last look at Cal, then at Adam, whose eyes were narrowed, fists clenched at his sides. The sight of him bloodied and bruised and caked with mud did something to her insides, twisting them into a knot.

"Please come now." Jade caught her hand, and motioned for Pearl to take her other hand.

With a sigh of confusion, Diamond allowed herself to be led away.

When the three women had returned to the house, Cookie lowered his rifle. But he didn't move away. Instead he stood his ground, determined to see the two men go their separate ways.

Cal picked up his gun and holster. "I don't want to see you come near Diamond again," he muttered. Without a backward glance, he strode toward the bunkhouse.

Adam buckled his gun belt, then retrieved his gun from the mud and jammed it into his holster. "You're a fool, McCabe," he shouted to the retreating back. "If you weren't so blind, you'd see that we're both on the same side."

"You heard me," Cal said sharply. "Stay away from Diamond."

With a sigh of disgust Cookie waved the rifle again.

Adam pulled himself into the saddle and disappeared into the darkness. Only then did Cal McCabe turn and let himself into the bunkhouse.

Diamond, flanked by Pearl and Jade, stood at her bedroom window and watched as Adam rode away. The sound of his horse's hooves faded into the distance. Seconds later, Cal retreated to the bunkhouse, and Cookie limped away.

"I don't know what's come over Cal," Diamond muttered.

"How long has your foreman known you?" Jade asked.

"All my life." Diamond moved away from the window and began to prowl her room.

Pearl took a seat in the rocker by the fire, and Jade perched on the edge of the bed.

"So he is like a second father?"

Diamond stopped in front of the fireplace. She shrugged. "I've never thought of Cal like that. He's just . . . a friend. My foreman. I depend on him to see that the ranch is running smoothly. But I don't think of him as a second father. I had Pa. I didn't need anyone else."

"But now our father is gone. An honorable man like Cal McCabe would see it as his duty to step into the role of protector, would he not?"

Diamond thought about it and slowly nodded. "I suppose so. But that doesn't explain the fight. Did you see them?" Her temper began to surface again. Her voice lowered with anger. "They were covered with blood and mud. That wasn't just a simple argument. They wanted to hurt each other. It's a wonder they didn't kill each other."

"But they did not." Jade smiled. "They did not wish to kill. What each wanted was to establish his own territory."

Diamond was clearly puzzled.

But Pearl, who had been listening in silence, suddenly nodded. "Of course. Oh, Diamond. Don't you see? They were fighting over you."

"Me?" But even while she protested, Diamond was recalling the looks on their faces. And for some strange reason, she was beginning to see a few pieces of a puzzle falling into place.

"Your foreman sees you as his responsibility. Not just your ranch, Diamond. You. Or rather, your virtue."

Diamond slowly nodded. "But what has that to do with Adam Winter?"

"Your foreman sees your neighbor as a threat to that virtue. Because it is clear, to those who will look, that Adam Winter also wants to be responsible for you. But not in a . . . fatherly way."

Diamond gasped at her outspokenness.

"Oh. Did you notice how he looked at her over dinner?" Pearl asked, clearly excited by the prospect of a romance.

Jade nodded. "And the way his voice warms when he speaks to her?"

"And did you notice how angry he became when he was ordering Diamond to remain in the house where it was safe?"

Jade laughed. "He is smitten."

"Stop this." Diamond pressed her palms over her ears as if to shut out the sound of their voices. "You two talk about me as though I'm not even here. And then you decide that a man I hardly know is . . . is smitten."

"Why else would a man like Adam Winter be goaded into a fight?" Pearl demanded. "Why, he's the most controlled, cool gentleman I've ever met. It has to be because he cares about you."

"You must trust me in this," Jade insisted. "My mother saw that my education delved deeply into all the mysteries of men, and their intricate relationships with women."

"Why?" Diamond asked innocently.

"Because men's pleasures, in all their forms, were my mother's business. And one day they shall be mine," Jade explained simply.

In that instant, Diamond understood just what the Golden Dragon was. She found herself thunderstruck.

"This much I know," Jade continued. "Adam Winter has feelings for you, Diamond. And those feelings are the cause of great distress for him."

Diamond rubbed at the throbbing in her temples. "I can't hear any more of this. If you don't mind, I need to sleep."

Jade nodded in understanding. "Come. Lie down. I will show you a lovely way to ease the tension you feel."

At Jade's urging, Diamond blew out the lantern and crawled into bed. Jade knelt beside the bed and pressed her fingers to Diamond's temples, massaging them gently. Within minutes the throbbing was gone.

"Umm. That's wonderful," Diamond murmured.

"It was another part of my education. Most men must be soothed before they can enjoy... other pleasures. Now you must rest," Jade whispered as she and Pearl made their way from the room.

The door closed softly behind them.

Diamond closed her eyes. But sleep eluded her. Instead, as she tossed and turned, she found herself brooding about Adam Winter. And seeing in her mind's eye the way he'd looked, bloody and battered. But unbowed. And darkly, tantalizingly dangerous.

Chapter Thirteen

"We've been waiting for you," Carmelita called as Diamond entered the kitchen and made her way to the table.

Diamond felt three pairs of eyes watching keenly as she sat down.

"How did you sleep?" Jade and Pearl asked in unison.

"Badly." Diamond wore her usual men's britches and shirt, with the sleeves rolled to her elbows. Her feet were encased in boots. At her waist was a gun belt. In the holster was a fully loaded pistol. Her hair streamed down her back in a tangle of fiery curls.

Pearl was dressed in a prim gown the color of buttercups, with a high neckline and a cameo pin at the throat. She had pulled her long hair back in a tight knot at her nape, and tied it with yellow ribbons.

Jade's tiny slippered feet peeked out from the hem of a long sheath of lush purple silk. It had a mandarin collar and frog closings, and was slit to her thigh on either side, for ease of walking. Her black hair fell long and straight to her waist.

"You were thinking about Adam Winter?" Jade asked in her musical voice.

"Don't be silly. Why should I?" Embarrassed, Diamond reached for a piece of Carmelita's corn bread and ducked her head.

"It is inevitable," Jade said with all the assurance of a headmaster. It was plain that she saw it as her duty to instruct this innocent in the ways of the world. "When a man fights for a woman, she cannot help but think about him."

"He didn't fight over me. And I wasn't thinking about him."

Jade smiled and sipped her tea.

"After breakfast, I'll help you with Daddy's ledgers," Pearl said. "That will help take your mind off Adam."

"My mind is not on Adam," Diamond said through gritted teeth.

"Whatever you say."

Pearl's determined attempt at cheerfulness only had Diamond's temperature climbing.

Carmelita kept her back to the young women at the table to hide the grin that split her lips. But every once in a while her shoulders shook in silent laughter. She'd never seen Diamond so flustered. It was most unusual. And quite appealing. Always, Diamond had been completely self-assured. A young woman who strode through life without fear, without question.

When she served the meal, Diamond stared at the platter of eggs that jiggled on squares of moist white bread.

"What is this?" she asked.

"Coddled eggs," Pearl said proudly. "I taught Carmelita how to make them the way my mother used to."

Diamond jabbed a fork into the center and watched as the egg bled all over the plate. When she tasted it she muttered, "It's so...bland."

"It's the way we eat them in Boston." Pearl pecked at her food like a dainty bird. "I hope you don't mind. I just wanted to repay you for all your kindness. I thought you might enjoy something new.''

''Thank you. They're...fine.'' Diamond choked down the egg, and watched as Jade did the same.

As soon as Pearl had finished her breakfast, Diamond pushed away from the table. ''Let's get to those ledgers.''

''May I join you?'' Jade asked.

''Of course. We'll work in Pa's office. It'll give you a chance to see something of his life. And afterward, we'll tour the ranch. I'm sure, like Pearl, you'll want to see how Pa lived before you return to San Francisco.''

Diamond led the way down the hall.

Inside her father's office, Pearl and Jade stood still as they took in the one single room in the house that best reflected their father. The office was big, as was everything in it, from the massive stone fireplace that dominated one wall, to the desk, piled with books and papers, and the overstuffed chair that had, over the years, taken on the imprint of his body.

The windows looked out over the ranch he'd loved, with a view of Widow's Peak, and in the distance the mirrored surface of Poison Creek. It was easy to imagine Onyx Jewel in this room, going over the ledgers, planning how to improve the livestock or enlarge his holdings.

''Oh.'' Jade hugged her arms about herself and gave a sigh. ''I feel Father here.''

Pearl nodded. ''More than in any other room, I can sense Daddy here in his office.''

Diamond found herself smiling. ''It's true. Since that first day after his...passing, I've always felt his presence here.''

It was strange, she thought, that all three of them should feel it so strongly. But then, weren't they all his daughters?

The thought should have shocked her. A day ago, it might have. But now, for some reason, she was beginning to accept the fact that they were all connected by a strong, invisible bond. A force stronger than her own will.

She lifted the ledgers from the desk drawer and opened them, then positioned a second chair alongside hers. "The sooner we get at this, the sooner we can take Jade on that tour of the ranch."

Pearl took the proffered seat and bent to the first column of figures. An hour later she threw up her hands in disgust.

"These figures are so jumbled, it will take forever to figure them out."

Diamond gave a sigh of relief. "I'm glad you agree. I thought it was just my lack of schooling that made them seem so muddled."

They looked up at a knock on the door, and opened it to admit Cal.

Though he was freshly scrubbed and his clothes were clean and pressed, his face still bore the ravages of last night's fight. He had a black eye and his right cheek was puffed and swollen.

"Carmelita told me where to find you," he said. Spotting the other two young women, he doffed his hat and nodded briefly to each of them. "'Morning, Miss Pearl. Miss Jade." He was always stiff and uncomfortable around women, except for Diamond, who didn't count because she was more like one of the wranglers than a female.

"What is it, Cal?" Diamond demanded.

"I want you to ride to town with me and report the shootings to the marshal."

"What good will that do?" Diamond frowned. "If you and the men couldn't find him, what makes you think the marshal can?"

Cal had come prepared for any argument. After all, the Jewels had always thought they were a law unto themselves, and the marshal merely a hired gun. And they considered all Jewel property sacred ground, and resented the thought of a deputy crossing their boundaries. And, though Cal would never admit it, Adam's words had kept him awake most of the night. *A wild creature like Diamond needs a keeper. That's the only way she's going to stay alive.* She was proving a handful since her pa's death. Cal wasn't certain he was up to it. But he had to try.

"For all we know, Diamond, Marshal Regan may have received some information on an outlaw loose in these parts. It's foolish to keep this from him."

"Cal is right." Jade crossed the room and paused beside the desk. "You need to confide in the marshal."

Pearl nodded her assent. "I quite agree. It would be foolhardy not to take the marshal into your confidence."

"But what about these ledgers?" Diamond's voice held the edge of impatience.

"We can do them later." Pearl patted Diamond's hand. "Your safety is more important than the books."

Diamond glanced from Pearl to Jade, then gave a sigh. "All right. First Marshal Regan. Then we'll tour the ranch. The ledgers will have to wait until tonight."

Jade and Pearl hurried away to fetch parasols. Diamond followed Cal to the barn to saddle her horse.

"Well, now, isn't this a coincidence?" Marshal Quent Regan looked up as Diamond and Cal strode into his office.

Seated across from him was Adam. And though he, too, had bathed and changed, his face bore the unmistakable bruises of his fight with Cal.

The marshal glanced from Cal's black eye and swollen cheek to Adam's cut lip and bandaged forehead.

"You here to report a fight with a grizzly?" he asked Cal.

The foreman shook his head. "Is that why he's here?" Cal asked, nodding toward Adam.

"Mr. Winter is here to report more gunplay out on your ranch. I assume you've come for the same reason."

Cal nodded.

"Tell me your story," Quent urged.

"I'll let Diamond tell it."

Diamond prayed she could find her voice. It seemed that whenever she encountered Adam, her throat went dry and her brain went numb. Damn the man. She hated the effect he had on her.

Marshal Regan listened quietly to Diamond's tale, his eyes downcast, his face impassive. When she was finished he stood and circled his office once before coming to a halt beside her.

His eyes, when they bored into hers, were narrowed in thought. "Is there something you aren't telling me, Diamond?"

"No, I..." She shook her head. "No."

"You and Adam Winter again. Every time you get shot at, he's there. In fact, it seems lately that every time you leave your door, he's there. What am I supposed to make of that?"

She brought her hands to her hips in a familiar stance, prepared for combat. "You can..." At a look from Cal, she bit back her temper. "I don't see what you can make of it. We're neighbors. We're bound to run into each other."

"Every time you walk out your door?"

Why did everyone insist upon making such an issue of her and Adam Winter? She took a deep breath and counted to ten, as Cal had cautioned her on their way to town. But it didn't help. If she didn't soon get out of this office and unleash this growing temper, she would explode.

"How about you, Winter? Do you have anything to add to the lady's story?"

Adam shook his head. And though he'd held his silence throughout Diamond's narrative, his gaze had followed her every movement.

"All right." Marshal Regan could see that his questions weren't getting him anywhere. "I'll look into it."

"Have you been able to identify any of those men who attacked us up on Poison Creek?" Adam asked.

"Not even one. I checked every Wanted poster for the past year, and sent their descriptions to towns across Texas. If they're outlaws, they aren't well-known." He held the door as they walked from his office. "It's almost as though someone brought together a whole gang of unknown criminals just for that one attack." He scratched his head. "But that doesn't make any sense."

At his words, Adam's frown deepened.

As they stepped into the morning sunshine, Quent looked up at the two young women seated in Jade's elegant carriage.

"'Morning, ladies," he said, touching the brim of his hat.

Diamond knew, by the way the marshal was standing there, that he was hoping for an introduction. By now, everyone in town was probably wondering what was going on at her ranch.

Out of the corner of her eye she saw Lavinia Thurlong and Gladys Witherspoon heading toward her. She felt her palms begin to sweat. It was common knowledge that these two gossips were only interested in learning all they could about everybody's business so they could repeat it all over town.

"Well, well. Diamond," Lavinia called, preventing her from bolting. Her words flowed like syrup. "Gladys and I have been wondering how you're getting along since the death of your father."

"Fine. Just fine," Diamond replied through gritted teeth.

The two women smiled and batted their lashes at the handsome marshal, then at Adam. But when they caught sight of Adam's face and Cal's matching bruises, their eyes widened. "Mercy. It must have been quite a fight. I hope it was worth it."

"It was," Cal muttered.

Realizing they weren't going to be offered an explanation, Gladys stared pointedly at the two young women. "I'm afraid we haven't been properly introduced. Diamond, will you do the honors?"

"I'd...be happy to." Happy? Diamond's scowl said it all. She was practically choking on every word. Ordinarily she wouldn't even suffer these two fools. But there were too many people around. She didn't dare tell them what was on her mind.

"Gladys Witherspoon, Lavinia Thurlong, Marshal Quent Regan, these are my..." Diamond realized that everyone was hanging on her every word, waiting to see how she would handle this. "This is Pearl Jewel and Jade Jewel."

"Jewel. Why, you two young women have the same last name as Diamond," Lavinia purred. "How did that happen?"

"We had the same father," Pearl said in her most proper Boston tones. She had met such women before in her young life. And had been the object of their scorn. But this time, she didn't mind for herself, since these people were strangers. But it hurt to know that Diamond was being mocked by members of her own town.

Marshal Regan removed his hat from his head in a courtly gesture. "Miss Pearl. Miss Jade. Nice to make your acquaintance."

"And yours, Marshal Regan," said Jade. "Thank you for the directions to Diamond's ranch. I would have been lost without them."

"I was happy to be of assistance, ma'am. After I gave you directions, I worried that I should have gone along with you to see that you made it all right. It isn't often," he added, "that the town of Hanging Tree is graced by such lovely ladies."

Pearl and Jade merely smiled. But Gladys and Lavinia, like dogs with a bone, would not give up yet.

"Do you two...ladies intend to make your home in Hanging Tree?" Lavinia asked.

"Oh, Lavinia," Gladys said, patting her arm. "Don't be impertinent. You know Diamond barely knows her own... sisters."

The two women covered their mouths and cackled at their clever remarks.

"I hope you were generously provided for in your father's will," Gladys said, assuming a sympathetic pose. "After all, Onyx Jewel was one of the richest men in Texas. It would be perfectly scandalous if all he left you was his...name."

Adam had been watching Diamond, and realized that she had reached the limit. Another word and these two gossips would be treated to the same sort of brawl that he and Cal had engaged in the previous night. Only this time, it would be witnessed by the whole town.

"If you don't mind." He maneuvered himself between Diamond and the two women. "I'll say goodbye now. I have chores to see to. Would you folks care to ride along?"

Diamond shot him a look of gratitude, and pulled herself into her saddle in one fluid motion. "That suits me just fine. I think our business here in town is concluded. Come on, Cal."

As the foreman started to mount, a crowd of men and boys approached, milling about a figure on horseback. The horse and rider drew near, and the crowd parted for a moment, revealing a stunningly beautiful young woman, seated sidesaddle on a strawberry roan. The woman was dressed all in red. The skirts of her red satin gown cascaded down the side of her mount in a riot of color. The neckline was daringly low, revealing an expanse of creamy flesh. A red satin hat with matching plumes adorned thick dark curls spilling around a face that would make men forget to breathe. Dark brows arched over liquid brown eyes fringed by long lashes.

The woman handed the reins to a young lad. Before she could alight, several men were jostling for the honor of helping her from the saddle.

"Mon Dieu," she said, sighing as her feet touched the ground. "It has been a long, tedious journey. But I have arrived at last."

The gown was molded to every lush curve of her body. When she walked, the narrow skirt was stretched tightly across her rounded bottom, causing the women in the crowd to gasp. The men couldn't hear over the pounding of their heartbeats and their involuntary sighs.

Catching sight of the marshal's badge, she made her way toward him. With every step, the hem of her gown swished around red satin slippers. Even the dust, which usually rose up to choke anyone who dared to walk the streets, seemed tamed by her presence.

"Marshal," she said in her heavy French accent. "I am hoping you can give me directions."

It took Quent Regan several moments to adjust his mouth and make it work. At last he managed to say, "I'd be happy to, ma'am. Where would you like to go?"

"I am looking for the Jewel Ranch."

Diamond felt a peculiar buzzing in her brain, and wondered idly if the earth might open up and swallow her. It would be far simpler than having to remain here and endure the looks from the crowd that had gathered. For even though the young woman hadn't yet finished her sentence, Diamond had the peculiar sense that it had all been said before.

Clearly visible around the woman's throat was a rope of gold on which were set two stones, one onyx, the other bloodred.

"My name is Ruby," the young woman said with a sultry smile. She offered her red-gloved hand like a precious gift to the marshal, who accepted it as though he'd never been given such a treasure before in his life.

"Ruby Jewel," she said, to the delight of the entire town of Hanging Tree, who hung on her every word. "I left my home in New Orleans as soon as I heard about the *mort tragique* of Onyx Jewel. You see, he was *mon père*. My papa."

The crowd erupted into chaos. Those in back jostled for a better view of the expected fireworks between Diamond and this latest surprise. The women of the town, shocked and scandalized by the stranger's earthiness, were struggling to subdue their husbands and sons. A few even managed to drag their errant men home. But most, intrigued by the scene unfolding, held their ground and watched in frank curiosity.

Lavinia and Gladys had the best spot of all from which to view the confrontation. They watched in openmouthed delight, their heads swiveling from Diamond, seated on her horse, to the woman in red, who seemed to be basking in the commotion she'd caused.

"Well now, ma'am," Marshal Regan began. "I guess the best one to ask would be—"

"Me." Diamond spoke the word without a hint of the inner turmoil she was feeling. "My name is Diamond Jewel. And I was just heading home. Would you care to ride along?"

Ruby's smile widened, revealing a most becoming dimple in her cheek. "It would be a pleasure. You do not mind, *chérie?*"

"Of course not." If the words stuck in her throat, Diamond gave no indication. "I would like you to meet Pearl Jewel and Jade Jewel."

As she indicated the two young women in the carriage, they nodded in acknowledgment.

"Pearl. Jade. *Enchantée*. This is more than I'd hoped for."

Adam watched from the back of his mount, marveling at the fresh new poise Diamond had acquired. Just days ago she had threatened to shoot Pearl if she set foot on her land. Now, in front of the entire town, she was acknowledging her, as well as Jade. And from the looks of things, she intended to welcome this latest stranger into her home, as well.

He could tell by the white-knuckled way her hands gripped the reins that she was seething inside. But to her credit, she gave away none of her feelings.

Ruby was helped into the saddle by half a dozen willing hands, all of whom were rewarded by her sultry smile and purr of thanks.

Then, with Diamond in the lead, and Cal and Adam on either side of her, the little party set off down the street, with most of the townspeople watching in awestruck silence.

Chapter Fourteen

"I guess you'd like to visit Pa's grave."

Diamond saw Cal and Adam glance at her in astonishment, but she kept her gaze firmly on the trail ahead. Right now she was weary of the fight. And wondering how many more surprises were in store for her. The best thing for all involved would be to get this over with as quickly as possible, and then send all Pa's...daughters packing.

"*Oui.* It is the sole reason for this arduous journey." Ruby touched a hand to her bosom. Her fingers closed around the band of gold that nestled in the cleft between her breasts. "My heart has been so heavy since I read about Papa."

With her attention drawn to the necklace, Diamond said, "I suppose that was a gift from Pa?"

"*Oui.* For my sixteenth birthday. Papa said that it would remind me that he would always be with me."

"He..." Diamond swallowed the lump in her throat. "He gave a similar gift to each of us."

Ruby slanted a look at the two young women in the carriage, who rode in silence. "I did not know of Pearl and Jade. And I knew of you only because of the newspaper account of Papa's death."

Once again Diamond felt a stab of pain at the many secrets her father had kept. "And what did you think when you read that he had a daughter?" Diamond asked.

Ruby's voice trembled with feeling. "That you were the luckiest daughter in the world. For you had Papa all the time, while I had only brief visits with him. But no matter how scarce, our time together was very precious."

How she must hate me, Diamond thought miserably. How they all must hate me. It was a shocking, sobering thought for someone who had always been so secure in her father's love.

And then she saw something that shocked her even more. In the pocket of Ruby's gown was the glint of something silver. Diamond kept her gaze fastened on the spot. At the horse's movements, the pocket opened to reveal a small silver pistol. Like the one Doc had said killed her father.

Odd, she thought, that all three of these women carried such weapons. Maybe it wasn't only strangers she ought to fear. Maybe her greatest danger lay within the circle of her family.

She studied the barren, windswept hill that loomed before them. Gathering her courage, she said, "This is where Pa is buried."

She and Ruby dismounted, and were joined by Pearl and Jade. The four climbed the hill and paused before the mound of earth.

Adam and Cal stood to one side, holding the reins of the horses, allowing the women their privacy.

Ruby took in the simple grave, topped with earth and stones.

"I know it must seem primitive," Diamond began, "but it was Pa's favorite place and—"

"On the contrary." Ruby spoke in hushed tones, as though in a house of worship. "I was afraid that Papa, being such a prominent man, would have an ornate crypt like those in my church. They are empty, impersonal slabs of granite and marble. But this…'' She indicated the tokens of love. Pearl's scroll. Jade's earthen jar of ashes. The view of sky and mountain. Her eyes filled. ''This is how I pictured Papa. The rugged, independent master of all he surveyed.'' Though her voice was choked, she managed to say, ''This is truly a resting place worthy of Papa.''

She dropped to her knees and folded her hands in prayer. Tears rolled down her cheeks, and she didn't bother to wipe them away. As she wept, she looked younger, more vulnerable, less self-assured, and far less sophisticated. She cried openly, allowing all her grief to pour from her heart.

At last she removed from her pocket a gleaming gold medal, on which was carved the faces of saints. She kissed it, then pressed it into the earth.

''Though you did not believe in our faith, Papa, you were very respectful of it, out of consideration for Mama and me. I have asked these saints to guide you on your journey into that other world, where I know you will find peace, and where you will be reunited with Mama and all those you love.''

Her words sent a shiver along Diamond's spine. She found herself looking, really looking, at this young woman. Not at the seductive gown or gaudy feathered hat. Not at the painted lips and heavily rouged cheeks. But at her eyes, brimming with tears. At her mouth, moving in solemn prayer. At the way her shoulders sagged as she gave in to her wrenching, agonizing grief.

Diamond had been prepared to dislike Ruby. In fact, she'd *wanted* desperately to dislike her, as she wanted to dislike Pearl and Jade. But each time one of them revealed the depth of her grief, Diamond found her heart betraying her. It wasn't resentment she felt for these three. It was a sense of shared loss and heartache. But that didn't mean she felt any sort of familial attachment, she reminded herself. These three were strangers, far different from her. The only thing that bound them was the Jewel name.

"Di, it's time to go," Cal called.

She nodded. Reluctantly, the other three turned and followed her down the hill. As she mounted, she saw Ruby's tear-filled gaze return to the mound of earth and stones.

On a wave of sympathy she found herself asking, "Have you someplace to sleep tonight?"

"I...did not think about such things. In my desire to find Papa, I gave no thought to where I would sleep, or if I would find food or shelter at the end of my journey."

"There's room at the ranch if you'd like to join us."

Ruby smiled, though her lips still trembled. "*Merci.* I would like to see Papa's home. He spoke of it with much love."

They rode some distance in silence. When they reached the boundary between Adam's land and Diamond's, he reined in his mount.

But before he could take his leave, Diamond surprised him by saying, "If you don't mind, Adam, I'd like you to see us home."

His eyes narrowed. "Why? You have Cal here."

"I..." She shot a sideways glance at Cal, who had paused alongside the carriage to speak to Pearl and Jade. "I'd like to talk with you. Alone."

He shrugged. "All right. I guess I can spare the time."

The ride seemed leisurely enough, with the horses setting a slow, steady pace in order to allow the carriage to keep up. But Adam sensed a tension in Diamond, and found himself wondering just what she wanted to talk about. He prepared himself for another one of her famous tongue-lashings.

When they arrived at the ranch house, Cookie and Carmelita were just walking up the veranda together, carrying several plucked chickens. Both looked up with a smile. But the smile faded on Carmelita's lips when she caught sight of the stranger.

"I'll leave you now." Cal addressed his words to Diamond, but fixed his sight on the man beside her. "I've got to ride over to the north range." He paused, then said meaningfully, "You'll stay close to the house, Di?"

"Yes. Of course." Diamond dismissed him with a wave of her hand and turned toward the others, eager to get these last introductions over with.

"Carmelita, Cookie, I'd like you to meet Ruby—" she paused, then continued in one quick breath, hoping to get through this with as few explanations as necessary "—Ruby Jewel. Ruby came all the way from New Orleans when she read about Pa. Ruby, this is Carmelita, our housekeeper, and Cookie, our ranch cook."

"Miss Ruby," Cookie said over the stump of a pipe in his mouth. "Nice to make your acquaintance. Fine little town, New Orleans," he added. "Just full of lovely ladies. Though not many of them as pretty as you."

The young woman smiled at his attempt to put her at ease.

"I will have a meal ready soon," Carmelita said, keeping a firm grip on the chickens' legs with one hand while she wiped the other on her apron. "Señorita Ruby, you will want to come inside and rest after your long journey."

"*Oui.* I would be grateful for a basin of water and a chance to refresh myself."

"Ruby will be spending the night, Carmelita. You can get a room ready for her." Diamond turned to the newcomer. "Pearl and Jade can show you around the house while I unsaddle my horse and take care of some...unfinished business with Adam.''

Adam slid from the saddle and helped Ruby dismount. Then he offered a hand to Jade and Pearl before leading the horses toward the barn.

Diamond walked ahead, leading her mare. Once inside she unsaddled quickly, then began to unhitch the horses from the carriage. She worked quickly, efficiently, deep in thought.

Adam worked alongside her, respecting her need for silence.

When the chores were done she crossed her arms over her chest and began to pace.

Adam lounged against a stall, watching and waiting. Sooner or later, he knew, she'd get to their...unfinished business.

"When is this nightmare going to end?" she muttered. "How many more surprises has Pa got in store for me? It's gotten so that I hate to ride into town."

"You can't let a few town gossips get you down."

She looked up. "Do you think I care what those fools say?" She shook her head and continued pacing. "Let them laugh. Let them all laugh. What do I care? I've never lived my life to please the people of Hanging Tree. But I do care about Pa's reputation. I don't like the thought of the whole territory of Texas smirking at the mention of his name. From now on, I'll be afraid every time the stage pulls up, or a new carriage rolls into town, wondering if it's another of Pa's surprises. This could go on for months. Years. And there's nothing I can do about it. Nothing."

She turned, her eyes glittering with repressed fury. Suddenly she focused on Adam. "But there is something I can do about you."

"I figured that sooner or later you'd get to the reason you asked me here."

"Jade said that the fight you and Cal had last night was over me."

She saw the flash of surprise, followed by a sudden darkness that came into his eyes.

"Jade says that Cal was only trying to protect me. In a fatherly way, of course."

"Is that so?" He gave her a dangerous smile. "What else did Jade say?"

"That your intentions are not at all fatherly."

His smile faded. He went very still, and she had the impression of a predator watching his prey.

"Damn it, Adam, say something." Without thinking, she grabbed his arm and jabbed a finger to his chest. "Is Jade right? Am I the reason you and Cal were fighting?"

He struggled to ignore her touch. "Is that the reason you brought me here? To satisfy some feminine need for compliments?"

She was outraged. "Is that what you think? That I'm just looking for some words of praise?"

"Well, aren't you?"

"Damn you."

She started to turn away, but he caught her by the shoulder and hauled her back.

Before she could react he caught hold of her other shoulder as well, nearly lifting her off her feet as he pinned her against the length of him.

"Would you care to tell me what else Jade said about last night's fight?"

"Only that…" Startled, and a little afraid, she ran the tip of her tongue over lips that had suddenly gone dry. The fact that he watched the movement through narrowed eyes only enhanced her fear. "That you wanted to establish your... territory."

His eyes darkened with a dangerous glint. His grasp tightened perceptibly on her shoulders as he drew her closer. He swore, softly and fiercely. "Jade was right." His voice was low and rough with feeling.

Diamond's heart began a wild flutter in her chest until she thought it would surely burst. This wasn't at all what she'd expected. She'd anticipated angry denial. Or a calm but heated explanation. But now she felt even more confused. And strangely elated.

With his mouth almost on hers, he paused, as though considering the consequences.

In that moment, she had a desperate need to taste his lips. More than anything in the world, she wanted his kiss. She raised herself on tiptoe, to claim what she desired.

A sigh seemed to well up from deep inside him. And with it, he gave up the fight. His mouth covered hers in a savage kiss.

A razor's edge of excitement sliced through her. She could feel his thighs pressed to hers, and his sudden, shocking arousal. She could feel the strength in the arms that held her. He could break her with no effort. And yet she sensed that he was holding back, as though aware of that very strength. It was comforting. And deeply erotic.

Roughly, almost savagely, he took the kiss deeper. Caught up in a blaze of passion, he forgot to be gentle. His kisses became more urgent, more demanding. Diamond found herself caught up in something more than she'd expected. This was no ordinary kiss, like the ones they'd shared before. This time, they were rushing headlong into something neither of them could control.

"Oh, God, Diamond," he breathed against her mouth. His fingers moved up her back and she felt splinters of fire and ice along her spine. "I've tried to deny it. Tried to tell myself that this was all wrong." He drew her even closer, until she could feel the thundering of his heartbeat inside her own chest. It matched the wild rhythm of her own.

He nibbled her lips until, on a sigh, they parted. His tongue explored her mouth, then withdrew, inviting hers to do the same. She was hesitant at first, then grew bolder as she reveled in the dark, mysterious taste of him.

His kisses were by turn fierce, then gentle. His mouth was bruising, then soft. His hands, too, gripped her fiercely one moment, then gentled, as he pulled himself back again and again from the brink.

He gave her no time to think as he took her on a wild, breathless ride, to the top of a mountain peak, then sent her plunging headlong into a bottomless canyon. With a wild rush of sensations, she followed where he led, clinging to him as her whole world seemed to tilt dangerously.

Lost in the wonder of their kisses, they dropped to their knees in the hay.

"I've been lying to myself. And to you. I want you, Diamond." His voice was thick with desire. He nibbled at the corner of her mouth, then trailed openmouthed kisses along the sensitive column of her throat. "I want you as I've never wanted anyone."

Thrilling to his words, Diamond moved in his arms, loving the feel of his lips on her flesh. She arched her neck, giving him easier access. He ran his tongue along the line of her collarbone until, with soft sighs and breathless whispers, her hand fisted in his hair.

"I never knew," she admitted. "I never even dreamed..."

He chuckled at her confusion. "Do you know long I've been fighting these feelings?"

She shook her head.

"Since the first time I saw you."

She shivered as his fingers fumbled impatiently with th
buttons of her shirt. He shoved it roughly aside and bent hi
lips to the soft swell of her breast, covered by a pale che
mise. Heedless of the delicate fabric, he began nibbling
suckling, until her nipples hardened and she moaned softly.

He drew her down in the hay and lay beside her. "Th
thought of you is driving me mad," he muttered as hi
hands followed the path of his lips and he untied the rib
bons of her chemise to tear aside the last barrier.

The feel of his callused hands against her soft flesh wa
more wonderful than anything she'd ever known. No mai
had ever touched her like this. Kissed her like this. And, sh
knew, no other man ever would.

"Do you know what I do when I can't sleep?" he mur
mured against her throat. "I lie awake and think about
hundred different ways I'm going to make love with you."
He plunged his hands into the tangles of her hair and plun
dered her mouth with savage kisses.

She'd faced snowstorms, avalanches and a thunderin
herd of cattle. But never before had she been caught up i
something so wild, so primitive, she could no longer think
All she could do now was feel. "Adam..." she murmured

"Shh." He silenced her protest with a deep, lingering kis
that had her heart racing, her head swimming.

He reached a hand to the fasteners at her waist. Througl
a haze of throbbing needs he whispered, "Tell me you wan
this, Diamond."

Her head was spinning, her pulse hammering. A part o
her was begging him to go on holding her, kissing her
stroking her. Another part of her was terrified.

"I'm afraid," she managed to whisper over the fear tha
clogged her throat.

He lifted his head. "Afraid? Of me?"

How could she make him understand her fears? Of losing control. Of being taken over by needs so demanding, they left her stunned and reeling.

"Of me. Of this." She turned her head, ashamed to have him see this weakness. "It's all happened so fast. I don't know...what's right anymore. I don't know what to do. Oh, I wish...I wish...Help me, Adam."

For long moments he studied her. How could he have forgotten how sheltered her life had been? It was true that she was a woman. But she was still clinging to yesterday, and the girl she had been when her father had been alive to shield her and make her decisions.

He felt her tremble and drew her into his arms with great tenderness. He held her against his chest, rocking her like a child. Suppressing his own needs, he stroked her hair, her back, until the trembling subsided.

"Come on, Diamond." He helped her to her feet and gently tied the ribbons of her chemise, then buttoned her shirt.

With each touch of her, the need was still there, raw and desperate, demanding release. But he managed to hold it at bay as he said, "You'd better go inside now. It's time you got to know Ruby."

"Come with me, Adam. It'll be easier with you there. You can talk to her, and I can just sit back and listen."

He shook his head. "It's time for me to head back to my place. There's work to be done. Besides, this is your business. You have to see to it."

He took a step back, and then another, feeling a sense of loss and pain as he peeled himself away.

"When will I see you again?"

He caught the reins of his stallion and pulled himself into the saddle. "Don't worry. I'll be around."

He rode away without looking back. It was the only way he could leave. If he chanced even one look, he'd never find the strength to ride out of here. Because the truth was, he still wanted her. Wanted her with a desperation he'd never known before. And there would be no relief for the raw, churning needs that clawed at him, fighting to be free.

So much for unfinished business, he thought. It was just one more thing that lay between them like a gaping chasm. Daring them to cross. Threatening to devour them if they did. Threatening to destroy them if they didn't.

Chapter Fifteen

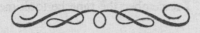

"Your home is lovely, *chérie*," Ruby said as she sank into a chair by the fire.

Diamond had to drag her thoughts away from Adam. All afternoon she had been subdued, while the others laughed and chatted. But though she'd been distracted, she had managed to digest bits and pieces of their conversation.

Ruby's life had proved to be as intriguing as the others'. Her mother had apparently been an earthy, passionate Creole, who was not above certain... indiscretions, such as stealing, lying or cheating to survive. Then she had met the charismatic Onyx Jewel. And her life had been forever changed. He had bought her a fashionable home, and had seen to it that she and Ruby lived a comfortable life. Still, Diamond sensed, there was a great deal of her mother in Ruby. She was a strong, capable woman who would do whatever was necessary to survive.

"Pa and I didn't care much about the house. Our only concern was the operation of the ranch."

"You speak of the ranch as one would speak of a lover." Ruby's gaze sought the distant mountain peaks, already cloaked in twilight.

Diamond struggled to ignore the trickle of ice along her spine. "I wouldn't know much about that. Tell me about . . . your life with Pa."

"He was so handsome and charming, all other men paled by comparison," Ruby said matter-of-factly.

"That's true," Pearl said with sudden animation. "I doubt there will ever be another man who can hold a candle to Daddy. I remember the time he took me to the circus."

She described, in vivid detail, her adventure with her father.

Almost at once, Jade jumped in with a story about her days in San Francisco with her father.

And then it was Ruby's turn again.

Diamond settled back, seeing her father through the eyes of these strangers. And then she was suddenly reminded of what Adam had said to her. Hadn't he told her that she could learn much about her father from these women?

Late into the night she allowed their stories to flow over her, seeing her father in a way she never had before. He had been much more than a Texas cattleman. He had been a world adventurer. A man of many moods. And many passions.

And when the fire had burned low, and they made their way to bed, Diamond realized that their stories had soothed some of the pain, and eased a little of her burden. But that was Pa.

What was she going to do about Adam?

"Another tour of the ranch, Di?" Cal gulped down his coffee and picked up his hat. "There can't be much left to see."

The foreman was worried about Diamond. It wasn't enough to lose her father. But he could see that the intrusion of all these females, and the attacks by a mysterious gunman, were beginning to take their toll. There were dark circles under her eyes. And her temper was on a short fuse. Even shorter than usual.

In the past few days, from dawn to dark, she had driven herself to the limit. She filled the hours with tours of the ranch, forcing Pearl, Jade and Ruby to endure far more discomfort than they would have wanted. With over a dozen wranglers to accompany them, they'd ridden over miles of rugged hills and rocky valleys. They'd viewed vast herds of cattle, and had visited a line camp. They had even spent one afternoon on the east range, eating from Cookie's chuck-wagon with the cowboys.

Several times Diamond had spotted Adam in the distance. Each time, her heart had leaped to her throat, leaving her feeling as though she'd just run a race with a mustang. But each time he'd spotted her and her party, he'd turned his mount in the opposite direction, as though determined to avoid her.

The first time it happened, she thought it might be a coincidence. But after the second and third times, she knew it was deliberate.

If being forced to view Adam from afar was painful, rejection was pure torture. It seemed that her heart was always either soaring or breaking. The strain was becoming too much to bear. She knew when she refused his advances that she might drive him away. But somehow, in the deepest recesses of her heart, she'd hoped he would give her time. Instead, he'd given up on her.

In an effort to erase his image from her mind and heart, she decided to stay as busy as possible. Hard, physical work had always been the solution to her problems. And so she plunged herself into ranch chores with a vengeance, hauling food and water, even mucking stalls alongside the wranglers, to keep from dwelling on Adam.

The days were tolerable, since she left herself little time to think. But the nights offered her no relief. Instead of sleep, she'd been plagued with images of Adam touching her, stroking her, kissing her, until she thought she'd go mad with the need for him.

Still, she had to keep running. She was afraid of what might happen if she stopped.

"There's so much the others haven't seen," Diamond protested.

"It would take months to see everything," Cal countered. "And then you'd probably miss half of it."

"That's just the point. No matter how much I show them, there's so much more they'll never see."

"I had no idea Father's holdings were so complicated," Jade said softly, interrupting their latest argument. "It is simply not possible to comprehend anything this big, until it is seen with the eye."

The others nodded their heads in agreement.

"When I was living in Boston and Daddy spoke about his ranch in Texas, I had no idea what he meant," Pearl mused aloud.

"Nor I, *chérie.*" Ruby laughed softly. "I think the entire city of New Orleans and the Louisiana bayou country could be swallowed up in these Texas hills."

"It's settled, then?" Diamond asked as she glanced from one to the other. "You're not tired of seeing the ranch?"

"I, for one," Pearl said sincerely, "would never tire of such breathtaking scenery."

With a sigh of resignation, Cal headed for the door. "I'll see which wranglers I can spare."

"Cal." Following him out the door, Diamond kept her voice low, so the others wouldn't hear. "It's been days now, and there hasn't been a single incident. Maybe the gunman has left."

"And maybe he hasn't," Cal said grimly.

"But I feel so guilty taking men away from necessary chores. I know you can't spare them. Why don't you just send one or two wranglers along with us?"

"Because," he said as patiently as if he were dealing with a child, "I'd rather send too many than too few. Look, Di," he said, catching her arm when she started to turn away in disgust, "the men aren't being wasted. I figure the reason there hasn't been another attack is because the gunman sees that the odds are against him. He might be willing to attack a couple of females, but he isn't going to plow into an army of men. Now, as long as you want to give your—" He caught himself in time, before he'd spoken the dreaded word *sisters,* and amended "—ladies another tour of the ranch, we can spare as many cowboys as you need."

Diamond smiled and touched a hand to Cal's cheek. Though he was younger than her father by a good ten years, there were times when she could swear he spoke with Onyx's voice. "Thanks, Cal. I appreciate it. And I won't forget this."

Stunned by her unexpected gesture, and more than a little pleased at the softening of her nature, he turned and watched as she returned to the house. Could it be that the ways of all these feminine creatures around her were rubbing off on her? If so, he hoped they'd stay a while longer. They were definitely good for Diamond.

He jammed his hat on his head and went in search of his best marksmen. Adam Winter would never again be able to accuse him of being careless about Diamond's safety.

It galled him to know that, even though Adam Winter wasn't here, his words had had a direct bearing on the decisions being made on this ranch. Cal hoped Adam's absence these past few days meant that Diamond had finally come to her senses and ordered him to stay off her land for good.

Adam knelt and studied what was left of the carcass of a bull. He'd pinned his hopes on this carefully bred stud, hoping to build a prize herd. The animal had set him back a small fortune. Had he lived, he'd have been worth every dollar.

It was unusual for wolves to attack such a ferocious creature, even when desperate. True, the weather had turned colder, with snow in the hills. Still, wolf packs usually searched out a more vulnerable cow, rather than risk being gored by a bull's horns.

The nighttime visit by nature's scavengers had left a bloodied mess. Mangled hide. Missing bones. The prints of wolf, coyote, fox, even vultures, mingled in the snow.

With a sigh of disgust, Adam started to rise. Just then he caught a glimpse of something shiny in the nearby brush. Sweeping aside a few branches, he stooped and picked up a spent bullet. He studied it for long minutes, then dropped it into his pocket.

Man was the only predator in these parts that fired a gun. Now all Adam needed to do was to figure out which man had fired this one. And why.

"You're awfully quiet," Pearl said over supper.

Diamond had pushed herself and the others all day, deliberately leading them toward the boundary between her land and Adam's in the hope of seeing him, even if from a distance. But the little cabin had shown no sign of life. She realized miserably that Zeb and Adam were probably with their herd on the banks of Poison Creek.

"I am certain it is the visit to Father's grave today," Jade said in her lovely, musical voice. "It affects us all in very strange ways."

Ruby nodded. "I feel . . . drained."

"And I feel tranquil," Jade said emphatically. "Father is at peace. And Father succeeded, in death, to bring us all together."

Pearl reached across the table and patted Diamond's hand in a show of sympathy and support. "It must be especially difficult for you, here in the home you shared with Daddy."

Diamond nodded, afraid to trust her voice. What a coward she was, she berated herself. She was actually allowing them to believe that Pa's death was the only reason for her discomfort. When all along it was also... Oh, Adam. What am I to do about you? I miss you so. I can't stop thinking about you. Could this feeling possibly be . . . love? The thought hit her with all the force of a thundering herd. Oh, sweet heaven. Not love.

"This will soothe you," Carmelita said, setting down a platter of tortillas filled with a chicken mixture. The fragrant aroma of rich spices filled the air.

Relieved that it wasn't another of Pearl's bland dishes, Diamond heaped her plate before passing the platter to Ruby, who followed suit. Even Jade seemed to enjoy the highly seasoned food. Pearl was the only one who merely picked at her meal while the others dug in.

"It is a shame Señor Winter has not come around to enjoy our fine food," Carmelita remarked.

At once Diamond's cheeks warmed. Carmelita took no notice, but the others did.

"I enjoy cooking for him," Carmelita continued as she moved around the kitchen. "Almost as much as I loved cooking for Señor Jewel."

"We could invite him for supper," Pearl said, watching Diamond's reaction.

Jade, seeing the way Diamond's color deepened, nodded in agreement. So, she had surmised correctly. Diamond wasn't as immune to Adam Winter as she pretended. "I quite agree. Adam is most pleasant company, is he not, Diamond?"

"I...hadn't noticed." Diamond was beginning to feel smothered by all these women and their attempts at kindness. Ever since their arrival she'd had to listen to their chatter, their laughter, their tales about their lives before arriving here in Texas.

"Would you like to ask Señor Winter to dinner?" Carmelita persisted.

"Not tonight." Diamond squirmed under the housekeeper's scrutiny.

"And why not?" Carmelita asked.

"Because..." Diamond's mind raced. She couldn't bear to face him so soon after... "Because of Ruby," she said. "I think she deserves a little of our time."

Ruby gave a wide smile, pleased at such generosity. "That is sweet, *chérie*. I have very much enjoyed getting to know all of you. I think we have much more in common than just Papa."

"There, you see." Diamond shoved aside her plate. Even Carmelita's spiced chicken couldn't hold her interest. It was another reason to resent Adam Winter. He was spoiling her appetite.

Oh, if only it were that simple. But the truth was, she couldn't find it in her heart to resent him. All she could do was want him. And berate herself for such a silly, feminine weakness. If this was love, she wanted no part of it. She had never felt so miserable in her whole life.

* * *

"Oh, Diamond. You startled me. I thought everyone was asleep."

Pearl, dressed in a prim nightshift and robe, paused at the foot of the stairs.

Diamond was wrapped in a faded army blanket, seated in her father's favorite chair pulled in front of the fire.

Pearl walked closer, lifting her lantern for a better view. "Can't sleep?"

"No."

"Neither can I. Do you mind if I join you?"

Diamond shrugged. "I'm afraid I won't be very good company." She looked up. "What brought you downstairs?"

"I thought I'd warm some milk. Mama used to give me warm milk whenever I couldn't sleep. Would you like some?"

Diamond couldn't manage to work up much enthusiasm. "I suppose."

Pearl padded away and returned a few minutes later with two glasses of warm milk. One sip, and Diamond wanted to set it aside. But she couldn't bear to hurt Pearl's feelings, so she drank it down in long swallows, before wiping her mouth on her sleeve.

"Thanks, Pearl. That was...that was real nice."

They both looked up as a delicate figure seemed to glide down the stairs. Jade, wearing a flowing silk robe, hesitated when she caught sight of the two.

"Please forgive," she whispered, folding her hands together. "I did not mean to intrude."

"Come and join us," Pearl called. "Diamond and I had trouble sleeping."

"As I did," the young woman said with a smile. "I was going to make myself a cup of tea. Would you have some with me?"

They both nodded, and she left, only to return a short time later with a tray of steaming cups.

The three women sipped in silence.

"Is that not soothing?" Jade asked.

"Umm. Yes," Pearl replied.

Diamond said nothing, but she drained the cup so that she wouldn't hurt Jade's feelings. And all the while, her misery grew. This longing for something she didn't understand and couldn't even name was driving her to distraction.

Within minutes a third figure descended the stairs. Ruby, wearing a scarlet velvet dressing gown and matching feather-trimmed slippers, paused when she caught sight of the others.

"Is this a party?" she asked, taking in the empty glasses and cups.

"We couldn't sleep," Pearl explained.

"Ah. Nor can I." She swept closer.

"We've tried warm milk and hot tea," Pearl said. "Have you a home remedy?"

"Oui." Ruby's glance swept the room and came to rest on the crystal decanter and glasses on a shelf in a cabinet. "Mama used to say that a glass of sherry was soothing nectar of the gods."

She filled four tumblers with ruby liquid and passed them around.

"Oh, my," Pearl said, feeling positively wicked. "The only time we ever drank spirits was when Daddy came to town."

"At the Golden Dragon, we saved the wine and whiskey for the patrons," Jade said softly. "The use of spirits was frowned upon by my mother. The women who worked for us were forbidden to indulge. Mother said it weakened the will of a woman and strengthened the resolve of a man."

"It wouldn't take much to weaken my resolve," Ruby said with a laugh as she sank down on the sofa beside Pearl and Jade. She glanced at Diamond. "You look very sad, *chérie*. Is there something we can do to help you?"

Diamond shook her head and took a sip of the wine. It was as smooth as the milk, cooler than the tea. And soothing. Definitely soothing. Unaccustomed to it, she drained the glass in one long gulp.

"Wine should be sipped," Ruby admonished as she picked up the decanter and refilled Diamond's glass.

"I'll remember." Diamond drank only half, then turned to stare into the glowing embers of the fire. "Have any of you ever had occasion to...kiss a man?" Now where had those words come from? She had no way of knowing. She only knew that the question had slipped unbidden from her lips.

The three young women glanced at one another, then turned to study her.

"Is that what troubles you, *chérie?*" Ruby asked. "Kissing a man?"

"Of course not." Embarrassed, Diamond emptied the glass and set it aside with a clatter. "I just wondered..."

"I once kissed Jeremy Peters," Pearl admitted shyly. "He was thirteen, and the handsomest boy in Boston."

"How old were you?" Ruby asked.

"Twelve."

"That doesn't count, *chérie*." Ruby filled Diamond's glass a third time. "Diamond is talking about kissing a man, not a boy."

"I suppose you'd know all about that," Pearl said with a trace of disapproval.

"As a matter of fact, I would not," Ruby admitted wryly. "I have learned many things. How to steal. How to cheat. How to attract a man's attention. But Mama warned me that if I were to play with a man's affections, I could find myself drowning in a bog of quicksand."

"That's...that's how I feel," Diamond said, suddenly getting to her feet. She felt as if she'd been prodded with a pitchfork. She began to pace while the others stared at her in surprise. "I'm not slow-witted. Pa always said I had a quick mind. That I could do anything I put my mind to. But this time..." She shook her head and continued pacing. "This time I just don't see a solution."

"Perhaps if you explained," Pearl began.

But Diamond wasn't listening. She had a need to talk. She found the words slipping off her tongue before she even had time to think.

"I certainly don't need a man. Never had any use for one. And if I were to choose one, it wouldn't be one who didn't want to put down roots here in Texas."

The other three nodded and wisely kept silent, trying to follow her line of reasoning.

"He's bossy and arrogant and...secretive. Why, I don't know a thing about him, except that he once owned a farm in Maryland."

"Maryland? Oh. Adam Winter," Pearl said as understanding dawned.

Diamond took no notice as she crossed her arms over her chest and paused to stare into the embers. "One minute he's in the barn, wanting to—" She caught herself in time, and glanced over to see the three women watching her intently. Pearl appeared scandalized. Jade was merely looking smug, as though she'd always known. And Ruby was grinning from ear to ear, eager to hear every juicy detail. "And then I don't see him again for days. And I know—" her voice dropped to a whisper, and she suddenly slumped in defeat "—he's avoiding me."

"Oh, dear." Pearl was on her feet first, clasping Diamond's hands in hers.

Jade followed, and dropped an arm around Diamond's shoulders. "Do not despair."

Ruby pressed her cheek to Diamond's. "Jade is right, *chérie*. All is not yet lost."

They led Diamond to her chair. When she sat down, they gathered around her, kneeling at her feet.

"Do you love Adam Winter?" Jade asked softly.

"Certainly not." Diamond was indignant at the question.

"If you think you are losing sleep over a man you hate," Ruby said, "you are only fooling yourself, *chérie*."

"Pa raised me to believe that I had to reach for lofty goals," Diamond said in defense. "And Adam Winter is a loner, a drifter, a..."

"A gentleman," Pearl said emphatically. "From the first time I met him, I sensed that he was a true gentleman."

"He doesn't kis—he's no gentleman," Diamond said firmly.

"Putting that aside for the moment," Jade persisted, "do you wish to see Adam Winter again?"

Diamond shrugged. "I suppose so. But just to let him know there are no hard feelings about—" she felt her cheeks burning "—what happened in the barn."

"What exactly did happen in the barn?" Ruby asked boldly.

"He... we... kissed. And then I... told him to stop."

Pearl gave a sigh of relief. "That's good."

"But I'm not sure I meant it," Diamond admitted.

"That is not so good," Jade said softly.

The others clucked in agreement.

"This is all so romantic," Ruby said with a sigh.

Jade nodded. "You must see Adam Winter again."

"How?" Diamond asked miserably. "Cal won't let me out of his sight without a dozen wranglers around me. And Adam turns the other way whenever he sees me anywhere near."

The three fell silent.

"Food," Jade said firmly. "Mother taught me that good food, fine spirits and lovely women, offered in an exquisite setting, are irresistible to a man."

The others merely stared at her. Then Pearl nodded. "He likes Carmelita's cooking. He'd come for supper, I think."

"But you can't be alone with him," Ruby added. When the others glanced at her, she explained, "In the bayou, a young lady and a gentleman are not allowed to be alone until they are wed."

"Then how did Pa and your mama . . . ?" Embarrassed, Diamond let her voice trail off.

"By now you must realize that Papa did not live by the rules of other men. Nor, it would seem, did our mothers."

Diamond rubbed her temples. Her head was spinning, and she found it difficult to follow a simple train of thought.

She yawned loudly. "He won't come. Even for Carmelita's cooking. I've driven him away. Now I have to learn to live with that and get on with my life. Without Adam." The very words brought a fresh pain to her heart.

She got to her feet and waited a moment until the dizzyness stilled. Then, surprising herself, she bent a kiss to each girl's cheek. "I never had . . . anyone to talk with until now. You've all been very kind and sweet, even if you can't help. Thank you."

They watched as she made her way slowly up the stairs, her hand firmly gripping the banister to keep from stumbling.

When they heard her door close, the three young women leaned close and engaged in a whispered, highly animated conversation.

Chapter Sixteen

"Señor Winter has accepted your invitation to dinner," Carmelita announced as Diamond walked into the kitchen.

The sun had been up for hours, and Diamond had just now been able to pull herself together. She couldn't recall ever having slept this late.

She gripped the edge of the table. "My invi—? I don't understand. When? How...?" Stunned, she wasn't able to gather her wits about her. All she had were questions. Too many questions.

It was the wine, she knew. She would never touch a drop again.

"The three lovely *señoritas* asked Cal to ride over to Señor Winter's ranch this morning with the invitation. Señor Winter sent his immediate reply."

With a little moan Diamond shoved aside the corn bread and coffee, and turned her head away from the sunlight streaming through the window, burning her eyes.

"Where are the—" her tone hardened "—three lovely *señoritas?*" She couldn't wait to give them a piece of her mind.

"They rode to town with Cal and several of the wranglers. They should be back any time now." The housekeeper turned around to see Diamond heading toward the door. "Where are you going?"

"Out to the barn. I need to work off some of my temper. Before I do something I might regret." Like send three busybodies packing, she thought miserably.

How could they have done such a thing without asking her?

She skidded to a halt. Or had they?

She wasn't at all certain just what she'd said last night. She remembered talking about Adam and the barn.... Her face flamed. How could she have made such a blunder? In the cold light of day it was inconceivable that she would reveal such an intimate secret. But last night, after several glasses of wine, it had seemed the most natural thing in the world to confide in her three sis—

She clamped a hand to her mouth. What in the world was happening to her? Next she'd start to believe they could all be one big happy family, and that she could talk to them the way she'd always talked to Pa.

She stalked into the barn. Snatching up a pitchfork, she walked to the first stall and set to work with a vengeance.

Pa used to say that there was nothing like being knee-deep in horse manure to clear the mind and sort through all life's puzzles.

"Diamond. Here you are. Phew." Pearl held her nose and stepped carefully through the straw. "Come out of that stall and see what we've brought you."

"A noose to hang myself?" Diamond was feeling mean. And the hard, strenuous chores hadn't helped to work it off.

"Don't be silly. Come on inside. The others are waiting to show you what we bought in town."

"I'm not interested."

"Carmelita said to tell you she made your favorite lunch. Tortillas and beef. With extra spices."

Diamond's mouth watered. She'd managed to work up an appetite. Besides, though she would never admit it, she was a little curious to know why they'd gone to town. "I guess I could manage to eat a little."

She followed Pearl from the barn and paused outside the kitchen door to pry off her dung-covered boots.

Inside, the others looked up from the table, where they were admiring an assortment of feminine frills.

"Look what we bought for you," Pearl announced as Jade held up a gown of shimmering white satin shot with silver thread.

"It was the finest gown we could find in a town the size of Hanging Tree," Jade explained. "Though we are not certain of the size, we will have time to tailor it to fit you by tonight. And we bought you dainty underthings to wear with it."

Pearl held up a beautifully embroidered camisole threaded with silver ribbons, and a delicate lace petticoat.

"Me? You expect me to wear…those?" Diamond's eyes widened.

"But of course, *chérie*." Ruby's gaze roamed Diamond from head to toe. "But first, you must bathe."

"The creek is too cold," Diamond began. "There's probably a layer of ice—"

Ruby stopped her with a wave of the hand. "You will bathe here in the kitchen, so that we can see that every trace of manure has been removed before these lovely things touch your skin. Also, we will want to wash and perfume your hair."

"Perfume my hair? I won't—"

"Ah, but you must, *chérie*," Ruby said with a laugh.

"And why must I?" Diamond stood with her hands on her hips, her chin jutting like a boxer's.

"Because, *chérie,* what we issued was not merely an invitation to Adam Winter to dinner."

"It wasn't?" She blinked, confused.

Ruby smiled and shook her head. "What we issued, on your behalf, was a challenge. And Adam Winter, being a man, has acknowledged that challenge. And accepted it."

A slow, lazy smile touched Diamond's lips. Nothing pleased her more than the thought of a challenge. Especially one involving Adam.

What she didn't realize was that the others could read her like an open book. And knowing her feelings, had taken advantage of them.

She turned to Carmelita. "Pearl said you've made tortillas and spicy beef. I hope it's ready. I'm starving." In fact, she was ravenous. And eager to gird for battle.

Concealing her laughter behind her apron, the housekeeper served their lunch, then filled every bucket and kettle with water and placed them on the stove. By the time they had finished eating, the kitchen had grown steamy, and the tub was filled with warm water.

"It's time to strip," Pearl announced.

"I will." Diamond cleaned her plate. "As soon as all of you leave."

"We are not going anywhere, *chérie,*" Ruby said. "We are here to help you."

"I've managed to take a bath by myself since I was able to walk."

"Perhaps," Jade said in easy agreement. "But you have never had a bath like this one."

She and Carmelita spread several linen squares on the floor around the tub. When Diamond had stripped off her clothes, she stepped into the tub and sank into the warm water with a sigh.

Jade handed her a cake of fragrant, lilac-scented soap and ordered her to scrub. She breathed deeply as she rubbed the soap over her skin. She hated to admit it, but this was just about the most pleasant bath she'd ever experienced.

When her skin was scrubbed clean, Ruby demanded that she duck beneath the water to wet her long hair. Diamond came up sputtering, and Ruby and Pearl proceeded to soap and rinse every strand until it gleamed.

At last Diamond stepped from the tub, dripping water on the towels. Carmelita opened up a clean linen that had been warming by the stove and Diamond snuggled into it.

"How do you feel, *chérie?*" Ruby asked.

"Delicious. Like some sort of princess in a storybook."

"But the story has just begun," Pearl said with a smile.

"Now we will go upstairs," Jade commanded. "And see what magic we can conjure."

Magic. That's what it was, Diamond thought as she sat in front of a looking glass while the three women fussed over her. Her skin was oiled and perfumed until it was as soft as a baby's.

Her fiery hair, which was long enough to sit on, was combed and brushed and blotted with towels. But no amount of brushing could manage the wild jumble of corkscrew curls that tumbled down her back.

"We should pin it up," Pearl suggested, lifting the heavy mass and studying Diamond's reflection in the mirror.

"Too severe," the others decided, shaking their heads.

"We should twist it into a crown." Jade fashioned a coronet of curls atop Diamond's head.

"Too regal," the others said, rejecting that as well.

"We will pull it over to one side." Ruby tied the hair with silver ribbons, allowing it to spill across one breast in a tangle of curls.

"Perfect," they agreed, ignoring Diamond's protest.

"Now the undergarments," Jade commanded.

Removing the towel, Ruby studied the slender figure with a critical eye. "With a body like that, there is no need for a corset."

"How scandalous," Pearl huffed.

But Ruby prevailed.

Diamond gave a sigh of relief, grateful for small favors. She was helped into the chemise and petticoat.

"Where are my boots?" she asked.

"We bought these instead," Pearl announced.

Diamond slid her feet into white kid slippers and stood, wiggling her toes. Everything felt so soft against her skin.

Next came the gown. It took all three women to lift it over her head, and a great deal of wriggling on Diamond's part. After the row of glittering crystal buttons had been fastened and the long full skirts smoothed down, the three stood back to examine her.

"It is perfect," Jade pronounced. "Except for the waist. It is too big." She tied a shiny silver sash around Diamond's middle, to hide the excess fabric.

"The neck is too low," Diamond protested. "I'll catch my death."

"It is just right, *chérie*," Ruby insisted. "But it needs jewelry."

Diamond retrieved her necklace from her dresser and held it up. Pearl fastened it about her neck, then studied her reflection in the mirror.

The simple gold rope, with its glittering diamond and jet black onyx, gleamed against her throat.

"Oh, my," was all Pearl could manage.

"You are . . . quite something," Ruby said with a sigh.

"I believe Adam Winter will find himself speechless," Jade announced proudly.

"Speechless? Adam?" Diamond smiled and studied her reflection. "Now wouldn't that be something?"

"One last thing." Jade removed the stopper from a small vial and touched it to Diamond's earlobes and throat, then lower, to the cleft between her breasts. "Whenever your pulse beats, it will heat your skin and give off a faint fragrance."

Diamond breathed deeply and thought it the most wonderful perfume she'd ever smelled. Like wildflowers on a warm summer evening.

"We must hurry and dress," Pearl called to the others. "Our guests will be here in a few minutes."

"Guests?" Diamond froze. "You mean there's more than one?"

"Oh." Pearl touched a hand to her mouth. "We forgot to mention. We also invited Cal and the marshal and your uncle Chet, so that Adam wouldn't feel outnumbered."

"You forgot to mention. Is there anything else you forgot?" Diamond started to sink down on the edge of the bed.

Pearl caught her by the arm and hauled her to her feet. "You mustn't sit down. You'll wrinkle the skirt."

"You mean I have to stand all evening?"

"Of course not. When it's time for supper, you can sit at the table. But until then, you should stand."

"What'll I do until Adam gets here?" she asked in sudden panic.

"Study yourself in the mirror," Jade suggested. "And practice smiling."

"Smiling?"

"Oui." Ruby touched a hand to her sleeve. "Smiling. Seductively," she purred.

They were gone.

Diamond found herself alone. And terrified. What had she done? How could she have possibly believed that this evening would be fun? An entire hive of hornets droned in her stomach. A knot the size of a doorknob had leaped to her throat.

Hearing the sound of hoofbeats, she flew to the window and watched as Adam tied his horse and made his way to the veranda.

In the distance she could make out the figure of Marshal Regan riding alongside Uncle Chet's rig.

But it was the sight of Adam that held her paralyzed.

She pressed a hand to her pounding heart, and glanced down in surprise at the touch of flesh. What had she been thinking of? Why, in this gown, she was practically naked. Half her breasts were exposed. And she would have to endure Adam's dark, burning gaze all evening.

She heard the knock on the door, and the sound of his deep voice as he was greeted by Carmelita.

"Señorita Diamond. Your company has arrived," came the housekeeper's voice.

At the door to her room she turned and stared longingly at the boots, britches and shirt that had been carelessly tossed in the corner.

"Señorita Diamond," came Carmelita's voice. "We're waiting."

She impulsively reached for the buttons of her gown, and turned back into her room. There was still time to correct the mistake. She would slip into her old comfortable clothes and pretend that this had never happened.

Just then she felt hands clutching her, and Jade, Pearl and Ruby dragged her from the room.

Pearl wore a modest gown of pale yellow, with high neckline and long, tapered sleeves. Her wheat-colored hair was tied back with yellow ribbons.

Jade wore a gown of green silk, with mandarin collar and frog fasteners. Her jet black hair streamed down her back like a silken veil.

Ruby's gown of red satin molded her lush figure. Her thick mass of dark hair was held off her face with jeweled combs.

Before Diamond could do more than mutter a few rich, ripe oaths, she was being propelled down the stairs by the three young women. And shoved toward the front parlor, where Adam was standing by the fireplace.

"Remember, *chérie*," whispered Ruby. "You issued a challenge. Now you must be prepared to duel."

Adam stared into the flickering flames, wondering what in the hell he'd been thinking of when he'd accepted the invitation to dinner.

The last thing he needed right now was this sort of distraction. He had all he could handle, with a crazed gunman loose somewhere on the range, and a predator out to ruin his herd. He had no idea if the two were somehow linked in a devious plot, or if they were random acts of violence. Either way, he needed his wits about him.

But the thought of seeing Diamond was too great a temptation. Besides, he consoled himself, it was only a dinner. He would enjoy Carmelita's good cooking, and the company of these fascinating women, and be on his way.

That was the last coherent thought he had.

When he turned, he saw the three beautiful women, like lovely butterflies, crowding through the doorway. Then he saw Diamond. And she was the only one he saw. He forgot how to swallow. His heart forgot to beat.

"Diamond." He took her hand. It was cold. Without thinking he pressed it between both of his. She was so lovely she took his breath away. She looked like a goddess. Aloud he said, "You look . . . lovely." The words sounded hollow and empty, and totally inadequate.

"Thank you. And you look very nice." She studied his dark suit and expensive shirt with starched collar and cuffs. She hadn't expected this. It was a side to Adam Winter she hadn't seen before.

"I've been admiring the portrait. Your mother?" He nodded toward the ornately framed picture hanging over the fireplace. The young woman, with green eyes and flaming hair, was a beauty. But she was no match for the flesh-and-blood woman beside him.

"Yes." Diamond followed the direction of his gaze. "I don't remember her at all. Every time I look at her, it's like looking at a beautiful stranger."

"You're the image of her."

"Really?" She brightened.

"Especially in that gown."

Her smile faltered. Was it just the clothes he admired? No matter, she reminded herself. This was war.

She could hear the sound of deep masculine voices at the door as the young women greeted their other guests. Within minutes they filed into the parlor.

When Quent Regan and Chester Pierce saw Adam, they stiffened for a moment, unsure how to react. But Cal, having had all day to get accustomed to the idea, stepped forward and offered his hand.

"Hello, Winter," he muttered.

"Cal."

Then Cal caught sight of Diamond, and his jaw dropped. "Di. What's happened to you? Why, you look like . . . like a queen. You're so pretty, I hardly know what to say."

Her reaction wasn't at all gracious or regal. Instead of being flattered, she brought her hands to her hips and challenged, "Well, I hope you don't expect to see me in this getup every day. I'd have a tough time riding and roping stray mavericks. And it's not quite up to mucking stalls, either."

Pearl, Jade and Ruby stepped between them and soon, in their roles of hostesses, put everyone at ease. With much good-natured laughter they passed around glasses of sherry. Gradually the tensions between the guests were soothed, and the conversation turned to mundane events.

"I know it isn't your birthday, Diamond," Chester Pierce said as he sipped his wine. "So what is the special occasion that brought us here?"

"It was..." Diamond swallowed.

"It was us." Ruby gave her most charming smile and every man in the room melted. "Diamond wanted to give us a chance to meet some of Hanging Tree's most prominent citizens before we return to our homes."

"It looks like you young ladies are getting to know one another," Marshal Regan remarked dryly. He'd been observing the easy friendliness between the four women.

In answer, Pearl slipped her arm through Diamond's in a display of camaraderie. "You'd never believe the things we've learned about one another."

Diamond blushed and studied the toe of her new slipper, while Pearl squeezed her hand. But when the young woman walked away Adam asked, "What sort of things?"

"Just...things." Diamond cursed the fact that her mind seemed to go blank every time Adam got too close.

When Carmelita announced that dinner was ready, Chester Pierce caught Diamond's hand and led the way to the dining room. She told herself that she was glad to put some distance between herself and Adam. But she glanced over her shoulder in time to see him offer his arm to Jade. A wave of pure jealousy washed over her, leaving her feeling ashamed.

"Why, I've never even been in this room before." Pearl paused on the threshold and studied a sumptuous table, covered in linen. Silver and crystal gleamed in the light of dozens of candles set in silver candlesticks. A glittering chandelier hung from massive beams. On a side table rested several large silver dishes. The fragrance of spices perfumed the air.

Diamond glanced at a faded tintype of her father and mother hanging over the sideboard. It showed a tall, handsome young man with his arm around a pretty woman. "Pa built it to please my mother, so she could have fancy dinner parties. When she died, he closed the room and never bothered with it again. He preferred to eat in the kitchen. And so do I."

Carmelita bustled about the room, pouring wine, passing platters of steaming tortillas and trays heaped with spicy meats and chilis, along with slabs of roast beef.

"You've outdone yourself, Carmelita," Cal said as he helped himself to more beef.

Beside him, Pearl picked at her food, avoiding the spicier dishes and relying on things that looked familiar.

Jade and Ruby, on the other hand, seemed to thoroughly enjoy Carmelita's hottest offerings.

"I will have to teach you about some of the spices used in my grandmother's province in China," Jade said as Carmelita offered yet another tray of food.

"It would never match what we use in the bayou," Ruby told her.

The marshal looked up with interest. "Is that what makes Louisiana women so spicy?"

Ruby shot him a dangerous smile. "It may be one reason, Marshal Regan. But I am certain there are others."

"Why, Quent," Cal said with a laugh, "I think you're the one who's blushing."

Quent Regan ducked his head. But not before he allowed one last admiring glance at the sultry Ruby. She was all woman. And all wrong, he reminded himself, for a man of his simple tastes.

"So—" Chester Pierce sat back and sipped his wine "—I suppose you young ladies are getting weary of this place and are eager to return to your own homes."

"Not at all." Jade's tone was sincere. "I could stay on forever."

The banker couldn't hide his surprise. "You don't find the days long? After all, there can't be anything to do way out here, so far from town."

"Ah, but there is much to do," Ruby said. "Diamond has taken us on tours of her ranch."

"And," Jade said quickly, "we have honored our father with daily visits to his resting place."

"And Diamond and I are working each night on Daddy's ledgers," Pearl added. "Although they're quite a mess. It would appear that Daddy was a very careless bookkeeper."

"Both of you are working on the ledgers?" Chet turned to Diamond. "Do you think that's wise, my dear?" He flushed. "What I mean to say is, Onyx never intended for strangers to view his private ledgers."

"Pearl isn't a stranger, Uncle Chet. She's family. After all, she is Pa's daughter, isn't she? And besides," Diamond added, without waiting for a reply, "Pearl studied mathematics at a fancy ladies' school in Boston. You ought to see her do sums. She's a hundred times better than I am."

"Is she?" Chester drained his glass of wine and twirled the stem between his fingers. "I'd hoped to take the ledgers home with me tonight."

"They aren't quite finished," Pearl said. "But if we're diligent, I think we could have them completed in a few days."

"Nonsense. Then you'd just have to make another trip into town to deliver them to the bank. I'll take them with me tonight and save you all the time and trouble."

"It's no trouble—" Pearl began.

Chester waved a hand. "I won't hear of it. You young ladies deserve these last few days to enjoy yourselves before you have to face the long journey home."

Diamond shook her head firmly. "I told you, Uncle Chet. I see the ledgers as my responsibility. Pa taught me to finish what I started. You'll get them in a couple of days."

"But—" He appeared as determined as Diamond. But his words were interrupted when Carmelita threw open the doors between the dining room and the parlor. On a round table in front of the fireplace was a silver tray on which rested a crystal decanter and several glasses.

"Pa always offered his friends brandy after dinner," Diamond announced. "So I thought I'd do the same."

She led the way into the parlor and began to pour brandy for the men, while Ruby poured sherry for the women. When the drinks were passed around, Diamond refused and sipped water, instead.

"I'd like to propose a toast," Cal said, clearing his throat in embarrassment.

Everyone waited.

"To Onyx Jewel," he said somberly.

Everyone drank.

"And to his legacy," Adam added.

"You mean the ranch?" Diamond asked in all inno cence.

"I mean," Adam said softly, "you, and Pearl, Jade an Ruby. I've learned that mere possessions can fall victim t the whims of fortune. But people have an indomitable wi to survive. Even after death, their legacy can live on. Th four of you are proof of that. You give testimony to the fac that Onyx Jewel lived. Through you and your heirs, he wi live on forever."

Diamond felt tears spring to her eyes and quickly blinke them away. Adam's words uncovered a truth that she ha been denying. But this time, she wasn't reminded of he terrible loss. Instead, she realized what a wonderful gift he father had left her.

His daughters.

Her sisters.

Because of them, she would never have to be alone again

Chapter Seventeen

"It's time I got back to town," the marshal announced. "I left Arlo in charge, and knowing him, he'll be asleep at my desk by now." He turned to the banker. "You ready, Chester?"

"In a minute." Chet crossed to where Diamond stood beside Adam. "My dear, I must insist that you allow me to take your father's ledgers with me. I could bring them up-to-date by tomorrow, and have the wranglers' payroll ready the day after that. It would certainly save everyone a lot of trouble. And Cal has mentioned that your men are getting restless for their pay."

Diamond brushed a kiss across his cheek. "That's true. And it's very sweet of you to offer, Uncle Chet. But the answer is still no."

She tucked her arm through his and walked with him to the door. "I'm so glad you came to my dinner. And you, too, Quent."

The marshal grinned and squeezed her hand before taking his leave, with Chester Pierce following.

"I will say good-night, as well," Carmelita called. "Rosario is here with the wagon."

"Thank you." Diamond gave her a wide smile. "I'll see you in the morning."

"I can't remember when I've had a better meal," Adam added. "Thank you, Carmelita."

The housekeeper's face was wreathed with smiles as she walked from the room.

"I'd better turn in, too," Cal announced. "I have to be on the south range by sunup."

"Would you mind if we walked with you to the bunkhouse?" Ruby followed him to the door.

"Whatever for?" Pearl asked.

Ruby shot her a warning look, then nodded toward Diamond and Adam, who stood apart, looking extremely uncomfortable.

"Oh, yes. Of course. A walk in the fresh air sounds like the perfect ending to this lovely evening." Pearl turned to Jade. "Let's get our shawls."

Within minutes Cal had taken his leave, surrounded by Pearl, Jade and Ruby.

"Well. It looks like we're alone." Adam couldn't help grinning at the less-than-subtle way the three young women had taken their leave. "Did you plan this ahead of time?"

Diamond blushed clear to her toes. "The others made the plans. I just . . . went along."

"So. What's the plan now?"

She stared at the floor. "I'm supposed to smile at you. Seductively."

"Ah."

He seemed to have spoken volumes in that single word. Diamond swallowed and turned away, idly tracing a finger around the rim of a vase.

"This could be dangerous." Adam's voice was closer now, and she knew, without looking, that he'd closed the distance between them and was standing directly behind her.

"Dangerous?" She lifted her head. "Why?"

He ran a finger lightly across her bare shoulder, feeling her flinch at his touch. "This is why. Even without the seductive smiles, the minute we're alone, I want to touch you." He closed his hands over her upper arms and drew her back against him. He bent his head and brushed butterfly kisses to her neck, sending spasms of pleasure curling along her spine.

His fingers tightened. "But I don't think I can be trusted to be alone with you, Diamond. The minute I touch you, I want more."

He slid his hands down her arms, then gathered her to him until his hands rested just beneath the fullness of her breasts.

"Oh, Diamond," he breathed against her ear. "What am I going to do about you?"

Pressed to the length of him, she was aware of his arousal. She could hear the torment in his voice, could feel the struggle he exerted to remain in control.

He ran soft wet kisses across her shoulder, then pressed his mouth to the sensitive hollow of her throat.

She sighed and moved in his arms, arching her neck to give him better access.

He continued raining kisses while his hands began a lazy exploration of her breasts until his thumbs found her nipples, stroking until they hardened.

"Dear God, Diamond." He turned her to face him and dragged her against him. His lips found hers and he savaged her mouth with kisses until they were both gasping.

His tongue tangled with hers and he drank in the sweet, clean taste of her. Then his lips closed over hers once more and he took the kiss deeper.

"Woman," he muttered against her mouth, "you've completely bewitched me. I can't think. And I can't stop. Ever since you walked into this room, I've been looking at an angel. A beautiful, beguiling angel." His eyes darkened as he allowed his gaze to move over her. His voice was a growl of desire as he dragged her closer and muttered against her lips, "I'd like to tear this gown off you and take you, here and now."

At his words she went very still.

Puzzled by her reaction, he lifted his head. "What is it, Diamond? What's wrong?"

"It's...me." She pushed free of his arms and took a step back. It hurt. Oh, sweet heaven, it hurt to push him away when she wanted him so. But she had to. She couldn't lie. Not to him. "It's...this," she said, staring down at the gown.

"I don't understand."

"Oh, Adam. Don't you see? This isn't me. None of this. The fancy dinner party. The polite conversation. And this. This gown. I didn't pick it out. Pearl and Jade and Ruby did. It looks like them, not me."

His tone softened. "I know that, Diamond."

Her head came up sharply. "You...do?"

"Of course. But what's the harm in a pretty gown? Or in a pretty illusion? As long as we both know who and what we really are, there's no harm done."

"But I feel like such a fool. I was trying to pretend that I could be a fancy lady like them. And I was trying to make believe that love was some kind of parlor game, to be played for the sake of winning."

"You know better." He touched a hand to her cheek in an achingly sweet gesture and kept it there, staring deeply into her eyes. "And so do I. Love, real love, doesn't care about clothes, or fancy dinners, or what others think. Real love seeks only the best for the other person."

Love. He was talking about real love, real caring. "Adam? Why...?" She felt her throat tighten, and swallowed before forcing herself to go on. "Why have you been avoiding me?"

He lowered his hand to his side. "Because we're—" his voice roughened with emotion "—not right for each other."

She opened her mouth to protest, but he silenced her with a finger to her lips. "And now that I've had a chance to see how your life really is, I'm even more certain."

"I don't understa—"

"Maybe it's because you've been sheltered in the past. Or maybe it's because there's too much in my past. Whatever the reason, it's better if I keep my distance from now on."

"But I don't want you to."

He shook his head. "Diamond, your instincts were right that day in the barn. You were right to be afraid. What almost happened between us would have spoiled something special about you. Don't you see? You need to save yourself for that one special person who'll be worthy of someone as wonderful as you."

"But what if I've already found him?" she asked miserably.

"Now who's being blinded by illusion?" His tone was harsh. "This fine suit is a remnant from my past. What I've become is a man only too willing to use a gun. And I've paid dearly for that. Don't you forget it." His voice softened slightly. "Don't let anyone change you. Just go right on being what you are, Diamond. A wild and beautiful surprise, as untamed as this land. You deserve only the best. I know someday you'll find it."

He lifted his hand, as if to touch her again. Then he seemed to think better of it and backed away.

"Thank you for a lovely evening. I'll see myself out."

He turned on his heel and crossed the room.

Diamond stood, rigid with shock. She watched him open the door, and listened to the sound of his footsteps on the veranda. A minute later she heard the sound of hoofbeats. And still she stood, unmoving.

A short time later, when Pearl, Jade and Ruby returned, the room was empty. Upstairs, Diamond's bedroom door was locked. And though they called her name and knocked repeatedly on the door, they heard not a sound.

Adam urged the stallion into a run and pushed him to the limit. His thoughts were as dark as the night that closed in around him. It was best this way. Clean. Quick. Final.

Tonight had almost been his undoing. She'd looked so beautiful. So alluring. So damned vulnerable. And when he'd said what he thought she needed to hear, she'd looked so wounded.

If only she weren't so easy to read. All her emotions were there in her eyes.

He'd have rather cut out his heart than hurt her like that. But one of them had to be strong enough, and smart enough, to see how wrong it would be to give in to these feelings. She deserved a bright and wonderful future with a man who could give her all her father had given her, and more. She deserved the best of everything.

At his ranch, he turned his horse into the corral and walked to the darkened cabin. He was glad Zeb was up at Poison Creek with the herd. He wasn't in the mood for company tonight.

Diamond knelt by the window, her head thrown back, staring up at the stars. She had no way of knowing how long she'd been there. Hours, maybe. Or mere minutes. It felt like forever.

The full skirt of her gown was crushed beneath her. She took no notice. The room had grown cold. The fire had long ago burned to embers. She didn't care.

This was worse than Pa's death, she realized. Then she'd been filled with a sort of raw fury, a thunderstorm of emotion, that drove her into action, seeking vengeance. But this. This pain in her heart was worse than any grief. It left her numb. And unable, or unwilling, to act.

And so she knelt, still and quiet, watching the night sky. Her eyes were dry. She had not wept. Nor would she. She felt...empty. Drained.

Adam Winter didn't want her. It was that simple. What she felt for him was not what he felt for her. Now she would have to accept that fact and get on with her life.

The numbness set in again. It wasn't possible to get on with her life. He had become her life. This man, this... silent, brooding rancher had taken possession of her heart, her mind, her soul. And then had callously rejected her.

He had awakened her to passion. And then had tossed her aside.

His words, cruel, hurtful, began to play through her mind. "We're not right for each other. Maybe it's because you've been so sheltered in the past.... Whatever the reason, it's best if we keep our distance."

"Sheltered," she muttered, getting stiffly to her feet. "Maybe I don't know as much about men and women as Jade, but I'm not a child."

She began to pace, feeling her temper beginning to return. And then she remembered some other words he'd spoken. "Or maybe there's been too much in my past.... Real love seeks only the best for the other person."

Was that what this was about? Had he somehow decided that he wasn't good enough for her? Of course. She should have seen it.

"Oh, Adam," she moaned aloud. "How could I have been so blind?"

She tugged frantically at the crystal buttons of her gown, ripping off several in her haste to undress. She slipped out of the petticoat and the soft kid slippers and picked up the pile of clothing in the corner of her room. Within minutes she had dressed in her old britches, shirt and boots. Gathering up her cowhide jacket and rifle, she turned toward the door.

Pearl, Jade and Ruby had stopped knocking and calling. But she could tell from the whispered voices beyond the door that they were still waiting for her.

Thinking quickly, she left the door latched and slipped out her window. Minutes later she was astride her mare, racing headlong over the hills to Adam's cabin.

Adam lay on his bed, one arm flung beneath his head. Smoke drifted from the cigarette that dangled from his lips. His eyes were closed, but he was as far from sleep as a man could be. In fact, every fiber of his being was alive with tension.

He had pondered every imaginable way to kidnap Diamond and flee with her to some distant place. A place where they could start over. In this imaginary place, she wouldn't own the richest cattle empire in Texas. And he wouldn't be a man who'd turned his back on everything that ever mattered, to become a loner and drifter. But each time he imagined such a life, images from his past intruded, haunting him as they haunted him every night of his life. He couldn't go back. He couldn't undo what had been done, nor change what he'd become.

He sprang to his feet and crossed the room, tossing the cigarette into the fire. Now who was playing games? He was as bad as Diamond, wishing he could be something he wasn't.

He heard the sound of hoofbeats and reached for his rifle. Peering through a crack in the door, he watched as the horse and rider came into view.

When he caught sight of Diamond, he let out the breath he'd been holding on a rush of air and threw open the door.

"What the hell are you doing out here alone? Where are your wranglers?"

Ignoring him, Diamond turned her horse into the corral before making her way to his cabin.

His temper exploded. "Damn it, you headstrong little fool. There's a gunman loose out here somewhere, just waiting for a chance like this." He caught her roughly by the sleeve. "You know the rules."

She gave him a sly, beguiling smile. "I decided to be like you and not play by the rules."

"What are you... ?" Seeing the look in her eyes, he released her and backed into the cabin.

She followed, pulling the door closed and leaning against it. Now that she was here, all the turmoil was gone. In its place was a strange sense of... anticipation.

He set the rifle beside the door, then, needing to put some distance between them, crossed the room. He picked up a log and tossed it on the fire, then wiped his palms on his trousers.

All the while, Diamond merely watched.

He was barefoot and naked to the waist, wearing only dark pants. His hair was mussed, as was his bed.

He'd been smoking. The faint whiff of tobacco still hung in the air, along with the scent of wood smoke and coffee.

"Does anyone know you're here?" He turned his back to the fire.

"No one."

"I'll get dressed and see you home." He picked up his shirt and managed to slip it over one arm before her words caused him to freeze.

"I'm not going home, Adam." She crossed the room and touched a hand to his naked back. "I'm staying here."

He stiffened, but didn't turn toward her. The shirt hung from his arm, forgotten. "That's impossible. You can't stay here."

"Why?" She brought her other hand to his shoulder and pressed her cheek lightly to his warm flesh. Oh, how had she lived so long without touching him like this?

He felt as though he'd been slammed into a wall of stone. His breath caught in his throat. "Because—" he forced his mind to work, choosing his words carefully "—I have better things to do than play nursemaid to some lovesick girl."

"Girl!" She pushed away from him and watched as he slowly turned. Her chin came up in the familiar pose, and she managed to ask, "Is that why you ran away tonight? You were afraid of a girl?"

A tiny thread of his temper came unraveled. "I'll remind you that I didn't run away."

She was on safer ground now. She'd always been able to handle a good fight. "Oh, you ran, all right. As fast as you could. You barely took the time to say good-night."

She was wearing the familiar rough shirt and britches, but all he could see was the lush body that had been revealed in that gown. He blinked, hoping to erase the image. "Well, it wasn't fear that had me running."

"Oh. That's right." She lifted a hand to his chest. The fierce pounding of his heart gave her renewed courage. He wasn't as immune to her as he pretended. "It was some noble desire to save me from myself."

He didn't know if he had any strength left, but he made one last heroic effort. He caught her wrist and pushed her hand away, as though the touch of her offended him. "I had no choice, since you don't seem to have enough sense to save yourself."

Her lips curved upward in a smile. She hadn't come all this way just to calmly accept defeat. "And what if I don't want to be saved?"

"That's just the point, Diamond. Somebody has to look out for you."

She moved so quickly, he had no time to react. Standing on tiptoe she brought her lips to his. "I think you're the one who's going to need saving, Adam."

His body reacted in a purely physical way. There was no way he could stop his arms from closing around her. And no way to keep his lips from melting against hers. But he had to act quickly to stop this storm of emotion that was brewing inside.

Calling on every ounce of willpower, he let his arms fall at his sides. Though his voice sounded hoarse in his ears, he managed to say, "All right, Diamond. You've proved your point. You're...pleasant enough to kiss. But you're hardly irresistible. I'll see you home now. I have a herd of cattle to see to in the morning."

She nearly reeled from the pain. She turned away to hide the hurt that she knew would be in her eyes. What a fool she'd been. Riding all this way, thinking she could walk in and seduce a worldly man like Adam Winter.

"You're right, of course." She swallowed. "I'll...wait out by the corral while you get dressed."

He felt like the lowest kind of snake. But, he reminded himself, this was all for her own good. What would happen to her reputation if the town gossips found out that she'd spent the night at his cabin? No matter what the cost to him, he had to get her out of here before...

At the door Diamond turned and watched as Adam quickly rolled a cigarette. He bent and retrieved a flaming stick from the fire, holding it to the tip before filling his lungs.

In that instant, she noticed that his hand was trembling. A surge of raw power streaked through her. She saw clearly now what she had to do.

Feeling steadier now, Adam turned. And was surprised to find her advancing toward him, with a gleam in her eye and a mysterious, woman's smile on her lips.

"You say you don't find me irresistible, but I think you're lying, Adam." She brought her hand to the buttons of her shirt and began to unfasten them.

His eyes widened in alarm. "What are you doing?"

"Proving that you're a terrible liar."

She slipped the shirt from her shoulders.

With an oath he tossed the cigarette into the fire and gripped her by the shoulders. "Stop this, Diamond." But it was already too late. The touch of her had him burning for more. The challenge in her eyes had needs pounding through his blood.

"Make me stop, Adam. If you can." Her voice was a low purr that wrapped itself around him like a caress. She touched a hand to his lips and he felt a blow to the midsection. Her fingers traced the outline of his lower lip until, on a groan, his mouth opened. "Wouldn't you like to kiss me, Adam, before you send me away? Wouldn't you like to taste my lips?"

He couldn't get enough air into his lungs. With every struggle for breath, he felt as though he were being crushed beneath a herd of stampeding cattle. Everything he'd ever wanted was here in his arms.

Without thinking he fisted a hand in her hair and drew her head back. "Is this what you want?" he demanded as he brought his mouth down on hers in a savage, punishing kiss.

If he'd thought to frighten her, it didn't work. Instead of backing away, she clutched at him and offered him more.

"Yes," she murmured against his lips. "Yes, Adam. This. And more."

"You don't know what you're doing." He dragged her close. His hands at her shoulders were rough and bruising as he kissed her with a hunger that matched her own.

"No. But you do. I'm sure you'll show me what to do." She reached for the ribbons of her chemise, but he stopped her.

Lifting her hands to his lips, he kissed them with a rare kind of tenderness, all the while staring deeply into her eyes. "Understand, Diamond. Once we do this," he murmured against her palms, "there's no going back."

"I'm never going back," she whispered. Her eyes were a deep, fathomless sea of green. And he was already drowning in them.

"Then God forgive us," he murmured. "For you have no idea what you've unleashed."

Chapter Eighteen

"I don't know if I can be gentle," he muttered. "I've wanted you for such a long time. And now that you're here, and willing—"

"Shh. I don't need you to be gentle. I just need you." She touched a finger to his mouth, then offered her lips.

He tasted, drawing the wild, sweet flavor of her into himself. He framed her face with his hands. With a sigh he brushed his lips over her forehead, across her closed eyelids, down her cheeks. He pressed a kiss to the tip of her nose, then nibbled the corner of her mouth until her lips parted. His tongue tangled with hers and she sighed from the pure pleasure of it.

"Diamond. Diamond."

He whispered her name like a caress. In his eyes she felt beautiful, desirable. For someone who had lived her life with no thought of such things, it was an intoxicating feeling.

With his tongue he traced the curve of her ear, nipping at her lobe with his teeth before darting his tongue inside.

She chuckled at the delicious tingles that raced along her spine. But a moment later her laughter turned into a moan as he trailed hot, wet kisses along her throat.

Even as she arched her neck for him, she clutched at his shoulders, afraid that her trembling legs might buckle at any moment.

As if reading her mind he lowered her to the floor. They took no notice of the coarse rug as, with soft sighs and tender words, they lost themselves in each other.

"I won't hold you if you change your mind," he whispered against her throat. It was a lie, he knew. He would bar the door, he would beg or even crawl, to hold her here with him. But he had to offer her one last chance to escape.

"I'm not leaving, Adam. This was my choice." *Mine*, she thought fiercely. *All mine.* She tangled her fingers in his hair and dragged his mouth to hers.

The cabin was quiet. So quiet that she thought he could surely hear the sound of her heart thundering.

The only light came from the fire. Flames hissed as they licked along the logs in the fireplace. An occasional draft of wind sent sparks flying, like a shower of stars.

Adam studied the woman in his arms. By the light of the fire, she seemed some ethereal creature, her hair more brilliant than the dancing flames, her eyes soft and seductive, pulling him in to her very soul.

He struggled against a raging passion that fought to be free. There was so little he could give her. But this much he could do. He would take care to see that this, her first time, was all she had hoped for. And more.

She felt the coiled tension in him as he struggled for control. It aroused her, excited her as nothing else could. And she responded with wild abandon.

Their kisses grew more heated as his hands began exploring her. He tugged impatiently at the ribbons of her chemise, then bent his lips to the soft swell of her breast.

She gave a gasp of surprise at the feelings that rippled through her. Feelings that quickly had her spiraling out of control.

He heard the alarm in her voice, saw the panic in her eyes. At once his movements gentled, until she relaxed in his arms.

His kisses, too, gentled, making no demands on her.

Steeped in pleasure, she lay in a dreamlike state, caught up in a silken web of feelings. She responded to his patient ministrations as he led her, with soft kisses and murmured words of endearment, to a new level of trust.

Trust. He sensed the change in her and thrilled to it. It wasn't surrender. With a fiery creature like Diamond, he would never want mere surrender. What he wanted was all the passion, all the promise, that he had sensed when first he'd seen her. Passion that had been slumbering, smoldering, until this first spark had ignited it into flame.

Now, as he undressed her, he felt the heat. She was no longer placid or cool. Now she was all fire and force and fury. And his, he thought possessively. His.

He studied her in the flickering firelight. The glimpse of body he'd seen in the revealing gown was nothing compared with this work of art. She was even more beautiful than he'd dared to imagine, with skin like alabaster, hair like fire, and a warm, sensuous smile that wrapped itself around his soul until he knew he was lost.

His heart was thundering as she reached for the fasteners at his waist. When her fingers fumbled, he helped her.

At last they knelt, facing each other. Heat rose up between them, their bodies already slick with sheen.

The exotic fragrance of her perfume filled his lungs until all he could smell, all he could taste, was her. He was mad to have her.

His hands tangled in her hair and he drew her head back while his lips covered hers in a savage, possessive kiss.

For a moment she held back, startled by this abrupt change in him. Then, as her own passions ignited, she leaned into him, eager for more. As she brought her arms around his waist, she felt his muscles contract violently. Then on a moan, he took the kiss deeper.

This wasn't what she'd expected. This darkness, this undercurrent of mystery laced with passion. It was a side he had kept carefully hidden. And no wonder. With a single touch he could make her shudder. With a single kiss he could make her moan. And as the touches became more intimate, and the kisses more savage, she found an even darker side to desire.

With her body a mass of nerve endings, there wasn't anything she wouldn't do for release.

"Please, Adam," she whispered, but he was beyond hearing.

With teeth and lips and tongue he drove her. With his fingertips he took her higher. He found her, warm and wet, and drove her to the first peak.

She clutched at him, touching him as he touched her. She was amazed at his quivering response. Exulting in her power, she grew bolder. She brought her lips across his shoulder and down his chest, then lower, to explore him as he'd explored her.

His body hummed with need. Desire clawed at him, demanding release. He had wanted to go slowly, to allow her to set the pace. But now, with her own passion unleashed, he was finally free. Free to do all the things he'd dreamed of since the first time he'd seen her.

It was no longer enough to want to please her, to make this first time satisfying. He wanted to give her so much more. Not just a moment of pleasure. He wanted to give her a lifetime. Not just a glimpse of paradise. He wanted to give her an eternity of love.

With exquisite care he laid her down and feasted on her like a starving man, his lips moving from one breast to the other until she writhed and moaned beneath him and clutched at the rug that cushioned her body. She sighed and whispered his name, and still he held back, learning all the new, intimate places of her body.

The heat from the fire mingled with the heat of their bodies, until it rose up between them, clogging their lungs, making each breath a struggle. And still they gloried in the wonders of their newly discovered passion, keeping release just out of reach.

For Diamond, the world had narrowed to this room, this man. She had slipped into a world of dark, forbidden desire. The touch of his rough, callused hands against her flesh was more seductive than the silk gown she'd worn this evening. He tasted of brandy and tobacco, and faintly of horses and leather. Dark, musky scents that she had known since childhood. But now they were no longer familiar, but new. No longer ordinary, but intoxicating.

She shuddered and strained against him as he moved over her, his flesh hot and damp and seductive. And still he gave her no release.

He had thought he was leading her, taking her to new places. But at the first touch of her, he realized he was the one being led. The student had become the teacher. The innocent had become the seducer. And he reveled in her mastery.

He struggled to hold back needs that were fighting, struggling, clawing to be free. He felt her stiffen as he brought his lips down her body.

This was a dark, sweet place she'd never been before. A place of exquisite pleasure that bordered on pain. She gasped as she rode the wave of pleasure to another crest. But he gave her no time to recover as he quickly drove her even higher.

Her eyes opened, and he saw himself reflected in those deep green pools as he entered her.

She didn't think it was possible to want more, but she did. Her deeper arousal startled both of them. She wrapped herself around him, wanting to hold him like this forever. Wanting to hold on to the moment, the feeling, the pleasure. Wanting it all.

And then she was moving with him, matching his strength, his rhythm, with her own. Such incredible strength. Climbing. Higher and higher, until they reached the highest mountain peak, and soared beyond, into a midnight sky lit by scores of stars.

A sound was wrenched from his lips that was both animal and human. And then he cried out her name as they felt themselves shattering, splintering into a million pieces. They touched a light more radiant than the sun. And drifted slowly to earth.

They lay, still joined, neither one willing to move. Their bodies were slick, their breathing ragged.

Slowly, gradually, their heartbeats began to return to normal.

"My God, Diamond." Adam rested his forehead on hers, then pressed his lips to her closed lids. "I'm sorry if I hurt you."

"You didn't. Much," she said with a soft chuckle.

But he was beyond hearing. "How could I be so selfish?" he berated himself. "You were sweet, untouched. A virgin. And I took you on the floor like some drunken cowboy."

"Oh, Adam." She touched a hand to his cheek. At once he stopped his protests and went still. "It was..."

He waited, feeling his heart stop.

"It was the most wonderful feeling. Is it always like that?"

His heart resumed beating. He felt a wave of triumph. His lifeblood surged through him, and he knew, at this moment, he could stop a stampede single-handed.

"Not always." He kissed the tip of her nose, then rolled to one side and drew her into his arms. "But when two people feel the way we do, it's always wonderful."

"How do you feel, Adam?"

"Like the luckiest man in the world. Do you know how long I've wanted you?"

"Since you first saw me."

He grinned and pressed his lips to a tangle of hair at her temple. "And how would you know that?"

"You told me so. That day in the barn."

His smile turned to a frown at the thought of that day. Walking away from her had cost him dearly.

"But how could you have loved me then?" she went on. "You were in jail for Pa's murder. And I came looking for revenge."

"Call me a fool," he said against her hair. "There's just something about a woman in a man's clothes, toting a gun in her boot, that makes my blood run hot."

She was laughing now. It was a sound that warmed his heart. She'd had so few reasons to laugh lately.

He drew her even closer, and pressed his lips to hers. If only he could always hear the sound of her laughter.

She pushed slightly away, so that she could look into his eyes. "I did intend to shoot you, you know." She closed her eyes against the knowledge. "I'm so glad you stopped me."

He grinned. "Not half as glad as I am."

She gave him a wicked, knowing smile. "Without you, I never would have learned all these new and wonderful things you just taught me."

"Oh, I'm sure there would have been some cowboy willing to take my place." But though his words were warm with laughter, he felt the twinge of pain at the thought of another man holding her like this, loving her.

She shook her head in denial. "I never would have let another man get this close, Adam. Pa used to say that some things were just meant to be. That's the way I feel about you and me. There was no sense fighting it. You're my destiny. And I'm yours."

"You mean—" he brushed his lips over hers and felt the curl of pleasure "—I'm stuck with you?"

"I'm afraid so." She nuzzled his lips and heard his low growl of pleasure. Growing bolder, she sat up. Her hair spilled across one shoulder, tickling his chest.

She idly traced the mat of hair on his chest and saw the way his eyes suddenly darkened with desire. It gave her a heady feeling to know that she held such power over him. This strong man, who would willingly face down a dozen gunmen, trembled at her mere touch.

Drunk with power, she moved her hands over him, then traced a path with her lips, determined to make him lose control.

Through lowered lids he watched her. Her body was young and lithe and perfect, with high, firm breasts and a waist so small his hands could easily span it. Her pale skin was dotted with freckles, and he had a sudden desire to kiss every one of them. Her fiery hair begged to be touched.

"Witch," he muttered. "Do you know what you're doing to me?"

She gave him a mysterious smile. "I hope I'm doing what I set out to do when I left home."

"What was that?"

"Seduce you."

His arms came around her, flattening her to his chest. His lips found hers. Against her mouth he murmured, "Then you've succeeded."

He rolled her over and they came together in a storm of passion more violent than the first.

He had seen both hell and heaven in one day, Adam thought as he brought his mouth, hot and demanding, on hers. But this . . . this was pure heaven.

And then all thought fled as he lost himself in the pleasures of loving her.

Darkness still hung like a curtain over the sky. But the first faint threads of dawn were weaving their way along the horizon.

Sometime during the night Adam had carried Diamond to his bed. But there had been little time for sleep. Their hunger for each other was insatiable. At times they had loved with a passion that was almost bruising in its intensity. At other times they had come together with a tenderness, an exquisite gentleness that soothed their hearts and healed their wounds.

Diamond lay with her back to Adam, snuggled to his chest. His arms were around her, holding her firmly against the length of him. He had thrown one leg possessively over hers. His face was buried against her neck, his breathing slow and rhythmic.

She lay in that strange limbo between wakefulness and sleep, feeling a sense of rare peace. She wanted nothing more than to remain like this, safe in Adam's arms, close to his heart. She sighed and snuggled closer.

At the slight movement, Adam came fully awake. His hands tightened perceptibly, drawing her closer still. His palm encountered the swell of her breast and he kept it there, loving the feel of her soft flesh against his rough skin.

At his simple touch her nipple hardened, straining against his fingers. He continued to stroke with one hand, while the other began a lazy exploration of her hip and the inside of her thigh. And all the while his lips nuzzled her neck.

She sighed with the pure pleasure of it, but her sighs soon turned to moans as the pressure of his touch increased and her need for him grew. She tried to turn toward him, but his leg pinned her, holding her still.

She was aware that he was fully aroused, yet he moved with deliberate slowness, drawing out the moment until her excitement matched his own.

"Adam."

"Shh." He ran nibbling kisses across her shoulder, then down her spine, and all the while his hands continued weaving their magic until her body was on fire.

He eased her thigh upward to allow him smooth entry. And while he filled her with himself, his fingers continued their exquisite manipulation until she shuddered and cried out his name.

She turned toward him and their mouths fused in a long, slow kiss. Still locked in a fierce embrace, they drifted back to sleep.

Morning light bathed the little cabin with golden rays that streamed through the tiny window and the cracks in the door. Seeing that the fire had burned to embers, Adam crossed the room and added a log, sending up a shower of sparks.

Then he returned to the warmth of Diamond's arms. As they snuggled beneath the covers she touched a finger to the raised scar that ran from his shoulder to his hip.

"What sort of wound would leave such a mark?" she muttered.

At once he went very still.

"I'm sorry," she whispered fervently. "Forgive me, Adam. I wasn't prying. I just can't stand to think about anyone hurting you."

"It happened a long time ago," he said against her lips. "It doesn't matter anymore."

She pulled back. "But everything that happened to you matters to me. Don't you see? I love you."

Love. He was thunderstruck. For the space of a heartbeat he couldn't speak. He marveled at the feelings that swirled through him at that simple word. Feelings he'd never expected to experience again in his lifetime.

At last he found his voice. "You shouldn't love me, Diamond. It isn't wise. And it certainly isn't safe."

"Because of the way the townspeople fear you?" she asked.

He shook his head and leaned up on one elbow, tracing the outline of her lips with his rough finger. "Because terrible things have happened to everyone I've ever loved."

"I don't understand." Her eyes clouded with concern.

He took a deep breath. It had been so long since he'd spoken of it. But now, seeing how much she trusted him, he realized he owed her the same trust.

"I spoke of family in Maryland."

She nodded, afraid to speak. There was something in his eyes she'd never seen before. Not just danger, for she'd seen that before. It was something else. Something so painful, it caused her heart to contract.

"My family had lived in the same community for three generations, beginning with my father's father. When the war started, my brothers and I chose to fight with the

North.'' His voice lowered. "The war was a hellish experience. But we were fortunate. My brothers and I survived. We returned home, eager to put it behind us." His voice lowered. "But we learned a hard lesson. The war wasn't over. Even after the guns fell silent, the hatred continued."

Diamond heard the pain and held her silence, afraid even to breathe, for fear of what was to come.

"Not long after we returned, we were attacked while we slept. I was slashed with an ax, and left for dead."

Diamond mentally calculated the length of his scar, and realized that he must have nearly bled to death.

"And your family?"

"All dead. My father and mother, my two brothers. And my wife and son."

Wife and son.

She absorbed the shock of this news and managed to say, "Oh, Adam. How horrible. I'd heard about the bands of roving soldiers who wouldn't accept the end of the war."

"My family wasn't killed by soldiers." His voice roughened with emotion. "I suppose I could have accepted such hatred and violence from strangers. They were killed by our neighbors. Men and women who had known us for a lifetime. My father had loaned them money in hard times. My mother had helped deliver their babies. My brothers and I had helped harvest their crops when rain threatened. My wife had sipped tea in their parlors."

She gasped in shock and horror. When she could finally find her voice she whispered, "But why?"

"Sometimes the reason is too simple to comprehend. They had chosen the other side in the war. They couldn't punish the whole country for their loss. But they could blame us. We were an easy target."

She fell silent for long moments. At last she said, "Thank heaven at least you were spared."

His eyes were bleak as he relived the horror. "That was the hardest part. Having to bury everyone I'd ever loved. And knowing I would have to go on living. But I wasn't prepared for what followed."

She sat up. "What . . . followed? I don't understand."

"I went off half-crazy, seeking revenge, and wound up in prison for attacking my neighbors. Afterward, the murderers were never punished. There was a trial, but it was my word against theirs. And the judge was not inclined to believe a man in prison chains."

At his words, she remembered his anger in the courtroom when he'd been brought in in chains. How helpless he must have felt. How desperate.

He took a deep breath and continued. "When I was released from prison, I couldn't bear to live among my neighbors. I turned my back on my country and lost myself in hard work in Mexico. That's where Zeb and I were reunited. We'd fought in the war together, and when I decided to try my luck in Texas, he decided to tag along."

"Oh, Adam." Her eyes filled.

He touched a finger to the moisture that spilled down her cheek. "Tears? For me? Diamond, I'm not worth them."

"Not worth them?" She sniffed. But it was too late to stem the flow. They spilled unchecked from her eyes. She loved this man. Desperately. Loved him with every ounce of her being. "You're finer than any man I've ever known except Pa. I can't bear to think how you suffered."

"Shh." He gathered her close and tasted the salt of her tears on his lips. "It's over now. The pain. The loss. The loneliness."

"Yes." She took the kiss deeper, seeking to comfort him, needing to comfort herself. "It's over. For both of us."

Their lovemaking took on a new urgency as they gave themselves up to each other, desperately seeking to heal forever all the old wounds.

Chapter Nineteen

"I've made coffee," Adam called as he picked up a clean shirt and headed toward the door. In his hand he carried his rifle. "Latch the door behind me."

Diamond stopped him at the door with a quick kiss. "If you take long enough with your bath, I just might surprise you with breakfast."

"I don't think I can spare that much time." He pulled her back with another hard, quick kiss. "Besides, maybe you'd better leave the cooking to me. I'd like to live long enough to enjoy another night of your loving."

The sound of their shared laughter warmed the little cabin. She latched the door and watched through the small window as he made his way to the creek. The sight of his slow, easy walk made her throat go dry. She could hardly wait for him to return.

She busied herself in the room, pausing to examine mementos from his past. A piece of fine linen, bearing neat, perfect stitches, and the names Caroline and Adam, and the date, May 1, 1860. His wedding date.

A mental image appeared, of a small, dainty woman, able to preside over a beautifully appointed home, cooking sumptuous meals and sewing fine clothes. Diamond was surprised that the thought caused no pain or jealousy. Car-

>line was his past. He was entitled to his memories. But from now on, she intended to be a special part of his future.

She leafed through his Bible, reading the names of his parents and brothers, his wife and son. It pleased her to know that he had been part of a loving family. She touched a hand to a wooden top and a child's slate. She could imagine Adam with a baby in his arms. Strange, just scant weeks ago, she would have found that image impossible. She had thought him to be a gunman, a man outside the law. But that was before she had come to know him. Now she thought him the most wonderful, the most noble, the most honest man she'd ever known. Because of his loss, he was better able to understand hers. He was truly a man of compassion.

She smoothed the covers of the bed, allowing her hands to linger over the warmth that still clung to the folds. Her heart was filled to overflowing for the man who had shared, not only his love, but his deepest, most intimate pain. She was certain that, together, they could put the past behind them and concentrate on the future.

Together.

The word made her heart soar. Together they could find out who had killed her father, and continued to stalk them. And why. If she could only figure out why her father had been shot, she was certain she would know who pulled the trigger.

At least now, with Adam's explanation of his past, she understood why he'd been so sensitive to her loss. The thought of having lost an entire family in a brutal, senseless murder caused her to tremble.

His words, spoken in pain, suddenly jolted her. "Sometimes the reason is too simple to comprehend. We were betrayed by people we'd known and trusted for a lifetime."

"...Known and trusted for a lifetime."

Sweet heaven. How could she have missed it?

She let out a string of oaths that would have made even her wranglers cringe. The reason for Pa's murder had been right there for her to see all along. And she'd been too blinded by loyalty and friendship.

She couldn't afford to wait for Adam. She had to move now, before it was too late. It wasn't only her life that hung in the balance. She had involved Pearl, as well. And Jade and Ruby.

She grabbed the slate from the shelf. Scrawling a note, she left it on the table and reached for her cowhide jacket. She ran to the corral, saddled her horse and took off at a gallop.

Adam stepped into the icy water and washed quickly. Come spring, when the weather gentled and the water was warmed by the sun, he intended to bring Diamond here with him. They would wash each other's backs. And make slow, delicious love along the banks.

At the sound of an approaching horse he strode from the water and took up his rifle. Spotting Zeb, he sent him a quick grin and set aside his weapon.

"I'd better warn you," he said as he started to pull on his clothes. "There's a guest in the cabin."

"A guest, hmm?" The old man knelt beside his horse and joined him in a long, soothing drink. When he straightened, he muttered, "It wouldn't be a fiery little wildcat, would it?"

"It is."

"I figured maybe the lady boss had spent the night. I just spotted her backside in a cloud of dust when I rode past the cabin."

Adam's hands stilled on the button of his shirt. His head came up sharply. "Dust?"

"Um-hmm." The old man scratched his beard. "She looked to be in a mighty big hurry. Had her horse pushed to the limit."

Adam snatched up his rifle and boots and started to run. Over his shoulder he called, "Which way was she headed?"

"She appeared to be headed home."

Adam crossed the distance from the creek to his cabin and charged through the open door. Spotting the slate, he read the message while he struggled into his boots. He filled a pouch with bullets, then raced to the corral and saddled his horse. And cursed every precious minute he wasted.

Diamond pressed herself low over the back of Sunrise, urging the mare to new speeds. She had to get home. Had to get to Pa's office before—

The gunshot echoed across the hills, and dirt exploded inches from her horse's hooves. Sunrise reared up. Though Diamond was caught unawares, she was too experienced to be thrown. With deft movements she wheeled her mount and drew her own weapon. Again the bullet landed mere inches from her, falling harmlessly in the sand.

"That was on purpose. The next one won't miss," came a man's voice. "Drop your gun."

With a hiss of frustration she did as she was told and watched as the gunman emerged from behind a rock.

"Who are you?" she called as he strode toward her.

"Name's Redmond." He snatched up her pistol and removed her rifle from the boot of her saddle. "Hold out your hands." With quick movements he yanked the reins from her, then tied her hands in front of her, leaving her seated helplessly astride her horse.

"Where are you taking me?"

"You ask too many questions." He shot her an evil grin before climbing into his saddle and catching up her reins.

"I know who hired you," she called.

"Then you know more than I do." His voice was flat, the tone ominous. He was a hired gun, willing to do whatever was necessary for pay.

He nudged his horse into a run, forcing her mare to follow.

Within minutes, they had left the familiar trail and were hidden in a maze of rocks and gullies.

"Cal." Pearl's face was flushed. Her usually calm demeanor was replaced by a sense of urgency.

Jade and Ruby stood on either side of her, wringing their hands.

The ranch foreman had been summoned from his bunk. His hair was mussed, his chin covered with dark stubble. On his face was a scowl of fury. "This had better be important."

"We can't find Diamond. We broke into her locked room. Her bed hasn't been slept in. We think she's been gone all night."

Cal looked from Pearl to Jade to Ruby. "Did she say anything? Do you know if she had any plans?"

The three shook their heads.

"She locked herself in her room right after dinner. She refused to respond to our calls." Jade's voice held a trace of sadness.

"Did you hear anything during the night?"

"Not a sound," Pearl said.

"I thought I heard a horse's hooves," Jade admitted. "But it could have been one of the wranglers."

"She may have gone to Adam Winter's place," Ruby suggested.

Cal's gaze narrowed on her. "Why would she do that?" His look was so fierce, she cringed.

"Because—" she moistened her lips with her tongue, considering every word "—she's sweet on him."

Cal swore loudly, fiercely. "That's just what I need. Damned female hasn't even got enough sense to be afraid. There's a man out there gunning for her, who might have been hired by Adam Winter. And she's off on some romantic midnight ride. Maybe with the very man who's out to kill her."

"I do not believe that of Adam Winter," Pearl said in her most injured tone.

"Then you're a fool, too." Cal turned on his heel and stalked out of the house. Minutes later he and the wranglers thundered past, headed in the direction of Adam Winter's cabin. A lone wrangler was dispatched to the marshal's office. Cal wanted it all nice and legal when he finally had his revenge on Onyx Jewel's killer.

Diamond lay at the base of several large rocks, roped as helplessly as a calf at branding time. Apparently her abductor had been warned of her prowess in a fight. He was taking no chances. She fought against her ropes, seething with anger and frustration. If she could get herself free, if she could get her hands on a gun...

She suddenly stopped struggling. Why had he left her here, in plain view? Why hadn't he hidden her behind the rocks?

The answer came to her in a flash of understanding. She wasn't to be the only victim this day. She was being used as bait. In a deadly trap. Bait to lure a second victim.

Adam. Dear God, Adam.

* * *

Carmelita and the three young women looked up at the knock on the door.

"Diamond," Pearl shouted as she got to her feet.

"Señorita Diamond would not knock," the housekeeper reminded her.

Deflated, Pearl and the others followed Carmelita to the front door. Chester Pierce stood on the veranda, his hat in his hand, a smile on his face.

"Good day, Señor Pierce," Carmelita said in greeting. "I am sorry that Señorita Diamond is not here."

His smile encompassed all the women. "That's all right, Carmelita. I'm not here to visit Diamond. I'm just here to pick up the ledgers."

"But Diamond told you last night that we haven't finished them yet," Pearl said.

"It doesn't matter." He strode past them into the house, then proceeded toward Onyx's office. "As a banker, I deal with figures every day. It will be nothing to finish the tally and prepare the wranglers' pay vouchers."

"But I don't think Diamond would approve." Pearl trailed behind him, wondering just how strongly she should protest. After all, this wasn't really her business.

Oh, if only Diamond were here to make a decision.

"Nonsense." Chester strode to the big desk and closed the ledger before tucking it under his arm. With a satisfied smile he turned toward the women clustered in the doorway. "I've been handling Onyx's business long before any of you were even born. Now if you don't mind, I'll be on my way."

The young women glanced at one another helplessly. They knew Diamond had wanted to handle the books herself. Yet none of them felt comfortable taking a stand against such a close friend of the family.

Taking advantage of their confusion, Chester made his way to the front door and tipped his hat. "Good day, ladies."

They watched as he climbed into his rig and flicked the reins. The horse started off at a run. Within minutes he had disappeared from view.

"What do you make of that, Carmelita?" Pearl asked.

The housekeeper wiped her hands on her apron and shrugged. "Señor Pierce has often come to take the ledgers. Especially whenever Señor Onyx was traveling." She walked away mumbling, "But I think Señorita Diamond will not like it. She was determined to finish the books herself."

"Maybe it's just as well," Pearl said with a sigh. "I came across so many discrepancies, it probably would have taken another month to figure out what was going on. Daddy was a very poor bookkeeper. And Diamond seemed not much better."

Adam was forced to backtrack, wasting precious time. But once he found the place where Diamond's stalker had dismounted, the trail was simple to follow. Too simple. He fought to ignore the little tingle along his scalp. The whole thing smelled of an ambush. But there was no time to stop and prepare a plan of counterattack. Diamond's life was at stake. His own safety meant nothing. Nor would his life ever again have meaning if he failed to save her.

He paused on the winding trail along the banks of Poison Creek. It was here that Onyx Jewel had been shot in the back. He glanced upward, toward towering Widow's Peak, and felt a sense of foreboding. Striding forward, he caught sight of a figure lying in the dirt, a hundred yards away.

For a full minute his heart stopped beating. Dear God, was he too late?

Then he heard the sound of her voice, and his pulse throbbed in his temples.

"Go back, Adam! It's a trap!"

He slipped his rifle from the boot of the saddle and dropped to the ground, seeking cover behind a rock. A stranger's voice had him taking aim.

"I'd enjoy nothing better than a gunfight with you, Winter. I've heard you're the man to beat in these parts. But I have my orders. Unless you drop your gun right now and come up here, I'm going to have to kill the woman."

The coldness of the words convinced Adam that the gunman meant what he'd said. Standing, he tossed his pistol and rifle aside and lifted his hands over his head.

"That's real good, Winter," said the voice. "I like a man who knows how to take orders."

When Adam reached the rocks, he dropped to his knees beside Diamond, ignoring the gunman who stepped from his place of concealment.

"Has that bastard hurt you?" he demanded.

"No. Oh, Adam," she cried, "I'm so sorry you got caught up in this. I know now who killed Pa. I was heading home for the proof when—"

They both looked up as a shadow fell over them. A figure dressed in a black suit and black hat emerged from behind a nearby rock. In his hand was a small, deadly derringer.

"You've known Pa and me all our lives. We trusted you." Diamond's voice trembled with passion as she stared up at her father's murderer. "How could you do this, Uncle Chet?"

Cal felt a wave of frustration when he found Adam Winter's cabin empty. Out back, he came across Zeb Forrest, just returning to the herd.

"Where's Winter?" he demanded.

The old man scratched his chin. "Don't know. He took off like the wrath of Jehoshaphat when he found the lady boss missing."

"Missing?" Cal's hand fisted in the front of the old man's shirt, dragging him close. "What do you mean?"

Zeb slapped his hand away and straightened with quiet dignity before answering. "He was washing in the creek when he learned she'd lit out for home. She left him a message. It's on the table."

"What does it say?"

"Don't know. Figured it was none of my business."

Minutes later Cal stormed out of the cabin and ordered his wranglers to mount up.

"Hold on," Zeb called. He checked the bullets in his rifle, then pulled himself into the saddle. "I'm riding along," he announced.

"I thought you said this wasn't your business," Cal said irritably.

"I'm making it my business."

"Answer me," Diamond demanded as Adam helped her to her feet. Her bound hands were balled into fists. "How could you kill your best friend?"

The banker refused to answer.

Adam kept his gaze locked on the pistol in Chet's hand. "It's a simple answer," Adam said. "And as old as time. Greed. Money. He wanted what your father had worked so hard to acquire. And he would take it any way he could."

Seeing the way Adam was watching his pistol, Chet signaled to the gunman to move closer, until his rifle was jammed roughly into Adam's back.

Ignoring Redmond, Adam added, "Even if it meant murdering his best friend."

"Why not?" Chet said with contempt. "Why should Onyx Jewel make all the money?"

"Maybe because he was willing to work hard," Adam said softly. "It takes a special man to turn this wilderness into a profit-making enterprise. And Onyx Jewel was a very special man. If you were jealous, why didn't you offer to give up banking and start ranching?"

"I didn't need to," Chet said with a laugh. "I let the poor ranchers do all the work, and I just helped myself to some of their money each month. And when they ran out of money, I was able to take over their land and milk the profits. You may not know it—" his tone was boastful "—but I own almost as much of Texas as Onyx Jewel did before he left this world. And soon, thanks to these," he said, pointing to the ledgers, "I'll own even more."

Adam's dark look challenged Chet's. "How much did you steal, Pierce?"

The banker shrugged. "A few hundred thousand."

Diamond gasped at the enormity of the sum.

Chet gave a mirthless laugh. "Onyx could afford it. Whenever he went off on a buying trip and handed over the books, I saw to it that his expenses were . . . very high. I managed to live very well . . . for a while."

"Then Pa discovered what you were doing," Diamond said flatly.

He nodded. "When Onyx first discovered the discrepancies in the books, I think he was more hurt than angry."

Knowing her father's generosity, Diamond nodded. "But he was your friend. He would have given you time to pay it back."

"A man like Pierce doesn't want to pay back his debts," Adam interjected. "I'd be willing to bet he wanted your father to forgive the debt."

Chet's voice deepened with anger. "He offered to, at first. But that was before he knew just how much was missing. I knew it was only a matter of time until he discovered how serious it was. So I began to make plans."

"Plans," Adam said with scorn. "That was when you started looking for a scapegoat."

Chet nodded. "I dammed up the creek and made it look like the work of his wranglers. That way, I hoped to start a public feud between you and him, so that, when the time came, the townspeople would believe you killed him."

When Diamond made a sound of strangled fury, he turned to her. "Too bad that traveling judge had to deprive the town of a good hanging."

Diamond closed her eyes against the pain, thinking how desperately she had wanted to see Adam hang. How would she have been able to live with the knowledge that he had been hanged for another man's crime?

"I knew my bank would fail if I had to make good on the theft," Chet continued. "So I concocted a little scheme to lure Onyx out here to talk about the payment."

"Why would he come all this way?" Diamond asked.

"I told him I didn't want anyone in town to know about this. He came, in order to protect my reputation."

"And even after all that, you killed him," Diamond said softly. She was feeling once again all the pain of loss and separation from the man who had been her whole life. But now the enormity of her loss seemed even more overwhelming, knowing that he'd been betrayed by his closest friend.

"Why didn't you let it end there?" she asked.

"I would have. If you had been willing to give up those ledgers. They were the only proof of my theft. When you refused, I hired an army of gunmen. Their orders were to find you alone and kidnap you. I would then pay the ransom, which would amount to exactly the amount I'd stolen. But I hadn't counted on Winter being so good with a gun."

"And the cattle?" Adam asked. "Why were you killing them off?"

"So that your ranch would fail. You see, I hold the mortgage. And your land is key to my plan to own this entire section of Texas."

"All of this because of money," Diamond said with a sigh.

"That's easy for you to say. Your father saw to it that you never had to do without anything. Ask most people here in Hanging Tree whether or not they'd kill for money, and you'd find that I'm not alone."

"You're wrong," Diamond said vehemently. "It takes a monster to do what you did." She shook her head in disbelief. "And now you intend to kill me, too. When will it end? How many people are you willing to kill in order to hold on to your precious money?"

He gave her a chilling smile. "As many as necessary, my dear." He turned to the gunman, who had been listening in silence. "Beginning with Redmond."

As calmly as if he were pointing a finger, he aimed and fired. A look of surprise was followed by a look of pain, as the gunman dropped to his knees. He managed to squeeze off a shot with his rifle, but the bullet went wide, missing its target. With a cry, the gunman sprawled facedown in the dirt.

Diamond bit back a cry of horror. This seemed like a terrible nightmare. One that would never end.

To add to her woes, she caught sight of Jade's elegant carriage heading directly toward them. Inside, their gowns fluttering like brilliant butterflies, sat Jade, Pearl and Ruby. As innocent, as unprotected, as babies.

Chet's jaw dropped at the sight of them. As the horses came to a halt, the three young women climbed out. Each of them was holding a small silver derringer like his.

"I finally figured out what was wrong with Daddy's bookkeeping," Pearl said softly. She glanced at Diamond and saw her stunned look. Turning to Adam, she said, "I know you said we weren't to ride without the wranglers accompanying us. But we couldn't wait. Especially fearing that you and Diamond might be in extreme danger."

"I should have known. It looks like none of the Jewel women know how to take orders," Adam said dryly.

"Fools," Chet said. "This was none of your concern." His mind seemed to be working overtime. His eyes glittered with sudden malice. "I am prepared to offer each of you a substantial amount if you leave now. You can return to your homes with a fortune. And no one will ever be the wiser."

The three young women stared at him in stunned surprise. This was not what they'd expected.

Diamond held her breath, wondering what was going through their minds. After all, their lives had not been easy. They had been forced to make do without the daily presence of a loving father. And they had no claim to his estate. The offer of a fortune must be tempting.

To further tempt them, Chet added ominously, "I warn you. If you refuse my offer, you must prepare to die along with these two."

"You are the one who must prepare to die," Jade said softly. "I do not know about the others, but I want no part of ill-gotten wealth. Furthermore, be warned. I know how to fire this weapon."

"So do I, *chérie*," Ruby said with a chuckle. "Many a man who has dared to cross me has found himself robbed of his... manhood. And you have made me very cross,

Monsieur Pierce.'' She took deadly aim with her pistol, and Chet flinched as she aimed directly between his legs.

"I'm not even sure how to fire this," Pearl said, her hand visibly shaking. "But I figure, if I fire enough times, I'm bound to hit something. And your offer has made me angry enough to try."

All the fear that Diamond had been holding inside suddenly dissipated. Her heart resumed beating. These three women, who had been strangers just scant weeks ago, were willing to risk death to stand by her side.

"I . . . can't believe it." Diamond's voice trembled with emotion. "Do you understand the danger you've just put yourselves in?"

"There is no danger I wouldn't face for you," Pearl said softly.

"Nor I," Jade added.

"We stand together, *chérie,* " Ruby said emphatically.

"How very noble." Chet's voice rang with disdain. "And how very foolish. Because now, you've given me another weapon." Instead of being afraid of their threats, his eyes suddenly gleamed. He pointed the gun at Diamond, standing tied and helpless before him. "Unless you throw down your guns immediately, I'll kill her."

The three looked at one another with uncertainty. "You can't kill all of us," Jade challenged.

"I don't need to. Unless you do as I say, Diamond's fate will be the same as his." Chet pointed to the lifeless figure of the gunman, whose blood mingled with the earth to form a mottled pool around him. It was a frightening scene. And a convincing one.

With a cry, Pearl tossed her weapon aside. Reluctantly, the other two followed suit.

Diamond felt tears sting her eyes. These three women, so very different, were willing to lay down their lives for her.

She had never known such love. Such devotion. They truly were her sisters.

"That's better." The banker turned to Adam. "Untie Diamond."

"Why?" Her heart quickened. "Have you had a change of plan?"

He merely smiled again. "On the contrary, my dear. I simply don't want any suspicious evidence left behind. When I lead the marshal to your bodies, it will be easy to explain. Everyone knows that you and Winter have been feuding. They will believe me when I say that I was on my way here with the ransom, after having been notified that you and your sisters were abducted by Winter and his hired gun. Alas," he said with mock sincerity, "I arrived too late. You were all dead by Winter's hand." He gave an evil smile. "It would appear that Winter and Redmond then fought to the death. A tragedy. But one that will soon be forgotten."

"And the ledgers?" Diamond asked as Adam untied her. She rubbed at her wrists, willing the circulation back into them. "How do you intend to explain them?"

"The evidence will be destroyed in my fireplace before dark tonight. And tomorrow I will lead the town in mourning the murder of my best friend's daughters. And when I take over the operation of your ranch for unspecified debts, as well as Adam Winter's ranch, no one will question it."

Diamond swallowed back the knot of revulsion that threatened to choke her. This evil man had stood at her father's grave pretending to grieve. And all the time, he had been gloating over his successful crime.

Beside her, Adam studied the pistol in Chet's hand. He was aware that it had taken but a single bullet to kill Onyx Jewel. Still, he had to take the risk. Not for himself. His own life had had little meaning in the past few years. But for Diamond's sake, he had to disarm this madman. He could still recall the pain he'd been forced to suffer when he'd finally returned to consciousness on his farm in Maryland, only to learn that all those he'd loved were dead. He wouldn't allow it to happen again. This time, he had a fighting chance. There was only one man and one gun.

He braced himself for the attack. As Chester Pierce leveled the gun, Adam leaped at him. He heard the sound of the gunshot, mingled with his cry of rage as his hands found the banker's throat. He felt a white-hot pain rip through his chest, and seconds later his legs refused to support him. But even as he stumbled and fell to the ground, he kept his fingers locked around Chet's throat, though he could no longer remember why.

And from a great distance came the sound of a woman's cries. Diamond's voice. Calling him. Weeping. Dear God, he realized. She was weeping. But she never cried. It could only mean . . . It could only mean the wound was mortal.

Chapter Twenty

The unmistakable sound of gunshots rumbled and echoed across the hills like thunder. Cal and his wranglers came to a sudden stop, then took off in the direction of the sound, with old Zeb following.

The marshal, coming from the other direction, pointed to a distant hill, then urged his mount to a gallop. His deputies had to race to keep up.

They converged on the winding trail along the banks of Poison Creek. And as they started forward, every man was recalling the horrible discovery of Onyx Jewel's body in this very place.

They rounded a bend, then stopped short at the scene that confronted them. At first glance it appeared to be four hysterical women, sobbing and weeping, clutching at the bodies of two men. But as they drew nearer, the scene became even more confusing.

Diamond and Pearl were struggling to pry Adam Winter away from Chester Pierce. The two men were drenched in blood, and Winter's hands were locked around the banker's throat. As they succeeded in separating them, the women's actions became even more astounding to the approaching riders.

Jade and Ruby scrambled to snatch up pistols from the dirt and, instead of aiming them at Adam Winter, aimed at the banker, forcing him to lie with his arms over his head. They were screaming at him in a most unladylike manner.

The prim and proper Pearl, unmindful of the dozens of men who were now circling on horseback, was frantically tearing off her lace petticoat. She gave no thought to modesty as she tugged the undergarment free.

Diamond was leaning over Adam Winter, sobbing and weeping as she tore his blood-soaked shirt away. Sobbing and weeping? None of the men could ever recall having seen such a thing before. It was so uncharacteristic, they thought that Diamond Jewel had surely lost her mind.

The marshal could see that he was going to have to take charge and bring order out of chaos.

"All right, ladies," he shouted as he dismounted and drew his gun. "I realize that you're not very good in a crisis. But that's understandable. After all, sweet little things like you probably never had to deal with a killer before. Now, step back and let me take care of this outlaw."

As he strode toward Adam, Diamond turned on him with a snarl. "Don't you touch him. Can't you see he's been shot? He may be dying."

"That'd serve him right," the marshal said smugly. "But Doc Prentice will keep him alive. And then we'll show him what we do to criminals in Texas."

"You don't understand," Pearl said, grabbing the marshal's sleeve. "That's the murderer over there." She pointed to the banker, who continued lying very still while Jade and Ruby stood over him with their pistols aimed and ready. Neither woman seemed the least bit reluctant to be handling weapons.

"What?" The marshal was clearly stunned. "Are you saying Winter is innocent?"

Cal and the wranglers added to the confusion by sliding from their saddles to form a circle around the others. They looked on as Pearl tore her petticoat into strips and handed them to Diamond. She, in turn, frantically worked to stem the blood that flowed from Adam's chest.

As she worked, Pearl explained, "Chester Pierce was cheating Daddy for years. That's why we couldn't get the books to balance."

Cal McCabe's face darkened with fury. Before anyone could react, he caught the banker by the front of his jacket and hauled him to his feet. "You killed my best friend? You murdered Onyx Jewel?"

Chester blinked a moment before Cal's fist smashed into his face, sending him sprawling backward against a rock. Before Cal could follow through with a second blow, Diamond stepped between them and lifted both hands to Cal's chest imploringly.

"Please, Cal," she cried. "I know how you feel. Everybody here feels the same way." Her voice trembled with passion. "More than anything, I want to avenge Pa's death. But if I've learned anything at all from Adam it's this. Don't take the law into your own hands. Let Marshal Regan handle this."

The crowd was stunned into silence. Could this possibly be Onyx Jewel's daughter displaying such humility?

"Looks like you've done a heap of growing up in the past few weeks, Diamond," the marshal said gruffly. "Adam Winter was right. Chester Pierce will pay. The way any murderer pays here in Hanging Tree."

The banker slithered to the ground and fell to his knees as the enormity of his crime and the manner of his punishment hit him.

Diamond returned to Adam's side. A moment later a cry was torn from her throat.

"Someone help me." Tears streamed down her face. "Adam's dying."

The gilded carriage, pulled by two matching white horses, moved smartly across the hills and valleys.

Adam lay on the cushioned seat, gritting his teeth at every jolt. At least, he thought, he wasn't dead yet. But he almost wished he were. Anything would be better than the pain he was enduring.

So many voices babbling. None of them made sense. Deep men's voices, all raised in anger. Higher-pitched women's voices, sounding like the chirping of birds. And one, close by, like the sighing of the wind. He knew that voice. Soft, breathless. He tried, but he couldn't speak to her. Couldn't give her any consolation. It seemed supremely important that he let her know that he was still alive. But all he could do was grit his teeth against the pain and feel the warmth of her arms encircling him, holding him close each time the carriage took another jolt.

"Don't leave me, Adam," she whispered. "I couldn't bear to lose you, too."

God, how he wanted to live. More than anything, he wanted to assure her that he would fight to stay alive. Instead, he closed his eyes as the carriage bounced over yet another gully, then landed with a thud.

"Stop the carriage. He's losing too much blood."

"Looks bad." Adam recognized Zeb's voice. "He'll never make it to town. Better take him to your place, lady boss. I'll ride ahead and fetch the doc." His voice faded in and out. "Hate to do this, my friend."

"What is it?" Diamond's words were spoken close to Adam's ear.

"Whiskey," came Zeb's voice as though from a great distance. "It'll keep him from getting infected until the doc can remove that bullet."

Adam felt something cold, which instantly set fire to his flesh. The flames grew, until they devoured him. And then he sank into blessed unconsciousness.

"It's a lucky thing you're strong and healthy." Dr. Cosmo Prentice affixed the last bit of dressing to Adam's chest. His soft, chubby fingers had all the grace of an artist. In a bloody dish nearby lay the small-caliber bullet, which had missed Adam's heart by inches.

"Thanks, Doc." Adam's tongue felt too big for his mouth. He couldn't seem to make his lips move properly.

He turned toward Diamond, who was gripping his hand so tightly he'd lost all feeling in it. Her shirt and britches were still smeared with his blood. Her face was pale, her eyes red rimmed from crying. She had wept buckets of tears. Even now, they were too close to the surface. The least little thing might set her off again.

In a daze she looked around her father's bedroom, which smelled of chloroform and disinfectant. The last time she'd been here, it had been to view her father's body. The thought caused her heart to twist painfully.

"You're sure you're..." She couldn't say the words. They were too important to her.

"He'll be fine." Doc Prentice's pencil-thin mustache twitched as he gave her a warm smile. "But he's going to need some time. And some care."

"We're going to take good care of him," promised Pearl solemnly. "I shall read to him whenever he is bored."

Adam tried not to groan.

"We will bathe him and dress him," Ruby said.

At that he flinched.

"I will burn incense and pray to my ancestors," Jade added. "And as he mends, I will teach him the ancient arts to help him grow stronger."

Carmelita's voice broke in. "I will personally prepare all of Señor Winter's favorite hot, spicy foods. Oh, it will be good to cook for a man again."

"My men and I will see to your ranch and herd until you're back on your feet," Cal said, grasping Adam's hand in a firm handshake. "I want you to know, Winter, how grateful I am. What you did, throwing yourself into the path of a bullet to save Diamond, was the bravest thing I've ever heard of. I was wrong about you. And, if you're willing, I'd like us to be friends."

Adam accepted his handshake and gave him a smile. But when he turned away, Adam hissed in pain. Zeb, who had been standing in the corner, walked closer.

"Something I can do?" he whispered.

"Get me out of here," Adam muttered.

"Sorry, friend. Doc says you can't be moved."

"Then get rid of them," Adam said through gritted teeth.

"Too much gratitude, huh? Not used to all this love and kindness."

Adam hissed again, and the old man looked up with a grin. "Come on, folks. I think it's time to go."

"But we must stay and take care of our hero," Pearl protested.

"I think your...hero's in good hands with the doc." Zeb herded them toward the door. "Besides, maybe he and Diamond would like a few minutes alone."

"Oh. Yes." Three heads bobbed in sudden understanding. Three pairs of eyes glowed with visions of romance. Three voices said in unison, "Of course. Alone."

The women began to file from the room, followed by Cal and Zeb.

In the doorway, Pearl turned. "How long must he stay in bed?"

The doctor snapped shut his black bag. "Until he's strong enough to stand."

"Then we will prepare a bath..."

"And incense..."

"And supper..."

The doctor pulled the door closed, shutting off the sound of their voices. At last, Diamond and Adam found themselves alone.

The silence was a welcome relief after all the madness of the past hours.

"You were very brave."

"Um-hmm." He frowned. "According to your sisters, a—" he bit back the epithet he wanted to hurl and finished simply "—hero."

Sisters. She was beginning to like the sound of that word more and more. Pearl, Jade and Ruby had been simply wonderful throughout the entire ordeal. They had stood by her side, lending their support, their strength. It felt good to know she had someone she could count on.

"You make the word *hero* sound like an insult. You were so noble, so—"

"I was scared to death."

She was shocked. "Of dying?"

"Of seeing you hurt."

At that she went very still. Those damnable tears were welling up again, blinding her. "I don't know what's come over me," she sniffed. "I never cry."

"That's all right. You're entitled."

She ran the back of her hand across her eyes, leaving a muddy, bloody smear that made her resemble a raccoon. "Are you truly all right?"

He gave her a lopsided grin and sat up, swinging his feet to the floor, even though the movement made him suck in his breath on a flash of white-hot pain. "I'll live."

"Oh, Adam." She started to hug him, then thought better of it. She leaned forward, afraid to touch him, and brushed her lips lightly over his.

At once he felt the flare of heat and cursed the fact that if he made any sudden moves, he would open up his wound.

"Think you could manage a better kiss than that?" he asked.

She sat gingerly on the bed beside him and wrapped her arms around his waist. "Isn't it lucky you fell in love with a big, strong, sturdy woman like me?" she muttered against his lips. "Instead of some pale, helpless little beauty?"

Lucky? He felt like the luckiest man in the world. But as she moved her mouth seductively over his, he couldn't answer. He was struggling to hold back, not only a rush of feelings, but a surge of pain.

The pain won.

The room tilted precariously. He wasn't even aware of falling back against the pillows. Or of the sound of Diamond's voice as she anxiously summoned the doctor back to the room.

The days passed in a blur of activity. From sunup until sundown, the ranch house was filled with visitors.

Carmelita was in her glory, cooking for all the men who seemed to have begun congregating since Adam's arrival. The marshal dropped by every day with new details of the crime. Cal and the wranglers visited Adam's bedroom in order to report to him and to Diamond, who was reluctant to leave his side. The doctor stopped by each day to examine his patient. He always seemed to arrive at dinnertime. Even the fiery young Reverend Wade Weston came by to say how grateful he was that the town hadn't hanged the wrong man. And to assure Diamond that her father's soul now rested in peace. That thought was a great comfort to Diamond.

As his wound healed, Adam's restlessness became apparent. Each day, when Zeb appeared, he bombarded the old man with questions about the ranch, the herd.

"What's the matter?" Zeb asked as Carmelita retreated with a tray of half-eaten food. "I would think all this fuss, all this pampering, would feel like heaven."

"Then you can have it, old man. If I don't get out of here soon, I think I'll go stark raving mad."

"Sounds serious." The old man sipped the coffee Carmelita had given him. She had added a splash of whiskey, just the way he liked it. "Maybe some men just aren't cut out for the good life." He glanced at Adam. "What are you going to do about the lady boss?"

Adam avoided his friend's eyes. "What do you mean?"

"Mean? Hellfire, it should be plain enough. You love her, don't you?"

Adam nodded. "With all my heart. But I can't ask her to give up all this for what I have to offer. And I can't stay here any longer."

"Sometimes," Zeb mused aloud, "loving a woman just isn't enough. I've loved a few ladies in my lifetime. But they always wanted me to put down roots, and live under a roof like other men. And I just couldn't. So in the end, I always had to leave them and move on. But I'll tell you, it gets to be a lonesome life."

Adam eased himself out of the chair and walked slowly to the window, staring out at the gathering darkness.

Zeb watched him for a few minutes, then stood. "I'll get back to the herd now."

Adam didn't move. Long after his old friend had ridden away, he continued staring out the window. And seeing only the reflection of his own bleak future looking back.

Diamond strode out of the barn, her boots covered with dung, her shirt and britches soiled and dirty. It felt good to be doing chores again. She'd missed the hard work. But in the beginning she had been afraid to leave Adam's side for more than a few minutes.

It occurred to her that love was very confining. At once she dismissed such a cold, heartless thought. She didn't mind the time spent with Adam. After all, he had risked his life for her. And she loved being with him. These past few days had been a special treasure. Except, of course, that there had been dozens of interruptions.

She didn't really mind, she told herself. After all, Pearl and Jade and Ruby had formed a special bond with her. Sisters. She smiled as she strode toward the ranch house. She was learning to love having sisters. But sometimes, she craved the privacy she'd once had. She thought it would be heaven to ride up with Adam to one of the line camps and spend the rest of the winter alone with him, snowed in until springtime. At once she cursed herself for such selfish thoughts. She ought to be thrilled to share Adam with the others, she thought as she pried off her boots. After all, weren't they one big happy family now?

As she entered the kitchen, she sensed the change. Carmelita was polishing a blackened kettle with such vengeance, she could almost see sparks coming from the housekeeper's fingers.

"Something wrong?" Diamond asked.

"Señor Winter does not want supper. He is upstairs preparing to leave."

"Leave. But..." Diamond turned toward the door. "Come with me."

She flew from the kitchen, followed by Carmelita, and made her way along the hallway. As she passed Pearl, she saw her lips pursed in a little pout.

"What is it?" Diamond asked.

"Adam doesn't want me reading to him today. He said he doesn't have time, since he's leaving."

"Carmelita just told me. Come on. We'll speak to him." Diamond continued along, trailed by Pearl and the housekeeper, until she came to Jade and Ruby, who were carrying a tub of steaming water between them.

"*Chérie*, you will never believe—" Ruby began, but Diamond stopped her.

"Let me guess. Adam doesn't want to take another bath."

"*Oui*. And he practically snarled at us when we entered his bedroom."

"Men," Jade said with authority. "Once they are strong enough to take care of themselves, they begin to resent all the things they once loved."

Diamond's heart skipped a beat. Was that true? Would Adam resent her now that he was back on his feet?

"I'll...we'll talk to him," she managed to say before she brushed past them. "Come on."

She knocked once, then pulled open the door.

Adam was fully dressed, and had pulled on his cowhide jacket. He was just buckling his gun belt when he turned and caught sight of her and the others.

"Going somewhere?" Her heart was hammering, but she was pleased to note that her voice was steady.

"I was just going to look for you." He took a step toward her, then stopped. It would be best if he didn't touch her. Especially in front of the others. What he had to say was painful enough. Touching her would make it impossible.

He turned to the others. "I was hoping to find all of you together. I want you to know how grateful I am for all you've done."

"Grateful." Diamond felt a flash of fire and bit down on her temper.

"Without all of you, I'm sure my recovery would have been much slower," Adam said. "And I know this hasn't been easy on any of you. But it's time for me to get back to my ranch. I've been letting Zeb carry the load alone."

"But you haven't...we haven't..." Diamond stopped, embarrassed. She was very close to crying. Or worse, begging. If it killed her, she wouldn't make a fool of herself in front of the others. Besides, they all seemed so calm, so resigned to his leaving. She was the only one who seemed at all flustered.

"I understand," Pearl said softly as she brushed a kiss over his cheek. "You have a need to return to your own ranch."

"And to get on with your life," Jade said as she followed suit and kissed his cheek.

"It is natural enough," Ruby added, brushing her painted lips across his, leaving a faint smudge. "It must seem strange, sleeping in another man's bed."

"I will miss cooking for you, Señor Winter," Carmelita said.

"Not as much as I'll miss eating your good cooking." Adam bent and kissed her.

At his words, she brightened. But only a little.

"Then why...?" Diamond stopped again, cautioning herself not to create a spectacle.

He steeled himself to kiss her cheek. When he did he felt the jolt and pulled back quickly. "You have an empire to see to, Diamond. And a lot of wranglers depending on you for work. I've kept you from it long enough. Now I'll bid you goodbye.''

He picked up his hat and headed for the door, with the four women following.

At the front door they crowded around, watching as he pulled himself slowly, painfully into the saddle. He tipped his hat and managed a smile. Then he was gone.

They watched until he disappeared over a rise. Then each one drifted away. All except Diamond. She continued standing at the door, staring into the distance. And praying that he would have a change of heart. And come racing back to her waiting arms.

The little cabin was silent, with only the crackling of the fire to break the stillness. Zeb was tending the herd. Adam lay on his bunk, smoke curling over his head from the cigarette in his hand. His thoughts centered on the night Diamond had come to him. He'd never known a sweeter seduction. Or a more powerful explosion of passion when they had finally come together.

He missed her. Missed her with an ache that tore at his heart. But he'd had enough of Onyx Jewel's home and bed and food. He'd had a need to be his own man again. In his own home. No matter what the cost.

The loneliness seemed all the more desolate now that he'd tasted family life again after all these years. It had reminded him how much he missed his own family. He and his brothers had been close. Closer than most. They had shared the same jokes, the same common thread of history. Though he'd been able to bury his pain, these few days with Diamond had opened up all the old wounds.

He could see that same closeness developing between Diamond and her sisters. Despite their differences, the four young women were beginning to forge a bond. One that would sustain them throughout the years.

If the timing had been different, he thought, he and Diamond might have been able to make it. But he had met her at a low point in her life. And now that she had discovered three sisters to fill the void left by the death of their father, he had no right to come between them. He had his life. She had hers. And the differences between them were too deep.

The wind howled, whipping a spray of snow and sleet against the north wall of the cabin. Winter was arriving with a vengeance, rattling the door, sending a shower of sparks up the chimney.

Over the sound of the wind he thought he heard hoofbeats. But a moment later there was only silence. Once again the door rattled, and he closed his eyes against the pain of loneliness.

"Adam."

At the sound of Diamond's voice, his eyes snapped open. He stood and caught sight of a vision in the doorway. A vision in man's britches and a weathered sheepskin jacket. A vision he knew he would carry forever in his heart.

"It...wasn't easy for me to come here like this again. But I had to... ask you one question."

He was alarmed by the abrupt tone of her voice. "What is it?"

"Do you love me?"

Without a word he crossed the room to the fireplace.

"Are you in love with me, Adam?" Her words seemed to hang suspended in the little cabin.

He could lie, of course. But he'd always been a man of integrity. And she was counting on that now. Hoping to ensnare him in his own web of honesty.

Tossing aside his cigarette, he kept his back to her. "Hopelessly."

At that single word, she let out a long, slow breath. All the way here, she'd been terrified of the answer. But now, everything was all right. Now they would find a way through this maze.

"Then, why did you leave me?"

He turned to face her. "It was time to get back to my own place, Diamond."

"Is there...room in your own place for me?"

He shook his head. "You don't know what you're asking. All I have ahead of me is hard work."

"That isn't an answer. Is there room here for me?"

"Diamond..."

She moved closer. In her eyes was that same determined look he'd seen the last time she'd come here. And he felt once again all the fear and uncertainty of that time. What if he hurt her? What if he selfishly asked more of her than she had to give?

"I can't cook," she said as she stopped inches from him. "And I'm better at mucking out stalls than cleaning house. But I can ride and rope and shoot better than most men. I don't know much about being a rancher's wife, but I do know how to be a rancher. If you let me, I'll be your partner, Adam. I'll sleep on the trail with you, and I'll ride herd with you all the way to Abilene and back."

Did she know that she'd just described heaven?

He could read the sincerity in her eyes, and he longed to touch her. But he was afraid, too. If he did, he knew he'd never be able to stop. And right now, one of them had to be sensible.

His tone roughened. "You don't know what you're saying. You own the biggest ranch in Texas, Diamond. And I own one of the smallest. All you'll be doing is taking on a lifetime of hard work. Don't you realize what you're giving up?"

"Oh, Adam. I'll be getting so much more than I'll be giving."

Before he could protest further, she added, "Besides, I'm not going into this blindly. I've already talked it over with Cal and my sisters. I've asked them to stay on. As equal partners."

"Cal and the women are your partners now?"

She nodded. "And I thought, since your ranch borders ours, that we could share some of the wranglers at roundup time. That is, if you don't mind."

He grinned. "It sounds like you're pretty sure of yourself, Miss Jewel. What if I say no?"

She touched a hand to his cheek, and he felt the purely sexual jolt all through his system. "I think you'll agree when you hear the rest."

"Are we back to the part about cooking and cleaning?" he asked with a smile.

"I'll love you, Adam," she whispered so fiercely he felt a shiver along his spine. "I'll love you better than any other woman ever could. I'll grow old with you, Adam. And I promise you, I'll love you until the day I die."

He shuddered at the intensity of her words. "Oh, God, Diamond. I don't deserve you."

"Does that mean you'll have me?"

"It means—" he drew her close and enfolded her in his arms "—I love you so much, I was willing to walk away rather than see you give up all you have for me. But if you're foolish enough to want to share my miserable life, I'm never going to let you go again."

"Promise?" she whispered against his lips.

"I promise you undying love, for all my life."

"Oh, Adam, let's go find the preacher right now," she said.

He caught hold of her as she started to turn, and dragged her into his arms. "In the morning. For now, for tonight," he murmured against her lips, "I just want to love you. It's been so long."

Her voice was warm with laughter. "Are you sure your wound is healed enough?"

He kissed her long, and slow, and deep. "I guess it's time to find out."

Diamond could hear the thundering of his heartbeat, and whispered a little prayer of thanksgiving for the courage she had inherited from her father. And the stubbornness. The ride here had been the longest of her life.

You kept your promise, Pa, she thought as she touched a hand to the rope of gold at her throat. You stayed right here beside me, guiding me to the right place, the right man.

She knew, as she melted against Adam, that she would never be alone again.

Epilogue

The little party stood on a windswept hill, dotted with four new mounds of earth forming a circle around Onyx Jewel's grave. The simple wooden crosses bore testimony to the women who had loved him, and whose remains had been moved here so they could join him in eternal rest.

Reverend Wade Weston wore his best white shirt and shiny black suit. Marshal Quent Regan had polished his boots and slicked back his hair.

Adam stood with his hands clasped behind him, staring at the sweeping vista spread out below him, a pensive look on his face.

"Having second thoughts?" Zeb asked.

Adam lifted his head. "Should I, old man?"

Zeb shrugged. "She's a handful. Your life will never be the same."

Adam's gaze moved beyond, to the gilded carriage moving toward them. His features softened into a smile. He clapped his old friend on the shoulder before turning away. "I'm counting on that."

Cal and a dozen wranglers dismounted and hurried forward to assist the women from the carriage. The hems of their pastel gowns fluttered in the breeze as Pearl, Jade and Ruby kissed Diamond, then preceded her up the hill.

And then there was only Diamond, standing alone.

She wore her mother's wedding gown of shimmering white, which sparkled in the brittle sunlight. A gossamer veil was attached with jeweled combs to her fiery hair. Hair that tumbled down her back in a riot of curls. At her throat was her father's necklace. In her hands was Adam's family Bible.

He stepped forward and caught her hand. "There's still time to run," he whispered as he placed her hand on his arm and took the first step.

"How far would I get?" She moved easily by his side.

"I'd catch you before you made it to your horse. And woman, I'd drag you back to me and chain you by my side forever."

"Promise?"

"I'm about to." He winked and her heart tumbled in her chest. "And it's a vow I intend to keep."

They paused when they reached the preacher. As the solemn words washed over them, Diamond clasped Adam's hand and stared up into his eyes. What she saw was a look of love that melted her heart and swept away whatever self-consciousness she had been feeling about all this pomp and ceremony.

This was where they had both chosen to speak their vows. On the land that nurtured them. Surrounded by the people who loved them.

Diamond thought again of how much both of them had lost. And how much more they had found.

Love. Enough to last a lifetime. Family. More than she

had ever dreamed of. And all the sweet tomorrows they would share together. These were truly treasures worth fighting for. And promises worth keeping.

* * * * *

UNLOCK THE DOOR TO GREAT ROMANCE
AT BRIDE'S BAY RESORT

Join Harlequin's new across-the-lines series, set
in an exclusive hotel on an island off the coast of
South Carolina.

Seven of your favorite authors will bring you exciting stories
about fascinating heroes and heroines discovering love at
Bride's Bay Resort.

Look for these fabulous stories coming to a store near you
beginning in January 1996.

Harlequin American Romance #613 in January
Matchmaking Baby by Cathy Gillen Thacker

Harlequin Presents #1794 in February
Indiscretions by Robyn Donald

Harlequin Intrigue #362 in March
Love and Lies by Dawn Stewardson

Harlequin Romance #3404 in April
Make Believe Engagement by Day Leclaire

Harlequin Temptation #588 in May
Stranger in the Night by Roseanne Williams

Harlequin Superromance #695 in June
Married to a Stranger by Connie Bennett

Harlequin Historicals #324 in July
Dulcie's Gift by Ruth Langan

Visit Bride's Bay Resort each month wherever
Harlequin books are sold.

Harlequin® Historical

This is what critics and award-winning authors
had to say about Nina Beaumont's
first time-travel novel—

ACROSS TIME

"...a tale to treasure!" —*Romantic Times*

"Truly spellbinding..."—Anita Mills

"...a reading trip worth taking." —*Affaire de Coeur*

"Exhilarating reading adventure!" —*Rendezvous*

"A marvelous read!" —Anita Gordon

"A breathtaking achievement." —Shirl Henke

And Harlequin Historicals is proud to be able
to bring you her second time-travel novel
coming this February—

TWICE UPON TIME

This is an exciting reading opportunity
that you won't want to miss!

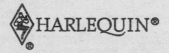

Yo amo novelas con corazón!

Starting this March, Harlequin opens up to a whole new world of readers with two new romance lines in SPANISH!

Harlequin Deseo
- passionate, sensual and exciting stories

Harlequin Bianca
- romances that are fun, fresh and very contemporary

With four titles a month, each line will offer the same wonderfully romantic stories that you've come to love—now available in Spanish.

Look for them at selected retail outlets.

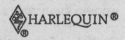
HARLEQUIN®

SPANT

INTRODUCING...

A collection of award-winning books by award-winning
authors! From Harlequin and Silhouette.

Heaven In Texas
by Curtiss Ann Matlock

National Reader's Choice Award Winner—
Long Contemporary Romance

Let Curtiss Ann Matlock take you to a place called
Heaven In Texas, where sexy cowboys in well-worn jeans
are the answer to every woman's prayer!

"Curtiss Ann Matlock blends reality with romance
to perfection!"
—*Romantic Times*

Available this March wherever Silhouette books are sold.